the GIRL who SPEAKS BEAR

the GIRL who SPEAKS BEAR

Sophie Anderson

Scholastic Press / New York

Library of Congress Cataloging-in-Publication Data available

ISBN 978-1-338-58083-9

10 9 8 7 6 5 4 3 2 1   20 21 22 23 24

Printed in the U.S.A. 23

First US edition, March 2020

Book design by Maeve Norton

TO MY HUSBAND, NICK, AND OUR
YOUNGEST CUB, EARTHA,
FOR HOLDING MY HAND
THROUGH THE FOREST

ANATOLY'S MAP OF THE SNOW FOREST

THE NORTHERN SEA

VILLAGE IN EAST

THE LIME TREE

SMEY'S CAVERN

THE FIERY VOLCANO

PRINCESS NASTASYA'S LAST ARROW

GREEN BAY

FISHING CABIN

THE BEAR CAVE

THE CRUMBLING CASTLE

THE BLUE MOUNTAIN

THE FROZEN SHIP

VILLAGE IN NORTH

THE SNOW FOREST

THE SILVER STREAM

THE GREAT FROZEN RIVER

YANKA'S HOUSE

SASHA'S HOUSE

ANATOLY'S CABIN

HOUSE WITH CHICKEN LEGS

YANKA'S VILLAGE

THE SNOW FOREST

N E S W

PROLOGUE

I remember the bear who raised me. Nuzzling my face into her warm belly. Huge furry limbs shielding me from the biting snow. I remember the deep rumbles of her snores through the silent winter, and clouds of steamy breath smelling of berries and pine nuts.

My foster mother, Mamochka, says I was about two years old when she found me outside the bear cave. She says I was standing naked in the snow, but with warm pink cheeks and the biggest smile. I walked right up to her, lifted my arms into the air, and made a soft barking sound. Mamochka picked me up and I laid my head on her shoulder, wrapped my legs around her waist, and fell straight to sleep. Mamochka says she knew right there and then we were meant to be together.

But if I don't know where I came from, how can I be sure where I belong?

Mamochka looked in the cave for clues about who I was or who my parents might be, but an old female bear was hibernating inside. Not wanting to disturb her, Mamochka crept away and carried me to her home at the edge of the Snow Forest.

I love living with Mamochka. She's the best mother I could have wished for, but I often wonder about the bear. I wonder if she remembers me. Maybe even misses me. I wonder about the bear almost as much as I wonder about my real parents. The ones who must have lost me—or left me—in the forest.

One day I'd like to find the story of my past, and I hope it's something more magical than being unwanted and abandoned as a baby. I hope it's a tale filled with wonder that explains who I am and why I'm different, why I hear the trees whispering secrets, and why I always feel the forest pulling me in.

CHAPTER ONE

YANKA THE BEAR

They call me Yanka the Bear. Not because of where I was found—only a few people know about that. They call me Yanka the Bear because I'm so big and strong.

I tower above all the other twelve-year-olds, and most of the grown-ups too. And I'm stronger than everyone. Even the ice cutters and the woodchoppers and the few hunter-gatherers who are brave enough to dip into the Snow Forest.

About one hundred people live here, in the village on the southern edge of the forest. And right now they're all squashed into the square, preparing for the festival tomorrow.

Snow sparkles and excitement fizzes in the air. For over six months, the village has been trapped by the fierce cold of winter. But tomorrow marks the start of the Big Melt. The Great Frozen River will thaw, and the Snow Forest will lose its blanket of white. I'll be able to wander beneath newly green trees. I won't wander far—Mamochka worries if I do. But just the thought of standing beneath swaying willows and chattering pines makes my cheeks tingle with happiness.

People call for my help as I cross the square. I stop to hold up wooden beams for the carpenters assembling the stage for the festival show. I help drive poles into the frozen earth for the climbing contest. And I haul creaking sleds up from the frozen river, loaded with blocks of ice for the ice fort. The fort is already as tall as the village hall, but children still clamber over its shining walls, building it even higher.

Finally, I reach the center of the square, where my best friend, Sasha, is stacking wood for the festival bonfire.

"Hey, Sasha." I smile and wave.

"Hey, Yanka." Sasha smiles back from beneath his huge furry hat. We've been best friends since I pulled him out of a nettle patch when I was three and he was five. I rubbed his stings with dock leaves and asked him to climb a tree with me. Mamochka says that was the first time I ever spoke.

Sasha is long and leggy as a heron. Until this winter we stood eye to eye, but after my latest growth spurt, I see right over the top of his head. I never imagined I'd grow this big, and I'm not sure I'll ever get used to it.

"Shall we carry this one together?" Sasha lifts one end of a long, cut tree.

"I can manage it." I swing the log onto my shoulder, and my feet sink deep into the snow. Sasha picks up another, smaller log, and we clump them side by side to the bonfire stack.

Sasha's youngest cousin, Vanya, rushes over with his arms full of twigs. He beams up at me, wide-eyed. "You're as strong as a bear, Yanka."

I lower the log onto the bonfire stack and smile. I don't mind my strength being compared to a bear's. Not really. But it does remind me how different I am—and not only in my size and strength.

Everyone else in the village was born here, and so were their parents and grandparents. They wear fur coats passed down from great-grandfathers and sleep under blankets knitted by great-grandmothers. But I don't know where I was born, or who my real parents are, or how I ended up in the bear cave. The not-knowing feels like a hole inside me that gets a little wider every year.

I heave another log up onto my shoulder and push away these wintry thoughts. Soon the bonfire stack is as tall as me, and I smile as I imagine the heat of it burning tomorrow.

Sasha is laughing with a group of children who have climbed down from the ice fort. His hat is in his hands and his feathery hair is sticking up at all angles. I recognize everyone in the group. There are only about twenty children in the village and we all go to the same school, and always have, so I shouldn't feel awkward around them. But I stumble as I walk over, then smile nervously. No one seems to notice. Maybe because they're busy making plans for tomorrow. Or maybe because my head is so much higher than all of theirs. I try slouching and bending my knees, but I still don't fit into the group. I feel like a cuckoo chick in a nest of wrens.

The pale gray sky darkens and frost bites into the air. Winter might be ending, but the warmth of spring still feels far away. It's always like this. Snow that melts in the sun refreezes in the gloaming, so the nights are full of ice and glacier sharp.

A bullfinch flutters past, so close that its feathers graze my cheek. It swoops up and away, toward the forest. I can only see a few spindly treetops from here, but they feel like thick ropes, tugging at my heart. I'm nearly at the top of the hill that rises up from the village before I realize I've wandered away from the others.

Sasha catches up to me and punches my arm as he falls into step beside me.

"What's that for?" I punch him back, as gently as I can, but still he wobbles away from me.

"Trying to get a head start." Sasha pulls out the blades that clip on to his boots to turn them into ice skates. "Race you to my house?"

"Yes!" My heart lifts, then sinks as I remember why I'm not wearing skating boots. I've outgrown three pairs this winter and can't face having more made. It scares me, thinking how fast I've grown this year—so much faster than other years that I get pains in my legs at night. I fumble with my pockets and sigh. "I forgot my blades."

"Again?" Sasha groans.

"I don't mind if you skate without me." I stop at the top of the hill. A track of sheet ice covers the path here and stretches all the way to Sasha's house, and then on to my and Mamochka's front door. I know Sasha loves to glide along the ice, graceful as a swallow in flight. But he doesn't clip on his blades.

"Let's go through the forest instead." He bounces over to the gnarly old elm we used to climb when we were little. There's a trail behind it that winds between the trees and loops around to our gardens. I've always preferred walking back that way, and Sasha knows it. Warmth floods through me. Sasha makes the best friend.

Stepping into the Snow Forest is like stepping into another world. The tall, tall trees make me feel small. My mind tingles and my senses come alive. Sometimes in the forest, I feel so close to the story of my past I can almost hear it on the wind.

"Are you excited for the festival?" Sasha asks, his eyes shining.

I nod, thinking of all the things I enjoy about the festival: the games, the music and the shows, racing on the freshly iced sledding hill with Sasha, and running through the fire maze to Mamochka.

The fire maze doesn't involve real fire. Huge sheets of flowing silks, cut and painted to look like flames, are draped over the stage. Everyone runs through them at the end of the night, laughing when they get tangled or lost in the sheets, and emerging with faces glowing like embers.

The first time I went through the fire maze, when I was

three or four years old, I was scared, so Mamochka stood on the other side and beckoned me through. I'm not scared anymore, but she still stands on the other side when I run.

"I can't wait for the siege game." Sasha beams. "Did you see how high the ice fort is this year?"

"Higher than the village hall," I murmur, distracted by the sounds of the forest. I duck under a branch, and snow shivers onto the back of my neck.

The forest has moods and at this moment it feels restless, with the snow dripping and the birds rustling, animals scurrying up trees and dashing along tunnels under the snow.

Sasha goes on about the games, but I can't concentrate. I feel on edge, like the forest is trying to tell me something.

"Yanka?"

"Sorry. What?"

"Were you listening to the trees again?" Sasha smiles. "Have they told you who you are yet?"

Blood rises into my cheeks. Me and Sasha have always told each other everything. Now, sometimes, I wish he didn't know quite so much about me—like how I hear things in the forest, and how much I wonder about my past.

"Shall I call for you tomorrow?" Sasha asks.

"I'm helping Mamochka carry her remedies to the square and set up her stall. We're leaving at first light."

"I'll come and help."

"You don't have to."

"I want to. My parents are sledding over to pick up my

grandparents, so I'm on my own in the morning anyway." Sasha runs off into his back garden. "See you tomorrow."

I walk on to my and Mamochka's garden and linger under the pines at the edge of it, to be near the forest a few moments longer.

Our garden, like Sasha's, runs straight into the forest, with no fences or gates to separate the two. At the moment, it's a flat patch of snow, but after the Big Melt we'll turn over the earth and plant seeds. By the time the long summer days arrive, it will be bursting with color: fruits, flowers, and hundreds of herbs, dancing with bees and butterflies.

The herbs are Mamochka's livelihood. She harvests them, dries them, grinds them up, and makes all kinds of remedies. Whenever I'm unwell, she has a tonic or a tea to make me feel better. This winter she even made a special ointment, just for me, when I complained that my feet ached from growing too fast.

People say Mamochka can cure anything—that if she wanted to, she could cure the sky from bleeding at sunset—because she has the wisdom of the Snow Forest inside her. Mamochka feels like the forest too, fierce and gentle all at once. Her hands are smooth but tough, like new bark. Her hair is dark, like the shadows between pines. And she smells sweet, like lime blossoms.

When Mamochka was younger, she'd walk deep into the forest, collecting wild herbs and berries for her remedies. That's how she ended up finding me at the bear cave. But these days, she stays in the village and grows everything she needs in her garden.

Like all the other villagers, she says it's dangerous in the forest and that her most important job now is to keep me safe. I wish she'd let me explore just a little farther, but she says I could get lost or frozen, or be attacked by one of the many predators that stalk between the trees.

A flash of pink on a snowy branch catches my eye. It's another fat, round bullfinch. I smile at him, slide my hand into my pocket, and pull out a few of the sunflower seeds I always carry for the birds. Holding my hand out flat and still, with the seeds on my palm, I whistle low and mournful.

The bullfinch tilts his head and edges down the branch. Then he jumps and flutters onto my hand.

"Yanka!"

My breath catches in my throat. I'm sure the bullfinch said my name.

"Yanka!" the bird calls again. "Yanka the Bear! Come back to the forest!"

I stare at the bullfinch, mouth open. I heard his words as birdsong, but they made sense in my mind. I lean closer, willing the bullfinch to say something else.

But tiny paws scamper up the back of my reindeer-skin coat, and Mousetrap, our house weasel, launches himself from my shoulder and dives straight at the little bird.

The bullfinch flaps away just in time and Mousetrap lands on my hand, sending the sunflower seeds raining into the snow. He coils around my wrist and looks up at me guiltlessly, licking his lips.

I frown at him and shake my head. "I wish you wouldn't hunt the birds I feed. Aren't there enough mice in the house for you?"

Mousetrap shakes himself, fluffing up his fur, then drops to the ground and sprints back across the garden, a streak of copper against the snow. Mousetrap's fur doesn't turn white in winter like other weasels' because he lives by our fire.

Mamochka knocks on the kitchen window. *"Sbiten?"* She mouths the word, holding up my favorite yellow mug. I smile and nod, feeling warmer at the thought of the hot honey drink.

I glance back in the direction the bullfinch flew, but he's gone. I tell myself I imagined understanding him, but my heart knows different. The treetops whisper and the snow drips secrets. I feel the pull of the forest, stronger than ever before. Somewhere, deep in the dark between the trees, hides the truth of my past.

My heart races and my toes twitch. I stamp the snow from my boots and brush off my coat, but I can't shake the restless feeling from my legs. And as the front door swings shut behind me, I hear the bullfinch once more, far in the distance.

"Yanka the Bear! Come back to the forest! You belong here!"

CHAPTER TWO

ANATOLY

Anatoly arrives at night, with ice in his beard and moonlit eyes. Excitement bubbles inside me as I watch him through the frost-coated window. He unharnesses and feeds his sled dogs, brushes each of them carefully, checks their paws, and whispers their names: Nessa, Bayan, Pyotr, and Zoya. Finally, he settles them into the shelter and comes inside.

He ducks through the doorway, huge as a bear in his deerskins and furs, but once he peels off his layers and sits by the fire in his threadbare *rubakha* tunic, he looks thinner and older than I remember. There are deeper wrinkles around his silvery eyes, and more white hairs in his lopsided beard, which doesn't grow evenly because of the burn scars on his cheeks. But his smile is the same. He looks down when he smiles, and flushes pink as a bullfinch's belly.

It's been two months since Anatoly last visited and though that feels like forever, it's not that long. Sometimes, there's half a year or more between his visits; other times, a few weeks. I wish he visited more regularly. I miss him when he's not here and spend too much time wondering when he'll come.

Anatoly lives alone in the forest, hunting, fishing, and trapping animals to survive. No one in the village knew he existed until about ten years ago, when he turned up on Mamochka's doorstep, asking for an ointment to soothe his burns. They were old scars, from a forest fire years before, but he said they still ached and itched at night.

Since then, Anatoly has visited at least once a year, and often many more times. Occasionally he stays for a night, sleeping by our fire, and people in the village tease Mamochka and say he's her sweetheart. She just laughs and says you can't have a sweetheart who spends all their time hiding in the forest. But her eyes shine brighter and her smile spreads wider when he visits.

"You look like you haven't eaten since we last saw you." Mamochka pours Anatoly a cup of tea with lemon and passes him a basket of *pryaniki*—soft spiced cookies with a glaze as white as the snow outside.

Mamochka is small—half the size of either Anatoly or me—but she takes up more space. She bustles around, strong and unstoppable, filling the room with as much movement and life as a flight of doves.

Anatoly sips his tea and bites a *pryaniki*, and color floods into his face. "I've eaten well, but I've been in the Far North these last months and the cold makes me thin."

"What did you find?" I ask, tingling with anticipation

for the story. When Anatoly comes out of the Snow Forest, there's always a story.

When I was young, I believed all of Anatoly's tales, whether they were about wolf packs hunting over moonlit snow or fire dragons leaping from volcanoes. Because his stories came from the forest—like me—they felt like clues to my past.

Now I know Anatoly's stories are just stories. Mamochka has told me often enough. But still I like to believe them, in the moments when he tells them and sometimes afterward—in the depths of night, when the branches outside my window shine silver and I can't sleep for thinking about what secrets the forest holds.

Anatoly smiles his shy smile, reaches deep into his pocket, and pulls out his map. He smooths the tattered old paper over the low table between us, and I search for the new mark. There's always a new mark, hidden somewhere among the inky trees, to show where the story begins.

"Here is the village." Anatoly points to the neat drawing of the village on the southern edge of the map. "And here is your house." His finger hovers over my and Mamochka's house, which is marked by two small hearts inside a square.

Anatoly always points out all the features on his map, even though I've seen it so many times I could draw it from memory. But I don't mind. I like listening to his gentle voice rumble against the crackling of the fire, and I like watching his callused fingers skate through the sketched forest.

It also gives me a chance to find the new mark on my own. The mark might be a large feature—like the picture of a crumbling castle that appeared last year to go with a story about a bear who had once been human. Or it might be a small feature—like the claw, hidden in a glade, that sparked a story about how a lone baby girl stood up to a pack of wolves. Anatoly told me that story when I was very young, and I still have the wolf claw he gave me under my pillow. Sometimes, running my finger along it makes me feel brave. But at other times, the sight of the thick, dark hook as long as my thumb makes me pull my blankets tight around me.

My gaze drifts across the map, north through the forest along a narrow, winding trail. Creatures hide among the trees: wolves and wolverines, badgers and bears, snakes and squirrels. Past the first of Anatoly's five cabins, the trail disappears, so I follow the Silver Stream instead, its rippled surface dotted with ice floes and leaping fish.

"The Yaga house has moved again." I point to a drawing of a house with chicken legs nestled in a pine thicket.

"Winter has been harsh this year." Anatoly nods gravely. "The house got so cold its knees splintered. It stood up in the middle of the night and the crack sounded like thunder. I heard it over ten miles away. It ran south, its feet pounding along the riverbank, until it warmed up and settled in this cozy thicket. The Yaga who lives in the house wasn't happy at all, as she doesn't like moving closer to the living. You know Yaga prefer dead souls."

"Dead souls and houses with chicken legs." Mamochka folds her arms over her chest and shakes her head. "You fill her mind with nonsense, Anatoly."

"There's truth in all my stories," Anatoly says quietly. He glances up at me with a look of such sincerity that I want to tell him I believe every tale he's ever told. Instead, I rise to my feet and open the long wooden box on the mantelpiece. Inside is my favorite ink pen and my own copy of Anatoly's map. I drew it myself the last time he was here, and although it's not as neat as his, I'm proud of it. I roll it out on the table and carefully draw the house with chicken legs in its new position.

Mamochka disappears into the kitchen, still muttering about nonsense. She only believes in things she can see for herself. But she wasn't always so dismissive of Anatoly's stories. When I was younger, she used to repeat them to me before bed in her matter-of-fact style. Or she'd sing me the songs of her ancestors, about the power of nature and the healing magic of the forest. But she seems to have decided twelve years old is too old for stories.

Last time Anatoly visited, after I went to bed, I heard Mamochka tell him she worries that his stories keep me wondering about my past. Anatoly told her I'm a magical bear-child who will always wonder where I came from. Mamochka replied it would be better if my heart was in the village, rather than getting lost in the stories of the forest. At that point I turned over in bed, not wanting to hear any more, and sang myself to sleep.

I finish drawing the house with chicken legs and lean back over Anatoly's map, to see what else is new. But my gaze lands on the Blue Mountain and I can't pull it away. Nestled high in a cliff is a sketch of the bear cave where I was found, with me as a baby inked inside, snuggling into the arms of the Bear Tsarina. Anatoly always refers to the bear who raised me as a *tsarina*, a queen of the Snow Forest.

My feet ache with the same restless feeling I had earlier, after I heard the bullfinch speak. Outside, the snow glistens, and an urge to make footprints in it swells inside me.

"The bear cave." Anatoly's voice cuts through my thoughts. He gently touches the map, right next to the cave. "Where your mamochka found the most precious treasure ever discovered in the Snow Forest."

Mamochka places a mug of *sbiten* in front of me and drops a kiss onto my head. She smiles at Anatoly and he smiles back without looking away, and for a moment I feel like the three of us belong together. Like a real family.

"How long are you staying?" I blurt out, then regret the question, because Anatoly's face burns bright red all the way to his ears and he doesn't answer.

Mamochka leans down and tops up the teapot with hot water from the samovar. Steam rises when she opens the tap in the shining brass urn, the heat in the air disguising Anatoly's blushing. "What's that?" she asks, pointing to a tiny triangular mark on the map.

I peer at the triangle embedded high in the trunk of a tall, slim birch. Inside the triangle is the letter *N*, with a crown on top. "It's the new mark!" Excitement rushes through me, washing away the twinge of disappointment I felt at not finding the mark myself. "And it has something to do with the Princess Nastasya." I recognize the crowned *N* as her symbol. Anatoly has told me stories about her before, and some of them have hinted that she might be my birth mother. The thought that might be true, and I might learn something about her, gives me a sudden, breathtaking thrill, like skidding, slightly out of control, on ice.

Anatoly pulls an object wrapped in cloth from his pocket and passes it to me. It's as big as my palm, is heavy, and feels cold through the cloth.

Mousetrap pokes his head out of his hole in the corner near the fire and sniffs the air. He's a fierce and proud hunter and never begs for food, unless it's freshwater cod brought by Anatoly. But it's not cod in the parcel.

Inside is a triangular ice-blue rock, smooth as glass, with a tip and edges as sharp as a knife. Anatoly has made a hole in the wide end and threaded it with a leather cord, so it can be worn as a necklace. The rock trembles in my hand. It feels unnaturally cold, like there's a snowstorm inside it.

The corners of Mousetrap's mouth turn down when he realizes there's no fish on offer, but perhaps he catches the scent of the story to come, because he edges closer, scoots up the back of my chair, settles onto my shoulder, and stares at Anatoly expectantly.

I breathe in Mousetrap's familiar smell of dust and earthy musk and reach up to give him a stroke, but he pushes my finger away. Mousetrap loves sitting on my shoulder, but he doesn't like being fussed over or petted.

"Is this an arrowhead?" I ask, holding the rock up to the window so it shimmers with starlight.

Anatoly nods. "It's for you. The Princess Nastasya's last arrow." His voice cracks a little and he takes another swig of tea.

"It's beautiful. Thank you." I lift the necklace over my head, being careful not to disturb Mousetrap, then turn to show Mamochka.

"It looks lovely on you." Mamochka smiles. "But with those sharp edges, it doesn't seem very safe to wear." She raises her eyebrows at Anatoly and he looks down apologetically.

"Would you like to hear the arrow's story?" Anatoly asks.

"Yes, please." Goose bumps shiver over my skin. Although I've heard stories about the Princess Nastasya before, I've not heard one about an arrow. Mousetrap lets out a squeaky yawn, stretches, and curls around my neck.

"Princesses and arrowheads." Mamochka tuts as she returns to the kitchen, where she makes a show of putting away the fish and game Anatoly has brought us. But I see her through the doorway, listening. Mamochka might not believe Anatoly's stories, but she's not immune to their magic.

Perhaps Anatoly's stories *are* too fantastic to be true, but wrapped up in one of his tales, with the fire crackling in the hearth, and ice glistening on the windows, I can believe that one day I'll find my own story, and it will shine as brilliantly as a clear night sky.

"There *is* truth in my stories," Anatoly whispers as he passes me a *pryaniki*. I smile and take a bite of the soft cookie. Then Anatoly begins, as he always does, with "Once upon a time . . ."

THE PRINCESS NASTASYA'S
LAST ARROW

Once upon a time, a great warrior came to the Snow Forest. Her name was the Princess Nastasya.

She carried a bow over her shoulder and a quiver of arrows on her back and with them she could shoot the twinkle from a star.

For many years the Princess Nastasya defended and protected the creatures of the Snow Forest. She drove the water demons from the river, calmed the wood spirits whose howls brought rain, and saved the soul of the Giant Deathless.

Then one day, she met a fisherman on the shores of the Green Bay. They fell in love and had a beautiful baby daughter.

But before the baby was one moon old, the Fiery Volcano in the north exploded into flames. Smey, a three-headed fire dragon, erupted into the sky, and Nastasya's husband, who was near the volcano at the time, became trapped by the furious beast.

Nastasya burned with rage. She shouldered her bow, held her baby to her breast, and climbed to a cave in the Blue

Mountain. There, though it broke her heart to do so, she left her beloved daughter in the care of the only creature she trusted to keep her safe: the Bear Tsarina.

And at the very top of the mountain, where the ancient peak is stained blue by the sky, Nastasya carved six arrowheads. Made from thick blue ice and hardened with stardust, they were strong and cold enough to cool the anger in a fire dragon's heart.

The sun set and the moon rose three times before Nastasya reached the Fiery Volcano and found Smey's cavern. Nastasya charged in and aimed an arrow at the dragon's heart, but Smey held her husband too close for her to take the shot.

Between two heartbeats, Nastasya fired five arrows at Smey's three heads, blinding five of his eyes. Nastasya smiled and drew back her final arrow, to blind the dragon's last eye. But Smey opened his great wings and flew from the cavern, still holding Nastasya's husband. Then Smey roared with anger and dropped him into a swirl of dragon fire.

Grief tore through Nastasya as she watched her husband disappear into the flames. Her chest crumpled and she struggled to breathe. She released her last arrow, but it missed its target. The arrow clipped Smey's wing, making him tumble through the sky. And spitting fiery bombs and cinders, he collapsed upon her. There was no escape.

High above, the last arrow flew on. It sailed over stars, carrying Nastasya's love and strength. It dipped under the moon, picking up moonbeams and magic, and it landed deep in the bark of a tall, slim birch.

Tears pooled in Nastasya's eyes, which shone with thoughts of her orphaned child. But her final breath was filled with hope that one day her daughter would find the last arrow, and then her story would be remembered.

CHAPTER THREE

THE FESTIVAL

The next morning, Anatoly is gone. Though I knew he would be, disappointment falls over me like a heavy leather cloak. There's a note from him on the table, saying the forest called him in the night, and two twigs of goat willow dotted with soft silvery catkins.

Mamochka shakes her head at the note but smiles at the twigs and tucks one into a buttonhole on her coat. I do the same with mine and we step out into the sharp air to load up a sled with Mamochka's supplies for the festival.

Mousetrap scampers around and over me, leaping from my shoulders to my hands to the sled and back again, sniffing all the bottles and jars and scowling at the ones filled with herbs and seeds that whisper and rattle as they move.

It's fun watching him, but I can't stop thinking about Anatoly's story from last night. I keep going over the details as if looking for clues, and I keep touching my arrowhead necklace, to feel its sharp edges and trembling cold. This morning it feels like there's more than a snowstorm inside it.

"You understand it was just a story, don't you?" Mamochka says, reaching up to straighten the buttons on my coat. She always knows what I'm thinking, and she always fusses with my clothes or my hair when she's concerned about me.

"Of course." I nod, but I can't help wondering, *What if there's truth in the story, like Anatoly said? What if Nastasya were real, and my birth mother?* The thought makes my heart skip and jump like Mousetrap on the sled.

"Come on." Mamochka finishes squashing cotton grass into the crates and covers it with furs. "Let's have a hot drink before we go. I have a surprise for you too." Her eyes sparkle with excitement, and curiosity rushes through me.

"Are you coming inside?" I offer my hand to Mousetrap, who is now stalking a fluffy seed head across the top of the crates. His whiskers twitch with annoyance, as if I've disturbed an important hunt, but he leaps onto my palm, scrambles up my coat, and squeezes into my collar. I smile at the feel of his tiny body, soft and warm against my neck, and follow Mamochka into the house.

She opens one of the drawers in her medicine-mixing corner, pulls out a large brown parcel, and passes it to me, beaming.

I take the parcel and unwrap it, then open out the vast folds of fabric I find inside. It's a long, dark skirt. I frown at it, because I like wearing my old, comfy trousers, but then I notice colors dancing on the hem.

"I embroidered it myself." Mamochka moves a pan of

sbiten onto the stove to warm up as I look at the delicately stitched pictures more closely. There's a forest filled with creatures and a blue mountain rising in the distance. A fiery dragon flies across a night sky and regal bears dance in a crumbling castle overgrown with vines. A house with chicken legs sprints along a riverbank and a pack of wolves hunt beneath a silver full moon.

"These are scenes from Anatoly's stories," I whisper, unable to believe Mamochka sewed this for me.

"I know how much his stories mean to you. That's why I made this. But I made it for you to wear today, in the village—the place where you belong, with those who love you." She looks me in the eye. More than anything, I want to believe she's right, so I push away thoughts of my own story hidden somewhere in the forest. But I feel my heart stretching.

Mamochka keeps staring at me, a huge smile on her face and a twinkle in her eye.

"What is it?" I ask, my brow furrowed.

"You've been chosen to carry Winter!" Mamochka throws her arms around me. I'm distracted by how they barely reach halfway, so it takes awhile for her words to sink in. Every year at the festival, a big straw doll called Winter is burned, to symbolize the end of winter and the coming spring. Carrying Winter to the bonfire is a real honor, usually given to one of the grown-ups who has contributed most to village life over the season.

"I'm so proud of you." Mamochka pulls away from me and puts her hand over her heart.

For a moment I wish Anatoly was here. I wonder if he'd have stayed and come to the festival if he'd known I'd be carrying Winter, wearing a skirt with his stories on. Then I realize what a silly thought that is. Anatoly never comes to the festivals.

"Go and try your skirt on." Mamochka nudges me out of the kitchen. "Then we'll have this drink and get going."

I go to my room and change into the skirt and my favorite pair of reindeer-skin boots. Anatoly made them from the softest, stretchiest leather, so they never pinch or rub. He always gives me a few pairs when he visits, some that fit and bigger ones to grow into. I make sure my arrowhead necklace is tucked safely inside my sweater. And before going back downstairs, I slide the wolf claw Anatoly gave me from beneath my pillow and put it in my pocket. Because even though Winter is only made of straw, I have the feeling I may need some extra strength today.

Sasha arrives, bouncing with excitement for the festival, and we set off, hauling the loaded sled behind us. Before we reach the bottom of the garden, Mousetrap stirs from his sleep around my neck, launches himself into the snow, and scampers off toward the pines. He rarely comes to the village with me, and like Anatoly, he never comes to the festivals. I lift my collar, trying to warm the cold space he's left around my neck.

The noise of traders setting up stalls rattles between the trees, and by the time we arrive at the square, musicians are tuning their instruments, and smoke is rising from steel-drum barbecues.

As we help Mamochka set up her stall, people fill the square until they're packed in tight as bees in a hive. I don't recognize everyone. People have sledded here from distant villages, nestled on other edges of the Snow Forest, to come to the festival.

Squeals rise from the sledding hill, cheers from the pole-climbing contests, and laughter from the stalls selling food and drink. A snowball whizzes past Sasha's head and lands at my feet. I look up to the top of the ice fort, where it was thrown from. A mischief of small children are hiding behind the battlements, giggling.

Little Vanya pokes his head out. "Look how many snow-balls we've made, Yanka." He gestures to a toppling pile and smiles proudly. "Will you be on our team for the siege game? We're defending."

"Me and Sasha already signed up to attack." I squish the snowball back together and throw it to him. "So you'd better save these for the game."

"Let's go sledding." Sasha punches my arm. I glance over the top of his head to Mamochka.

She's serving a customer, but she winks and waves me away. "Go and have some fun."

Sasha leads the way across the square, weaving through crowds that part ahead of me. People always move out of my way, because I'm so big. They look at me differently too, staring a little longer, smiling a little more stiffly. To Sasha they just nod a greeting. To me they say "Yanka the Bear," either whispered in awe or shouted too loud. Today it's worse than ever, because the visitors from distant villages haven't seen me since the last festival, and I've grown over a foot in that time.

I wonder if as much space would widen around a real bear in the village, and for a moment I want to roar, just to see people's reaction. But when Sasha stops to talk to some children from school, I only hang back silently, fiddling with the wolf claw in my pocket.

Liliya, one of the girls my age, turns to me and smiles. "I heard you're carrying Winter." I feel a fleeting flush of pride, but it disappears when I notice the sharpness in her eyes and the sting in her smile. "It's strange they chose you," she continues. "I don't think you've done much for the village this season. You hardly talk to anyone apart from Sasha and you spend most of your time in the forest."

"And carrying Winter is a *village* tradition," Liliya's friend Oksana chimes in. "And you weren't born in the village, were you?"

"I've lived here nearly all my life." I shrug, pretending not to be bothered by their words. But anger prickles beneath my skin. Why do they have to remind me how different I am when it's so obvious anyway?

"They were probably forced to choose Yanka." Liliya waves her hand dismissively in my direction. "Winter is massive this year and they've tied her to a heavy birch pole. No one else would be strong enough to carry her."

"That's true." Oksana nods and they turn away to carry on the conversation they were having before I arrived.

"They're just jealous," Polina, another girl from school, mouths behind their backs. I return her smile. Polina is always nice to me, though she's not really a friend. Like Liliya said, I don't spend enough time talking to anyone in the village to make friends. I only grew so close to Sasha because we live next door to each other.

It's a relief when Sasha finishes talking and we move away from the others, on to the sledding hill. I pick the strongest-, sturdiest-looking sled from the jumble at the bottom and drag it up the steep slope.

Sitting at the top, high above the village square, the forest at my back and the Great Frozen River stretching all the way to the horizon, I take a long cool breath and my muscles relax.

"Race you!" Sasha shouts, and shoots off ahead of me.

I lean back on the sled, pull tight on the rope, and speed down the hill. For a moment my whole body lifts into the air and I gasp in a cloud of ice. Then I bump back onto the track, jolting my heart into my throat. I overtake Sasha and skid to a halt in a flurry of snow. I rise to my feet, legs shaking, skin tingling hot and cold, and a huge smile making my cheeks ache.

Sasha swooshes into powdery snow next to me and rolls

off his sled, laughing. "No one else races like you, Yanka. You're fearless!" He scrambles to his feet and grins. "Again?"

I nod. Even though I've grown taller than Sasha this winter, as we tramp back up the slope, I feel like we still fit together somehow.

We race down the hill, over and over, until my lungs are raw and my legs burning from dragging the sled back up.

Then a drumroll sounds—quietly at first, building until it reverberates like thunder around the square. Sasha and I abandon our sled and join the crowds flowing toward the stage. My skin tingles with excitement, because the festival show is about to begin.

CHAPTER FOUR

THE SHOW

The main feature of the festival show this year is a puppet show, but not like one I've ever seen before. I helped build the scaffolding behind the stage and glimpsed some of the marionettes. They're bigger than real people—bigger even than me—and it takes three or four puppeteers to control each one.

Sasha moves closer to the stage, but I stand at the back. Being so tall, I can easily see over everyone's heads. The drums stop, and a hush falls over the square. I hold my breath as I wait for the show to begin.

On the stage is a forest made from real trees dusted with real snow, and real snowflakes dance down from high in the scaffolding.

My heart leaps as *kalyuka* flutes swing into song and three marionettes appear: two wooden children dancing jerkily between the trees, and their father walking solemnly behind them.

Drums roll again, deeper and more sinister than before,

and the father abandons his children in the darkest part of the forest. My face tightens into a frown as I wonder if my birth parents abandoned me in the same way. But I can't stop watching.

The biggest marionette of them all jumps out from behind the trees, accompanied by the screech of violins. The flock of tiny children sitting cross-legged in front of the stage jump too, because it's a house with chicken legs, and a Yaga—a terrifying witch who gobbles up lost children with her iron teeth—is leaning out its window, cackling.

"Yanka," the lady beside me whispers. It's Inga, who always buys Mamochka's chamomile tonic for her nerves. She points to where Mamochka is waving, beckoning me over to her stall. I glance back at the stage. I know this story already, but I want to watch the puppet children trick the Yaga, and I especially want to see the children's father find them at the end and apologize for leaving them in the forest. But Mamochka is flapping her hands frantically.

I sigh and wander over to her stall, which is cluttered with remedies. Woodsmoke from the nearby barbecues swirls around me, mingling with the scents of melted cheese and butter from sizzling stacks of pancakes.

"It's nearly time." Mamochka smiles as I draw close. "Are you ready?" She brushes the snow from my skirt.

A kaleidoscope of butterflies hurtles through me, but then Mamochka reaches up to tuck my hair behind my ears and her familiar fussing calms me. My hair is thick and brown, with flecks of yellow and black. I like the colors, but

I don't often get to see them because my hair doesn't grow past my chin—though I hardly ever trim it.

"You look beautiful." Mamochka lifts one of her necklaces of strung *sushki*—the hard, sweet little bread rings she gives customers to dunk in hot tea—and I duck so she can loop it over my head. It falls next to my arrowhead necklace, which has bounced free of my sweater. "Enjoy this moment." Mamochka cups my face in her hands and kisses my cheeks. I kiss her back, wishing I was still small enough to be enveloped in one of her hugs. There was a time when I fit perfectly in her arms.

The crowd around the stage applauds the end of the puppet show and music swells, faster and louder. People surge toward us and a babble of babushkas—the grandmothers who organized the festival—jostle me across the square while singing loudly about the end of winter and the coming spring. My heart races. Everything seems too loud and everyone seems to be moving too fast.

Winter looms above me, straw sticking out from beneath her blue dress. She has round pink cheeks and a wide smile drawn on her sackcloth face.

"Lift her up," the babushkas sing. "Burn Winter to bring on the spring."

I wipe my sweating palms on my skirt, place my hands on either side of the birch pole, and lift it into the air. It's heavier than I expected, and I take a step back to balance myself.

The crowd cheers and blood rushes into my cheeks. I'm

right in the center of the square, hundreds of faces staring up at me.

"Yanka!" A chorus of voices sings in tune with the music. "Yanka the Bear!"

My stomach tightens, and my legs give way. The pole wobbles.

"Sasha!" one of the babushkas shouts. "Come and help Yanka."

"Yanka doesn't need help; she's as strong as a bear." Two girls giggle behind me and my jaw clenches, because it's Liliya and Oksana. Their voices are soft as sable, but their words are hornets, full of venom.

The crowd cheers again and the music swells louder. Drums pound and feet stamp, jouncing my heartbeat. *Kalyuka* flutes scream into my ears and accordions play faster and louder. The crowd bounces like a stormy ocean. Everyone is clapping and yelling. My ears ring and my vision blurs. Then a flash of pink crosses the white sky, and the bullfinch sings, "Yanka! You don't belong here! You belong in the forest!"

Liliya and Oksana laugh and I'm sure they're thinking the same thing.

"Yanka the Bear!" the crowd roars. "Strong as a bear."

All of a sudden, I want to run to where the trees are tall and I am small and there are no crowds of people, no drums, no bouncing babushkas, and no giant straw doll needing to be burned.

"Hey, Yanka." Sasha puts his hand on my arm, and his

calm, gray eyes swing into focus. "We'll do it together." He moves opposite me and grips the pole, his hands below mine.

My heart stops racing and the urge to run fades away. But my face burns. I should have been strong enough to do this on my own.

Sasha helps me carry the pole through the noise and the chaos, and then we lift it high and slide it into the bonfire stack. I try to back away, but the crowd won't give. Smoke rises from the bonfire and flames lick up Winter's skirts. Just as the straw doll erupts into a towering blaze, a deafening crack echoes through the air. It takes a moment for me to realize it's the Great Frozen River—the ice is splitting and the water is starting to flow. With perfect timing, the Big Melt has begun.

There's a roar of excitement. Then people link together in great circles and spin this way and that, dancing in celebration, dipping and bobbing gracefully under raised arms. Trapped among them all, I try to follow their steps, but when I duck under arms, I bump them, and when I jump and spin, I pull the elegant dancing lines out of formation.

Sasha is swept away from me, and my chest tightens as I lose sight of him. I turn around, looking for him or Mamochka or even Polina's friendly face, but all I see are too-wide, unfamiliar smiles. I fight another urge to run away. People laugh and sing as Winter's cheeks blacken above me and her arms shed sparks into the wind.

The flames dance into the shape of a dragon and I think

of Anatoly's story from last night. If it was true and my birth mother was a great warrior who fought a fire dragon, what would she think of me not being able to carry a straw doll on my own?

I touch my arrowhead necklace and it shivers, like the forest whispering secrets. Until Sasha grabs my arm.

"Come on." He pulls me toward the ice fort. "The siege is starting."

Snowballs rain down from the glistening turrets and I lift my arms over my head to protect my face. A mass of bodies flows toward the fort and shouts rise from every direction.

"Storm the walls!"

"Lift me up!"

"Yanka, help me!"

I duck down and link my hands together so some of the younger, smaller children can use them as a step to climb onto the walls.

"Yanka!" Sasha calls. He's reached one of the turrets already. "Climb up!"

I dig my foot into a gap between two ice blocks and start to scale the sheer, icy walls. People clamber around me, quicker and lighter on their feet, but I'm strong. I can do this. I push my gloved fingers into cracks and heave my body up and up, until I'm high on the wall, near the battlements.

Sasha and some of the other children reach down to help me. "Grab on!" they shout, but I shake my head. *What if they can't pull me up? What if they drop me, or I accidently pull them over the edge?*

I look around for another handhold, but snowballs rain down, splattering my face.

The block I'm holding lurches, and my blood runs cold as I think I might fall. I grip on tighter, but the block keeps shifting and sliding.

"Grab my hand!" Sasha shouts. "Let me help you."

But I shake my head again. *I'm too big.*

I reach for the edge of another ice block, curl my fingers around it, and pull as hard as I can. But my body doesn't rise. My feet scramble against the wall, but they only weigh me down, and they ache and burn inside my boots.

Then the wall buckles and my heart stops. *I'm too heavy.*

"The wall is collapsing. Grab my hand. *NOW!*" Sasha leans farther until his fingers are almost touching mine.

I look down. Children scream as they scatter from the tilting section of wall. I look back up, at the long line of arms reaching for me from the safety of the turret, Sasha in the middle of them.

"Come on, Yanka!" he yells, and finally I reach for him— but it's too late.

My fingers slip through his as the wall drops away and I fall through the air.

I see the bullfinch, flying through a wolf-gray sky, and I hear him call my name. Then I see my boots as my head drops back and I wonder why the soft leather is splitting along the seams. And finally, I land hard on my back, and am swallowed into a thick, dark silence.

I wake hot, cloudy headed, and too heavy to move. Curtains ripple in the faint breeze drifting through the open window. I'm in my room, back in my and Mamochka's house, bathed in morning light. I wonder how I got here and how long I've been asleep. It feels as if a thousand years have passed since I was last awake.

The scuffle of Mousetrap hunting vibrates through the floorboards and the sounds and scents of Mamochka cooking breakfast rise from the kitchen below. I lie in bed, enveloped by the familiar feel of our house, and slowly the events of the festival come back to me: sledding with Sasha, struggling to carry Winter on my own, the bonfire blazing and the frozen river cracking, climbing the walls of the ice fort. Falling . . .

A groan rumbles in the back of my throat. I'm embarrassed for falling and upset to have missed the rest of the festival. I didn't realize how much I'd been looking forward to running through the fire maze to Mamochka, and later walking back with her and Sasha through a glowing sunrise.

I sit up and slide my legs out of bed. Several of Mamochka's herb compresses fall to the floor and a minty smell fills the air. My legs feel huge, and so, so heavy.

I'm still wearing the skirt Mamochka embroidered and

large furry boots. I frown at them in confusion. These aren't my boots. They're made from thick brown fur and have what look like long, dark claws on the toes.

The boots touch the floor and I lift them straight up again with a start. *I felt the floor!* The cold of the floor hit me as if these boots were my own skin. I peer at them closer. I wiggle my toes and the claws on the ends of the boots wiggle.

Hands trembling, I pull my skirt upward. The boots go on and on. Past my ankles, past my knees. Blood drains from my face and my heart thunders in my chest. These aren't boots. Or trousers. *These are my legs.*

CHAPTER FIVE

BEAR LEGS

My body locks up tight with horror, and the room sways. I gasp for air, feeling dizzy and sick. My legs are enormous. Thick and muscular. And covered in *fur*. My feet are so wide they're almost round, with great claws on the toes. Like a bear. *I have bear legs.*

I lie back and close my eyes. *This is impossible.* I open my eyes again and blink at the ceiling. *I'll sit up and my legs will be fine.*

But they're not.

I open my mouth to shout for Mamochka but end up holding my breath instead. I'm not sure why. I always go to Mamochka when I'm unwell, but this isn't aching feet or stomach cramps or chapped lips. *These are bear legs.* I brush my legs with my hands, desperately trying to sweep them away. But nothing changes. Touching them only makes them feel more real.

The fur is coarse and bristly and smells of the forest in spring. It's chestnut brown with flecks of yellow and black—like my hair. A cold wave of panic crashes over me as I wonder if the hair on my head has changed to fur. I shoot up to look in the mirror, but my balance is all wrong. My legs are too heavy, and my knees don't bend as I expect them to. I tumble forward, smack into the floor, and wail, even though I'm not really hurt.

"Yanka?" The stairs creak under Mamochka's feet. "Are you all right?"

I scramble back onto the bed and cover my legs with blankets. My face burns with shame.

Mamochka opens the door and smiles too wide. It reminds me of the way the people at the festival smiled—the way people smile when they're wondering why I'm different—and I realize Mamochka has already seen my legs. Tears well in my eyes. I didn't think Mamochka would ever look at me like that. I didn't think a smile could hurt so much.

"Oh, Yanka." Mamochka sits next to me and strokes my hair with trembling fingers. "I know this is strange, and you must be scared, but you're going to be fine. I promise." Her voice shakes like a nightjar's and anger burns inside me, because her words and body don't match—and that feels as wrong as my legs.

"How is this fine?" I throw back the blankets and glare at my feet. The sight of my legs and the sharpness of my words sting my throat. This isn't Mamochka's fault. I shouldn't be shouting at her. "What's happening to me?" I bury my face in my hands.

"You fell from the ice fort yesterday and were knocked

unconscious. Sasha and his parents helped me bring you back here and get you into bed. Then, during the night, your legs swelled and . . ."

"Became bear legs?" I feel my forehead crumple in confusion.

"They're not bear legs." Mamochka tries wrapping an arm around my shoulders but settles for hugging an elbow when she can't reach. "They're just injured. I've tried compresses for the swelling, infusions for the excess hair, and poultices on your thickened toenails, but . . ." Her voice trails off and she bites her lip.

"But what?"

"I think we should go to the hospital, in the town across the Great Frozen River."

I pull away from Mamochka and stare at her in shock. "But nobody from the village *ever* goes to the hospital. You can cure anything."

"I thought I could." Mamochka twists her hands together in her lap. "But I've never seen anything like this. I've tried birch buds and mustard, nettle seeds and charred pine cones, whitlow grass, bilberries, horsetail, bladder wrack . . . I even tried the ant oil and earthworm salve passed down from my grandmother. Nothing is making any difference."

My nose wrinkles at the thought of Mamochka smearing my legs with earthworm juice.

"I don't know what else to do." Mamochka's eyes fill with tears and fear creeps through me. Mamochka doesn't look like herself anymore. She isn't strong and unstoppable. She looks like a branch weighed down by too much snow. I feel my own eyes welling up.

"Oh, look at us, on the brink of tears." Mamochka flaps her hands in front of her face. "There's no need. I hear the doctors in the hospital can cure things herbs can't. They have special equipment, clever machines. Sasha will be here soon and—"

"Sasha?" My eyes widen in panic. "Why is he coming? Does he know about my legs?" Sasha is the only person who makes me feel like I fit into village life. If he sees me with bear legs, that's bound to change. I won't be Yanka the Bear because I'm big and strong. I'll be Yanka the Bear because I fell off an ice fort and grew bear legs. No one, not even Sasha, could ignore that.

"No one else has seen or knows about your legs," Mamochka says gently. "Not that it would matter if they did. The villagers care for you. Sasha came to ask after you at first light. I told him you were still sleeping and that I wanted to take you to the hospital, so he's gone to arrange transportation. The Great River won't have thawed enough for boats to cross yet, but maybe we could travel in one of those old biplanes that occasionally flies over the river."

The fear creeping through me bursts into a run. We've *never* left the village, never needed anything the forest couldn't provide. I'm scared—of what's happening to me, and of people seeing me like this, and of traveling to be poked and prodded by strange doctors far away. But before my thoughts can form into words, there's a knock at the back door and Mamochka jumps to her feet. "That'll be Sasha."

"Don't let him in!" I reach out to stop her rushing off. "I don't want him to see me like this."

"All right." Mamochka squeezes my hand before disappearing down the stairs. I hear her talking to Sasha, then the back door closes. "A plane will take us tomorrow morning," she shouts up the stairs. "They're sending a special one that can land on the river in melt." Mamochka pauses, as if waiting for me to respond, but too many fears are stuck in my throat and the thought of leaving is tearing me apart.

The day passes in a blur. Mamochka brings up a breakfast I don't eat and endless cups of heather tea I don't drink. Though she said her remedies weren't working, she still covers my legs with so many different herbs that I end up smelling like her medicine-mixing corner. She checks my pulse and temperature over and over and keeps telling me I'm going to be fine. But her too-wide smile and too-busy hands give away her worries.

I stare out the window, fiddling with my arrowhead necklace. I can't stop thinking about Anatoly's tales, and my own story wavering beyond my reach. These legs feel like more than something that needs to be cured. They feel like a clue to my past.

I want to talk to Mamochka, to tell her how I feel, but

she's cooking food and packing clothes for the trip tomorrow, rearranging things that don't need tidying, and dusting things that don't need cleaning.

Finally, when the sun sets, throwing long shadows across the garden, Mamochka stops bustling around and sits in the armchair beside my bed, sipping valerian root tea.

"Do you remember the story of the Lime Tree's curse?" I ask.

Mamochka frowns and shakes her head.

"Anatoly told it to us a few years ago," I press, willing her to remember. "It was about an enchanted tree, and a woodsman and his family who were cursed to be bears. I've been thinking about it all day and I'd love to hear it again."

"I'm not sure now is the time for one of Anatoly's stories." Mamochka sighs.

"But don't you think it's a strange coincidence? How that story was about people turning into bears and now my legs have become bear legs?" I look out the window, to the chattering pines at the bottom of the garden. "Maybe the answer to what's happening to me lies in the forest . . ." I whisper the suggestion, but it reverberates around the room like a shout.

"Your legs are *not* bear legs," Mamochka says firmly. "You're just injured in an unusual way. Falling from the fort must have triggered some kind of imbalance. I'm sure the doctors in the hospital will know how to treat you."

"How can you be sure?" My voice rises. I pull back the blankets and point at my feet. "Look at them. They're bear feet! They *must* have something to do with where I came from—the bear cave and the forest."

Mamochka's teacup wobbles in her hand. "Growing bear legs doesn't make sense. It's impossible. I don't know what this is, but it isn't bear legs, and there are no answers in the forest. There's only snow and ice, teeth and claws, and a million other dangers. I love you. I need to keep you safe. And that means dealing with this in the most sensible, rational way. We need to go to the hospital—not wander around the forest, chasing the stories of an old fool."

"Anatoly is not an old fool!" I yell. "Why do you refuse to believe his stories? Even now, when I have *claws*."

"Thickened toenails," Mamochka corrects, covering up my feet. "I'm sorry." She fusses with my blankets and blushes. "I shouldn't have called Anatoly an old fool. I care for him, and I like his stories. But they're only fanciful tales to fire the imagination. It's important to stay rooted in reality. Illnesses and injuries are things that need treatment with medicines, not stories." Mamochka cups my face in her hands and kisses my cheeks. "We should get some sleep. It's going to be a busy day tomorrow."

I open my mouth to argue with Mamochka. But I can't. She looks so small and tired and far away. I feel like there's an ocean between us, and my words wouldn't reach across it.

I lie in bed after Mamochka has gone, watching the last rays of sunlight fade and the moon rise over the treetops. Stories of the forest spin through my mind, especially the story of the Lime Tree's curse. I give up trying to sleep, and sit up.

Mousetrap emerges from a gap between the floorboards. He shakes the dust from his coat and sweeps a tuft of mouse fur from his nose. Then he scampers up into my lap and stares at me, his whiskers twitching expectantly.

"Do *you* remember the story of the Lime Tree's curse?" I ask.

Mousetrap shakes his head. Or at least I imagine he does.

"Then I'll tell it to you." I kick off my blankets and wiggle my toes. The long, dark claws on the end of my feet spread out . . . and right now, alone with Mousetrap in the moonlight, having bear legs doesn't feel so strange.

Mousetrap curls up and rests his chin on his rump, and I begin the story, as Anatoly would, with "Once upon a time . . ."

THE LIME TREE'S CURSE

Once upon a time, a woodsman found the soul of the forest. His axe fell from his hands and his eyes opened wide as he gazed at the tree that stood there. It was tall as the sky and wide as the sunrise, and it sang and danced with the wind.

From its branches grew birds, from its seeds sprouted streams, and from its leaves lifted lyrical poems.

With trembling fingers, the woodsman picked up his axe. *One branch*, he thought. *I'll take one branch of this enchanted tree and carve my son a cot to give him sweet dreams.*

But when the woodsman lifted his axe, the tree spoke in a voice of rustling leaves. "Don't cut me," said the tree, "and I'll give you a wish."

The woodsman's brow furrowed. He had everything he needed: freedom, food and shelter, the beauty and stories of the forest, and the love of his wife and son. Finally, an idea shone in his eyes.

"I wish for my family to always be healthy and strong."

The tree shivered, and seeds rained into the woodman's hands. "Plant these around your home, and fruits and herbs will grow to keep your family strong."

The woodsman thanked the tree and raced home to

plant the seeds. A garden bloomed, so full of health-giving foods that the woodsman's family would always be strong. The woodsman glowed with satisfaction, but he also started to wonder. What else could he ask of the tree?

Wants crowded the woodsman's mind, and desires ached in his chest. Before one moon had passed, he stood before the tree once more.

"Tree," said the woodsman, "I'm pleased my family is strong and healthy, but I'm poor. I wish for riches to give my son a bright future."

The tree swayed, and berries fell that hardened on the ground into luminous jewels. The woodsman rushed to gather the treasure and flew home feeling light as air. But after he stored the jewels, he yearned for something more. Before another moon passed, he was back at the tree.

"Tree," said the woodsman, "my family and I live in a small cabin. I wish we had a bigger home."

The tree shook, and a golden nut dropped. "Plant this and a castle will grow."

The woodsman's heart leaped. He beamed as he found a clearing in the forest, planted the nut, and then watched a castle rise from the earth, with rainbow walls and a shining golden domed roof. Delight bubbled in the woodsman, but still he itched for more. So he went back once again.

"Tree," said the woodsman, "my child is but the child of a woodsman. I wish to be a tsar, and my wife a tsarina, then our child would be respected and revered."

The tree shook its leaves and sighed. "Go home and be content."

But greed clawed inside the woodsman like a hungry wildcat, and his hands twitched upon his axe. "Give me what I ask, or I'll chop you down."

But the tree only turned to the sky and sang.

Consumed by greed, the woodsman roared in anger and chop . . .
. . . chop
. . . CHOPPED down a branch.
And the tree cried out in pain.

The woodsman froze, but it was too late. Tears of sap dripped onto the woodsman, cursing him forever. He ran home, filled with remorse, and held his family close.

And the tears of sap upon the woodsman touched his family too.

The next morning, the sun shone on the castle, and the woodsman and his wife woke with heavy heads—for he was a bear, and she was a bear, and their son was a fluffy bear cub.

Many moons passed before the woodsman and his wife grew accustomed to their new lives, but when they did, they found they were happy. They had freedom, food and shelter, beauty, stories, and love, and as the Bear Tsar and the Bear Tsarina, they were respected and revered by all the creatures of the Snow Forest.

Memories of their human lives faded, and their souls became the souls of bears. But their cub kept the soul of a human and often wished to be part of the human world once again. And so a battle began between a wish and a curse, one that goes on and on to this day.

CHAPTER SIX

THE BULLFINCH CALLS

I finish the story, look down at Mousetrap, and bristle with annoyance, because instead of listening to me, he's fast asleep. His head has fallen back, and a tiny thread of drool hanging from his mouth wobbles as he snores.

A breeze blows through the still-open window and washes away my irritation. I imagine leaving the house and breathing in great lungfuls of the cold night air, walking across the sparkling snow and slipping into the shadows of the forest. I imagine finding my story there: one that explains where I came from and what's happening to me now.

The thought stirs a deep longing inside me, but I push it away. Because it would be wrong to leave Mamochka. And it would be dangerous to go into the forest, alone, at night. But the idea is already growing, shivering in the air like an electrical storm.

A bullfinch lands on a branch at the bottom of the

garden and snow cascades to the ground. He ruffles his feathers and stares straight at me, and I wonder if he's the same bullfinch who has spoken to me.

"Yanka!" he calls, as if in answer to my thought. "Yanka the Bear!" He flutters up to my window and perches on the sill. "Come into the forest?" His head tilts in a question.

The urge to go outside is overwhelming, but I force my head to shake. "I can't leave Mamochka. I shouldn't," I whisper. "Please be quiet. Don't say anything else."

"Would you like me to silence him?" A small but mighty voice sounds in my ear. I whip my head around and nearly knock Mousetrap off my shoulder. I hadn't felt him climbing up there. I stare into his shining black eyes, my mind whirling in confusion.

"What did you say?"

"Would you like me to silence the bird?" Mousetrap repeats slowly, running his tongue over his tiny pointed teeth.

"No!" I exclaim, horrified by the suggestion.

Mousetrap slouches with disappointment. "Let me know if you change your mind." He sprints down my arm, leaps off the bed, and disappears into a gap between two floorboards. I stare after him. *Mousetrap talks too?* He made a series of squeaks and squeals, but I understood every word.

The bullfinch flutters away and I rub my eyes as if I've just woken. The moon shines high over the Snow Forest, turning everything silvery blue. The trees reach up to the stars, and secrets whisper between their branches. The bullfinch has stopped calling, but something else is drawing me toward the forest. Something far more powerful: answers to who I am and what's happening to me. I can't resist anymore.

My mind buzzes with plans and ideas. I have a copy of Anatoly's map. I could use it to find my way in the forest, to explore the places mentioned in his stories, and to look for clues to my past. I could take some food with me, and shelter in Anatoly's cabins when I need to rest. Anatoly has five cabins, scattered throughout the Snow Forest, and they're all labeled on my map.

Another gust of wind comes and ruffles the fur on my feet, and I can't wait any longer. I have to go. I lower my feet to the floor and tiny vibrations run into my swollen soles. It's Mousetrap, pattering beneath the floorboards. I can feel where he is, and something else too . . . the trembling of a mouse or a vole hiding from him. It's incredible, like having another sense, and I wonder what it will be like to walk over snow.

I stand and wobble across the bedroom, still not used to the feel of my legs, slip through the door, and emerge onto the landing, holding my breath. I'm not worried Mamochka will wake; she looked exhausted when she went to bed, and she always sleeps deeply after valerian root tea. But I still tremble with the thought of getting caught. If I don't reach the forest now, disappointment will crush me.

The size of my feet and the strangeness of my legs make the stairs a challenge. I end up sitting and half sliding, half bumping down them, like I used to do when I was little. At the bottom, I lift my coat off the peg by the front door and shuffle through the living room, pausing to collect my copy of Anatoly's map from the box on the mantelpiece.

All the food Mamochka cooked today is laid out on a marble slab in the kitchen. I slide a couple of *piroshki* pastries stuffed with cabbage and egg into my pocket and add a handful of dried apricots.

Then I lift a pencil and piece of paper from Mamochka's medicine-mixing corner and write her a note:

Dear Mamochka,

I can't go to the hospital. I'm sorry. I need to find more than a cure for these legs. I need to understand why they have grown, and how they relate to my past, and I think those answers lie in the forest.

I'll be careful. I have my map and some food, and I can shelter in Anatoly's cabins when I need to.

Please don't worry. I'll be back in a day or two.

I love you,

Yanka x

I stare at the note and frown. It's not a very good note, but I have no idea how to express the feelings I have inside. It would take a thousand words, and even then Mamochka wouldn't understand. And she'll worry no matter what I write.

My gaze drifts through the window to the garden beyond.

The moonlit snow is crisscrossed with small animal tracks running into the forest, and the branches of the pines at the bottom of the garden curl, as if beckoning me toward them.

The thought of Mamochka waking to find me gone tugs at my back, but the pull of the forest, and my story inside it, keeps growing stronger. I need to go. So I take a deep breath, place the note on the table, and walk out the back door, trying to ignore the stretching sensation in my heart.

CHAPTER SEVEN

INTO THE FOREST

I stand on the porch, feeling more awake and alert than ever before. Every drip and rustle echoes loud in my ears, and every scent sets my nose twitching. Tonight, the forest feels full of promise.

I lift the hurricane lamp from the hook outside the door. The moon is so bright I don't need to light it yet, but farther into the forest it will be dark. My claws click across the porch floorboards. I raise my toes to stop the noise, then take one last step into thick snow.

The ice crust prickles against the soles of my feet. Although it's cold, it's not uncomfortable. It feels fresh and exciting. I lift my skirt a little and watch my furry feet make giant bear tracks as I sway across the garden, trying to figure out the best way to move my legs and keep my balance. A smile creeps across my face and I suppress the urge to laugh. It's just so ridiculous and impossible. Like one of Anatoly's stories.

If a person can grow bear legs, then *all* the magical things

Anatoly has told me could be true. The arrowhead around my neck shines like the stars, and hope shivers inside me—hope that in the forest all the questions swimming through my mind will dry up with answers.

At the bottom of the garden I step beneath the trees and a gust of wind swirls around my ankles. Its icy fingers rake through my fur and I shudder. Branches snap in the cold, and shadows crowd me. Something scurries away through the dark, tangled undergrowth and the screech of an owl pierces the night.

My mind whirrs with thoughts of other things I might find deep in the forest too. There are dangerous things in Anatoly's stories—fire dragons who would burn your life away and Yaga who would steal your soul. But more frightening than them are the ordinary dangers I've been warned about since I was little: wolf packs on the hunt, steadfast and silent; angry boars that charge with the ferocity of rockfalls; vipers that dart from below; lynx that pounce from above; and wandering bears that might be startled into wild uncontrollable storms. And there are the tiny things that sneak up unseen: ticks and karakurt spiders, and though spring is coming, frostbite still crawls through the air. I suddenly feel as vulnerable as a chick fallen from its nest.

The safety and warmth of my and Mamochka's house tugs me back suddenly and I fight the urge to turn around. Because if I see the window behind which Mamochka lies sleeping, I won't be able to do this. And if I don't leave now, tomorrow I'll end up far from the forest, with doctors in an unfamiliar town. The answers I seek won't be there.

So with trembling fingers I check my map. Then, though it makes my eyes burn, I stare straight ahead and take the trail that runs north, deeper into the forest.

"You don't usually walk at night." Mousetrap leaps onto my shoulder, making me jump. "Where are you going?"

I frown at Mousetrap in confusion. "How is it I can understand you?"

"It's impolite to answer a question with a question," Mousetrap trills.

"Sorry," I say, almost more confused by Mousetrap correcting my manners than I am by him speaking. "It's just strange to be talking to you."

"Considering how long we've lived together, it's rather rude that you haven't before."

"I've talked to you lots of times," I protest. "It's *you* who has never talked to *me*."

"Of course I have." Mousetrap twitches his nose in irritation. "You just weren't listening."

I step around an aspen with a deeply curved trunk. "That's not true. I've always listened to you, and the birds, and the forest, but none of you have made sense to me before. Not like this."

"You obviously weren't listening hard enough."

I shake my head and sigh. This is about more than listening. Something about me has changed, beyond just my legs. Something deep inside. The thought is both exciting and nerve-racking, because although understanding animals could be wonderful, and all this change might help me discover the story of my past, I don't know what it means for my future.

"Don't feel bad about it." Mousetrap squeezes himself into my collar and curls around my neck. "Hardly any humans listen. At least you've tried. And you've always been kind to me, if a little overprotective of your garden birds." He smacks his lips together. "So if you're walking alone in the forest at night, I shall accompany you. You may need my protection."

A snort escapes from my nose.

"You find me amusing?" Mousetrap rises and rests his claws on my cheek. His black eyes flash tiny daggers of reflected moonlight.

"I don't mean to offend you," I say, "but I'm the biggest, strongest person in my village, and you're a tiny house weasel. How can you protect me?"

"You, human girl, know nothing of the Snow Forest. My ancestors hunted here long before humans came to this region, and their knowledge is in my blood." Mousetrap lifts his chin high and his tiny nostrils flare. "Just because my great-grandmother chose to move into your house to help with your mouse problem doesn't make her, or her descendants, lesser weasels. Do you know how skilled you have to be to hunt prey beneath your creaking floorboards?"

"I know you're a fine hunter." I nod. "I just wonder how you think you'll protect me in the forest."

"I have faced enemies more terrifying than you could imagine." Mousetrap settles back onto my shoulder and inspects his claws. They glint like metal and are needle sharp. "Once I was in your garden, stalking a rabbit, when an owl swooped down. He was three times the size of you. Talons, longer and fiercer than your boning knives, were poised to snatch me up. I leaped, twisted in the air, and landed on the owl's back. My teeth sank into his neck and he screeched with pain. The owl flapped frantically, trying to escape my attack, but my grip didn't weaken. Not even when the owl rose into the air. I clung on tight, and the owl carried me across the Snow Forest for three days and nights."

"Really?" I raise my eyebrows. There are no owls that big, and even if there were, I can't imagine Mousetrap riding one.

"You don't believe me?" Mousetrap puffs out his chest.

My face flushes. Considering I have bear legs and am talking to a weasel, it seems unfair I should doubt Mousetrap's tale. "I'm amazed, that's all."

I clamber awkwardly on all fours over a fallen cedar blocking the trail. Because my legs are so much bigger and stronger than my arms, I worry I'm going to tumble head over heels.

"I saw the whole of the Snow Forest in those three days, laid out beneath me like a blanket." Mousetrap waves a paw over an imaginary world beneath his nose. "This forest is so vast that when it's morning on the east side, it's night on the west side. It's so far-reaching that you could walk all day every day for months and never find the end of it. Which brings me back to my question—where *exactly* are you going?"

I slide a hand into my pocket and curl my fingers around my map. Feeling the paper is a comfort. The forest might be immense, and I might not know *exactly* where I'm going, but I have my map to guide me. "This trail runs north," I say confidently, "and Anatoly has a cabin along it. I'll probably stop for a rest when I reach it."

"And get some of his freshwater cod?" Mousetrap licks his lips. "That's a fine mission. How far away is it?"

"I thought you knew all about the forest." I glance at Mousetrap, suppressing a smile.

"I do." Mousetrap jumps off my shoulder onto a nearby branch. "But I don't bother myself with trifles such as the exact location of human cabins."

"I think we should get there in an hour or two," I say, hoping it's true. I'm not sure of the scale or distances shown on Anatoly's map.

"You think?" Mousetrap stops in his tracks and stares at me. "You mean you haven't been there before?"

"I have, but it was a long time ago." I think back to the last time Mamochka took me to visit Anatoly. I was about five years old and I ran off after a bird. Mamochka couldn't keep up and panicked, thinking I'd be lost forever. She found me, of course, but after that, she said it was safer for us to stay in our house and let Anatoly do the visiting.

My stomach tightens at the thought of Mamochka waking to an empty house. She was already upset about my legs, and me disappearing into the forest will give her even more to worry about. I look up into the canopy, hoping something will distract me. But guilty feelings are like thirst or hunger—they gnaw away at you and are almost impossible to ignore.

Mousetrap jumps back onto my shoulder and shakes the snow from his paws. "If the cabin is that far away, wake me when we get there." He scampers down the front of my coat and squeezes into my fur-lined pocket.

"What happened to protecting me?"

"This is a safe part of the forest," Mousetrap says in a muffled voice, and ends the conversation with a drawn-out, high-pitched yawn.

Trees close around the strip of star-filled sky above and I slow down to let my eyes adjust to the darkness. I don't want to light the hurricane lantern yet—I don't want the hiss and stink of the burning oil to overpower the sounds and scents of the forest.

Now that Mousetrap is quiet I realize how much I've been ignoring my surroundings. I need to pay more attention, be alert for dangers. I stop, hold my breath, and listen. Leaves rustle above me. A small bird hops along a branch, then flutters away. Frost crackles and icicles creak. Something scratches, scrambles, darts up a tree. The nighttime noises are unfamiliar. They move differently through the trees and echo louder in my ears. Fear tingles all around me.

I stand tall and take another few steps. The new weight of my feet and the feel of my claws are reassuring. They remind me I'm strong. Even stronger than before. I can cope with whatever dangers lie in the forest.

But then the trail dips into a tight knot of pines and every drop of starlight vanishes. I stop and squint into the darkness, fumbling in my pocket for matches. I stifle a groan as I realize I forgot to pick some up.

Then something moves ahead of me.

Something large.

It knocks a branch, sending a flurry of snow to the ground. My muscles tense.

The howl of a wolf, far in the distance, cuts through the air and shatters the strength I felt a moment ago.

"Mousetrap," I whisper, poking my pocket.

"Are we there yet?" he asks without moving.

I swallow back the lump that has formed in my throat. Asking for help feels like lifting a heavy log. I should be strong enough on my own. I peer between the trees again, but all I see is darkness. "I need your help," I say finally. "To see."

"To see what?"

"Something moved up ahead."

Mousetrap peeps out and sniffs the air. "It's a deer."

I sigh with relief and take a step forward.

Right into the path of a large gray wolf.

CHAPTER EIGHT

IVAN THE GRAY

My jaw drops open and I gasp at the sight of the wolf in front of me. He's enormous, larger than I imagined a wolf could ever be. His massive head is level with my chest, and his shoulders are broader than my own.

The wolf stares up at me. His golden eyes narrow, his ears fall back, and a growl rumbles from deep in his chest. The sound rolls over me like icy water, freezing my muscles.

"Leave!" the wolf barks. "I'm Ivan the Gray, and this is *my* part of the forest."

My mind sparks with a fleeting excitement that I can understand him. But then Ivan's dark lips scrunch upward, revealing long shining fangs, and he lets out an echoing snarl that seizes my heart.

One of the first things I was taught in the village, even before I learned to read or write, was what to do when faced with a wolf. So I know I'm meant to avoid eye contact, lower my head, and back away. But I've lost control of my body.

My eyes are locked on Ivan's and won't shift, and my claws sink deeper into the snow to root me in place.

"Leave!" Ivan barks again. Muscles ripple across his back, and his fur lifts, making him look even larger.

I draw myself to my full height and glare down at Ivan. It took enough strength and heartache to make the decision to leave Mamochka, so I'm not retreating now—not for a wolf or anything else.

"Let me pass!" I shout as loud as I can, but Ivan tilts his head, and when moonlight glints off his teeth, my voice cracks and wavers.

Ivan's mouth widens into a mocking grin. "You're weak. You don't belong in the Snow Forest." He prowls forward until his snout is less than an arm's length away. His fur smells like old rain and leaf litter, and his breath has the edge of something rotten.

Mousetrap trembles in my pocket and I'm overwhelmed by an urge to be strong for both of us. "Let me pass!" I repeat, and this time my voice holds steady.

Ivan stops still. He lifts his snout and breathes in, and recognition flashes in his eyes. But then he seems to shake it off—and he lunges, mouth open, straight toward my neck.

I drop the lantern and raise my arms to protect myself. Ivan bites down on my elbow, crushing it between his powerful jaws. I yell in pain and fall back. My spine smacks into the ground, punching the breath from my lungs.

Ivan's dark, wet nose is right above mine. Drool drips from his teeth onto my cheek. My muscles become quivering leaves. I push back with all my might, but Ivan presses down and bites harder. I struggle, trying to roll over or kick him off, and my arm knocks something. *My lantern.* I grab it and swing it at Ivan's head.

The metal base hits Ivan above his eyes. He yowls in pain and releases my arm. I scramble back against a tree and stagger to my feet, holding my throbbing arm against my chest. The skin on my elbow aches and burns, but I can't feel any blood trickling from the bite.

I stare at Ivan and he stares back. So many thoughts flicker in his eyes, and I wish I could read his mind as well as understand his words. Neither of us moves for what seems like an eternity. White clouds plume from our mouths and mingle in the icy air. Hot blood pulses through my veins, and my elbow pounds.

Finally, Ivan curls back his lips and snarls. He lifts a paw hesitantly, like he can't decide whether to attack again or dart away. His claws twitch. They're thick, dark hooks, as long as my thumb.

"You have a claw missing!" I exclaim. Pain and fear vanish as one of Anatoly's stories jumps into my mind—the story of the wolf claw he gave me.

"What of it?" Ivan growls.

I slide a hand into my pocket, and my fingers close around the claw. "I have it!" I'm so pleased it's still there that a smile bursts across my face.

Ivan's growl deepens but stops when I hold up the claw for him to see. "Where did you get that?" He leans closer and sniffs the claw, and his ears dip forward with curiosity.

"Someone gave it to me. They told me a baby girl tore it from a wolf." My cheeks flush with embarrassment because, standing here, in front of the mountain of muscle and fang that is Ivan, the story sounds ridiculous.

Ivan laughs, a throaty chuckle like cracking ice. I'm so relieved his attack seems to be over, a laugh rises in my own throat too.

"A human baby could not tear a claw from me." Ivan sits back and licks his paw. A shaft of moonlight falls over him, highlighting patches of white hairs in his gray fur that dust his muzzle and chin. He looks old, and so much smaller now.

I relax a little and look at the claw in my hand. "No, I don't suppose they could." I sigh and slide the claw back into my pocket. "It was just a story, made up to entertain me when I was young."

"I haven't heard a story in a long time." Ivan leans sideways and yawns. "Tell me."

Delight bubbles through me. To be fighting off a wolf one moment and then asked to tell him a story the next is as strange and magical as growing bear legs. And as I love telling stories so much, the words tingle on my tongue.

I lean against the tree behind me and slide down until I'm crouched level with Ivan. My elbow aches and I cradle it with my hand. Mousetrap pokes his head out of my pocket, then darts through my sleeve up to my shoulder. I lower my chin into the familiar feel of his soft body, no longer trembling but warm and relaxed as he waits for a tale to be told.

If Ivan notices Mousetrap, he doesn't say anything. He just stares into the forest like he isn't bothered whether I tell the tale or not. But his ears are turned to me. It reminds me of how Mamochka listens to Anatoly's stories while pretending she isn't.

I wonder, *If Mamochka was here, would she pretend I wasn't talking to a wolf?* I smile at the thought, then open my mouth and let the words of the story tumble out.

THE WOLF'S CLAW

Once upon a time, a wolf pack hunted beneath a high pearl moon. They stalked through the shadows, paws silent on the snow, and when the thrill of the hunt became too much to contain, they threw howls into the sky that splintered the night air.

The pack leader, a gray wolf with golden eyes, stopped still, one paw hovering above the snow. His ears turned to the faraway crunch of a tiny footstep and he lifted his snout high. Then he grinned a fangsome grin, because he smelled prey, plump and weak. Anticipation fluttered through the wolf. He took off after the prey, and in a whispering whirlwind his pack followed.

The wolves sped through the forest, swerving around trees and leaping over shrubs. But as they approached a sparkling glade, they slowed to a gentle sigh. They glimpsed a human child, not four seasons old, standing naked in the snow on pink, fleshy legs. The child giggled at icicles clinking in the boughs and burbled to the high, swaying branches. Leaves chattered back in the language of the forest.

But then the wolf stepped into the glade and all was silent. From behind the trees crept the rest of the pack, black and white and silver in the night. They watched their leader closely, shivering with excitement, waiting for the signal to attack.

The gray wolf licked his fangs and smiled. "Child," he growled, "you should not be here alone. My pack and I are hungry, and it's our duty to eat the weak so only the strong creatures of the forest survive."

The child turned to the wolf and spoke in the language of the forest. "I am strong, so I will live."

Laughter rumbled from the gray wolf. "Fight if you wish. If you're strong enough, you may earn your place in the Snow Forest." And he prowled forward, fangs bared.

But the child stared into the gray wolf's eyes with such courage and determination that the wolf stopped, dipped his head, and took a step back.

"Our leader retreats," whispered the wolves of the pack. "He fears the child."

"I have no fear," snapped the gray wolf. His fur bristled and he glowered at the child. "You're not stronger than me and my pack."

The child looked at the wolves to her right and to her left, and she lifted her chin high, for she felt the strength of the forest inside her.

"Attack!" snarled the wolves to their leader. "You must lead the attack."

The gray wolf hesitated again, confused by the strength radiating from such small prey. But the child was alone, and he was the leader of a pack. He darted toward the little girl, his lips drawn back, and the other wolves followed in his wake.

The child stood tall, raised her arms, and, in the moment before the gray wolf's paws landed on her chest, closed her fingers around one of his claws and pulled. The claw ripped free, and the wolf yelped as he fell to the ground in shock. The child giggled, and the wolf's golden eyes burned with anger and shame.

The wolf pack scattered in dismay that their leader had been overpowered by such tiny prey, and the gray wolf limped into the forest alone. That night, while licking his tender, injured paw in the shadows beneath the trees, the gray wolf vowed he wouldn't return to his pack until he had proven himself strong enough to be leader once more.

CHAPTER NINE

ALL BEAR

I finish the story quickly, leaving out the last bit. In Anatoly's version, the child wanders back to the cave where she lives with the Bear Tsarina, snuggles into her thick, warm fur, and falls asleep. That part feels too personal to share with Ivan.

Mousetrap wriggles deeper into my collar, and tiny snores drift up to my ears.

Ivan releases something between a snort and a sneeze. "Your story is impossible. A human child is not capable of ripping out a wolf's claw."

"The story might not be completely true, but maybe there's some truth in it," I suggest, echoing what Anatoly has always told me.

"Maybe." Ivan licks his lips and turns away. He looks as if he's about to leave and suddenly I want him to stay more than anything. I feel like he knows something that might help me.

"How *did* you lose your claw?" I ask.

Ivan's fur bristles. "A bear took my claw. A cub. But it was stronger than it should have been for its age. Unnaturally so." Ivan glares at my bear feet and I shift uncomfortably. "I lost the respect of my pack that night and—like the wolf in your story—I've vowed not to return to them until I've proven my strength." Ivan's eyes glow and tension chokes the air between us. "I never forget a scent. As soon as I breathed yours, I remembered you. It was long ago, and you've changed, but I remember."

"What do you remember?" I whisper, confusion whirling through me.

Ivan grins, all fangs and bloodred gums. "I remember you, but you don't remember yourself."

A howl rises, followed by another, and another. They echo from far in the distance, but goose bumps still crawl across my flesh. The ache in my elbow intensifies and I stand, pick up the lantern, and hold it in front of me like a weapon. I've been so foolish, staying and talking to Ivan when I should have continued toward Anatoly's cabin. I could be there now, safe and warm. But instead I'm here, chilled by cold winds and Ivan's words and the howls of dangerous wolves.

"My old pack is hunting." Ivan lifts his head proudly, but there's something sorrowful in his eyes. "If I were you, I'd find somewhere safe to shelter. You aren't stronger than my pack. And you won't be, even when you're all bear."

"All bear?" The confusion whirling through me escalates into a tumultuous storm.

Ivan looks at me pityingly. "Go deeper into the forest, then you'll understand."

I flinch as another chorus of howls soars over the tree-tops. Ivan's ears turn to the sound, followed by his whole body. He shudders, as if it's taking all his effort to stop himself from chasing after his pack. Finally, he bounds off in the opposite direction. I stare after him, cold inching down my spine. But it's not Ivan or the distant wolves that have scared me. It's Ivan's words: *even when you're all bear.*

He's wrong. I'm not turning into a bear. I push the thought away and listen for the howls or footfalls of the wolf pack. But I can't concentrate. Ivan's words have thrown me into chaos.

A small bird flutters above. "Yanka!" it calls. "Home in the forest!"

I shake my head and look back in the direction of the village. I don't want to hear the bullfinch, and I don't want to feel the snow against my bear feet anymore. I lift a foot, to take a step back toward Mamochka, but it's huge and heavy, with long claws at the ends of my toes. I can't go back like this.

"Yanka!" the bullfinch sings. "Yanka the Bear!"

I turn to the dark trail, touch my arrowhead necklace, and imagine it filling me with the courage of a warrior princess. The answer to what's happening to me lies deeper in the forest. I know it, the bullfinch knows it, and Ivan the Gray knows it too. Although his words have shaken me, they feel like proof I'm heading in the right direction. So I take a deep breath and walk on into the darkness.

I scratch my neck above where Mousetrap is huddled,

thinking it would be nice if he woke to keep me company. He stretches and yawns into my ear. "Is Anatoly's cabin close?"

"I hope so." I nod. "We walked a good distance before Ivan stopped us."

"The wolf." Mousetrap's nose twitches as he sniffs the air. "It was interesting how you dealt with him: a scuffle and a story. Not what I'd have done, but it was good of you to take control. I'd have hated to silence him."

"Silence him?" I raise my eyebrows. "Up until I told the story, you were hiding in my pocket, shaking like a leaf."

"I was not hiding." Mousetrap rises onto his hind legs and flashes his teeth. "I was assessing the danger before I attacked. I never silence a creature unnecessarily."

I press my lips together to stop from laughing as I picture Mousetrap fighting a wolf.

"And"—Mousetrap lifts his snout high—"just so you know, I never shake with fear. I shake with fury."

A snort of laughter escapes from my nose and I try to hide it by coughing.

Mousetrap's fur prickles against my neck. "You're being very impolite. But I'll forgive you because you don't yet understand how exceptional my hunting skills are."

"You said it was a deer." I glance sideways at Mousetrap.

"A deer?"

"When I asked you what the noise was, you said it was a deer. Not a wolf."

"You misheard me. I told you before, you don't listen

properly." Mousetrap squeezes back into my collar and starts snoring immediately.

I groan in frustration. I wanted Mousetrap's company, but I've only managed to offend him. He wriggles around so his back is pressed against my neck and I decide to settle for the comforting feel of his warmth instead.

The trail is narrow, barely visible in the darkness. With no way to light my lantern, my eyes ache from straining to see, and it takes all my concentration to make sure I don't drift from the path. Hours seem to pass before the trail twists out of the pines and becomes lit by moonlight.

A sled track scars the surface of the snow, and my heart lifts as I think of Anatoly riding across here. I wonder if he's in the cabin I'm heading toward. He'd be so surprised to see me! I imagine him taking me in to be warmed by his fire, maybe offering me some broth and bread. He might help me plan where to go next in the Snow Forest, to look for clues to my past. Energized by these thoughts, I walk faster.

Soon I spot Anatoly's cabin in a clearing at the top of a steep slope. It's as cold and dark as the night around it. No light from the small windows. No chimney smoke curling into the air. I know before I reach the door that he won't be here.

"Where do you think Anatoly keeps the cod?" Mousetrap sits up on my shoulder as I unbolt the door. There's no need for locks in the Snow Forest—people rarely wander this far from the village—but bolts keep out wolves and bears. The thick wooden door creaks open and Mousetrap runs down my arm, jumps off my elbow, and disappears into the pitch-black.

I step inside too, bolt the door behind me, and let out a long sigh of relief. Anatoly might not be here, but at least I've found somewhere safe to rest. I lean back against the door and so much tiredness crashes over me I nearly sink to the floor. But I need to get warm and check my wound from Ivan.

"Mousetrap?" I call into the darkness, and he scampers up my coat and rests a paw on my cheek.

"What is it, human girl?"

"Just checking you're all right."

"I'm fine, but I can't smell any cod." Mousetrap's furry face furrows.

"What about candles and matches?" I ask.

"Beside the log burner." Mousetrap points with his nose and I shuffle forward as my eyes adjust to the darkness. I find candles, light them, and spread them around until the shadows fall back and the room fills with a warm yellow light that reminds me of my and Mamochka's house. The sun will rise in a few hours and Mamochka will wake to find me gone. I look around to distract myself from the thought.

Anatoly's cabin is smaller than I remember but hasn't changed otherwise. It's neat and tidy and filled with practical things: pots and pans, metal tools and wooden hide-stretching frames, piles of leathers and furs, and sacks of grains and salt that hang from the rafters so mice can't reach them.

The cabin smells of Anatoly—of tea with lemon, fresh snow, woodsmoke, and old furs. I inhale to catch more of his scent and wonder when he was last here. Kindling and logs have been stacked in the burner and a tinderbox has been placed in front of it. It feels like he was expecting me, although it's more likely he leaves the cabin ready for his own return.

I light the fire and lift the already-filled kettle on top of the burner. Flames curl around the logs, and warmth ripples through the air. My hands itch as blood flows back into my fingers, and my elbow throbs where Ivan bit it. I peel off my coat and roll up my sleeve to examine the wound. The skin is blotched purple and blue but isn't broken. If Mamochka was here, she'd apply a Spongilla grass poultice. I pull my sleeve back down. *It's only a bruise.* I wonder if it was my coat that protected me, or whether Ivan chose not to bite too hard. His fangs were certainly sharp enough to pierce my flesh, if that's what he'd wanted to do.

"I still can't find any cod," Mousetrap grumbles from a high shelf stacked with jars and tins.

"Maybe there's something else you'd like?" I wander over and read some labels. "Pickled herring?"

Mousetrap screws up his nose. "I'm going hunting." He dives off the shelf and sprints toward a crack between the floor and the wall.

"Don't leave the cabin," I shout after him.

He pokes his head out of the crack. "I can take care of myself, you know."

"I know. It's just . . ." I want to ask him to stay, to keep me company, but the words won't form. "I'm sure I heard a mouse under the floorboards," I say instead.

"If there's a mouse, I'll catch it." Mousetrap nods and disappears into the crack. Emptiness swells in the room until I sense the tiny vibrations of Mousetrap's pawsteps through the soles of my feet.

The kettle whistles. I make a cup of tea while eating one of the *piroshki* I brought with me. Then I remember the necklace of sweet *sushki* that Mamochka gave me at the festival. It's still dangling around my neck, so I break off chunks of the hard, sweet bread rings and soften them in my drink.

I don't want to sleep until Mousetrap returns, so I sit in a chair by the fire and look at the stack of books on the table next to me. They're mostly tattered old volumes about hunting, fishing, and trapping. Loose pieces of paper poke out of them, covered in sketches of trap designs and small-scale maps. I notice a book of poetry and another of short stories at the bottom of the pile. As I move the uppermost books to get to them, a few pieces of paper drift free and float to the floor.

I lean down to pick them up and stop still when I read Anatoly's neat handwriting on the top of the nearest piece: *The Bear's Child.*

Ivan's talk of a bear cub and me not remembering myself

echo through my thoughts, and my fingers tremble as I pull the paper closer. It's one of Anatoly's stories. One I haven't heard before. His voice rises in my mind as I read the words, and with every sentence my heart beats faster—because maybe this is the story that will explain everything about me.

THE BEAR'S CHILD

Once upon a time, the Bear Tsarina, the strongest and gentlest creature in the Snow Forest, was asked to care for a newborn cub.

The Bear Tsarina's heart swelled with love and she promised to raise the cub as her own. Every day, the Bear Tsarina carried the cub on her back and showed her all the wonders of the Snow Forest, from the sunlight glittering in the canopy to the moonlight dancing on the streams. She showed her how to catch tender fish and find the sweetest, juiciest berries, how to dig dens among roots and make leafy beds that smelled of autumn all through the icy winter.

The cub loved all these things, but what she loved more was to watch the humans who visited the forest—the woodcutters, the trappers, the fishermen, and the gatherers of healing herbs. The cub was pulled toward humans as the river is pulled downstream.

No matter how much sunlight glittered in the canopy or how much moonlight danced on the streams, no matter how tender the fish or how sweet the berries, the cub always wandered away, distracted by the crunch of boots or the humming from a human throat.

Seasons passed, and the cub began to look and act like a

human too. She stood on two paws, laughed like a woodpecker, and sang strange, babbling songs. The Bear Tsarina's heart cracked open, because she feared she'd lose the cub to the human world altogether. As she had lost her own cub, many years before.

The Bear Tsarina watched from a distance, swaying from one great paw to the other, not knowing how to keep the cub, or how to say goodbye.

Sometimes the cub would roll in pine needles or talk to a bird, and the Bear Tsarina's heart would leap at the thought she might stay. But these moments were more and more fleeting . . . and then the Bear Tsarina realized it was too late. Winter was coming, yet the cub was losing her fur.

Cold, wet leaves gathered in mounds, and worry settled heavy on the Bear Tsarina. How could she prepare the cub to live in a world she didn't understand?

Then with the first deep snow, a lady came into the Snow Forest, collecting frosted hawthorn berries. The Bear Tsarina read the lady's soul and learned the lady had a kind heart and endless love to give. The cub's eyes lit up at the sight of the lady, and the Bear Tsarina knew it was time to say goodbye.

When the lady wandered close to the bear cave, the Bear Tsarina whispered into the cub's ear, "This is your mother. She'll take care of you now," and she nudged the cub out into the snow.

Though the Bear Tsarina knew the lady would care for the cub and help her live in the human world, her heart split in two. She rolled over, closed her eyes against the pain, and pretended to sleep as the cub stood on her back paws and walked away.

The last of the cub's fur fell and a smile warmed her cheeks as she looked up into the gentle face of the lady. Their souls swirled together, and the bear-child lifted her hands into the air, wanting to be held by the lady more than anything else. The lady picked her up and the child fit perfectly into her arms.

A tear rolled into the fur of the Bear Tsarina's cheek as the scent of the cub drifted away. She didn't know if she'd ever see the cub again. But as the Bear Tsarina sank into the deep sleep of winter, she heard echoes of the cub's laughter and she smiled, because then she knew that though the cub was gone, something of their souls would always be joined together.

CHAPTER TEN

YURI

I lean back in the chair and imagine Mamochka, arms folded over her chest, telling me the story is nonsense. A bear cub turning into a human child—it's impossible. But then I look down at my legs.

There's a blanket on the arm of the chair. I pull it over me, but it doesn't hide the shape of my legs, and my claws poke out. So I close my eyes.

A memory climbs into my mind, of standing on the Bear Tsarina's back, on *four paws*. I tell myself it's my imagination— that I'm fired up by what Ivan the Gray said and this ridiculous story. But it feels real.

The fur on my legs rustles and my claws splay wide as I stretch, and the sensations are suddenly familiar. Lost memories force their way to the surface . . .

I remember rolling over to cover my fur with the scents of dry earth; licking my snout with a long, wet tongue; my ears swiveling to the sounds of fish splashing.

I remember being *all bear*.

Cold creeps over me, and though I'm sitting still, I feel as if I'm falling through the air, about to crash into the ground.

I've spent my whole life feeling unsettled in the village, like I didn't fit. But it never occurred to me that might be because I'm not meant to be with people—with humans—at all. Maybe I'm meant to be alone in the forest. *As a bear.*

Tears spill down my cheeks. For Mamochka. For Sasha. For all the things I love about the village but didn't realize until now: the squat wooden houses that line the square; the hall with its carved, painted roof; the way everyone works together to build things for the festivals . . . even the way the villagers compare my strength to a bear's. It might have made me feel different, but it was usually meant as a compliment.

For the first time since I entered the forest, it occurs to me that I might never be able to go back . . . and that makes me feel more alone than ever. I open my mouth to call for Mousetrap, but the words stick in my throat and I find all I can do is squeeze my eyes shut and cry myself to sleep.

I'm woken by Mousetrap's whiskers tickling my cheek. I open my eyes and flinch as a dead mouse swings into focus right under my nose.

"I brought you breakfast." Mousetrap nudges the carcass closer. "You were asleep when I returned from my hunt last night, so I caught this one fresh for you this morning."

"No thanks." I wrinkle my nose and sit up.

Mousetrap looks from me to the mouse. His mouth draws into a thin, offended line. "What's wrong with it?"

"Nothing. I'm just not hungry." I slide my legs out from under the blanket and look at my bear feet. I knew they would still be there—I felt their weight—but that didn't stop me from hoping they might have disappeared. I wish none of this had happened. I wish I was in my house, with my own legs, having breakfast with Mamochka. My stomach rumbles at the thought.

"Not hungry?" Mousetraps looks at my belly accusingly.

"Not for mice." I snap a couple of bread rings off my *sushki* necklace and pop them into my mouth, then shuffle across the floor, getting used to the feel of my new legs again. I unbolt the door, eager to breathe in the morning air and clear my head of gloomy, fruitless thoughts.

Sunshine dazzles on the snow outside. I step into it, and the cold makes me feel awake and alive. A mouse darts through a tunnel beneath me, and the sensation is so magical I feel foolish for wishing away these feet. I lift my head into the air and laugh. "I have bear legs!" I shout at the trees, and my voice echoes back to me from every direction. Suddenly, I'm bursting to know more about my legs, and why I have them. I close my fingers around my arrowhead necklace. *Where shall I go today?*

I rush into the cabin, have a quick tidy-up, throw on my coat, and step back outside, unrolling my map. The sketch of the Blue Mountain pulls my gaze like it has its own gravity. *That's where I need to go.* The Bear Tsarina will be there, and I'll be able to talk to her, like I can talk to Mousetrap.

Meeting Ivan, hearing his words, and reading the story of the Bear's Child has convinced me there *is* truth in Anatoly's tales. And if anyone knows the truth, it would be the Bear Tsarina. She raised me for the first two years of my life, so she'll know who or what I am, and hopefully know why I'm changing now too. I need to find her.

The sun is high in the sky and I curse myself for sleeping in. Mamochka could be on her way here now, determined to find me and take me to the hospital. And the Blue Mountain looks far away, more than a day's walk. After struggling to see in the dark, and hearing the howls of the wolf pack, I'd rather not travel at night again. Which means planning a route that will get me to another of Anatoly's cabins before dusk.

I look at my map again. If I walk north along the banks of the Silver Stream, I'll pass two of Anatoly's cabins. It's a winding, indirect route, but it's easy to follow. And if Anatoly is in one of the cabins, he could sled me to the bear cave.

"Human girl," Mousetrap shouts, and I turn to see him hanging over the edge of the roof. "There's a store up here. It might hold Anatoly's cod, but I can't get into it."

I squint at the viewing platform Anatoly built on the roof. I had forgotten all about it. The last time I came here, when I was five years old, I was small enough for Anatoly to lift me onto it. The platform is the perfect place to get a look at the route I've planned, and it might give me an idea of exactly how far away the bear cave is.

"On my way," I call to Mousetrap, and bound through the snow to a ladder fixed to the far end of the cabin. I step onto it tentatively, worried it won't hold my weight, but each rung is thick and holds firm.

The view from the roof whips my breath away. The snowy forest stretches out as far as I can see. The enormity of it makes me giddy.

"Mousetrap, look!" My hand flies up when I spot the Blue Mountain in the distance, rising from the forest like a tooth.

But Mousetrap isn't paying attention. He's trying to break the lock on a small store while still babbling on about cod.

I unroll my map again and try to match it up with the landscape. The Silver Stream shines as it cuts through the forest. Though it's called a stream, it's actually a long, braided river—and in places it is as wide and deep as a lake. Its icy surface is breaking up, crumpling and shifting as channels of water start to flow. I can't believe it's already two days since the festival, when the Big Melt began.

I'm jolted by an echoing crash, a splash, and a piercing scream. My gaze darts along the riverbank below. The scream rises to an earsplitting screech and finally I spot the creature in distress—something large and leggy, maybe a deer or an elk. It's fallen through the ice at the river's edge and is thrashing around, trying to pull itself out.

"Help!" The creature's cries become words in my mind and I rush to the ladder, pushing my map back into my pocket. It takes too long to climb down, so I jump into the snow and run across the clearing. "I'm going to help," I call back to Mousetrap, but he's streaking alongside me already.

I pick up speed as the ground slopes away, and skid down the hill, snow avalanching ahead of my feet. Then I pause at the bottom to listen for the cries again.

"This way." Mousetraps sprints ahead of me and I follow him off the trail, through tightly packed pines, until the shrieks are so loud I know we must be close.

Bright light shines ahead, reflecting off the ice on the river. A young elk is struggling in the water at the edge. I can just make out his long brown face, two short velvety antlers, and two gangly legs skidding around in front of him as he fails to get a grip. His whole back end has fallen through the ice.

"Help!" he wails, and I rush toward him—but I stop in my tracks when I see a person behind a tangle of branches, kneeling next to the elk. They are wrapped in a huge coat with a fur-lined hood that covers their face. Mousetrap leaps onto my shoulder and squeezes deep into my collar, out of sight.

"Get off!" The elk shrieks as the person tries to loop a rope under his front legs. He cries for help again, his voice panicked and confused. I groan as I walk over because I don't want the person to see me like this. I'm scared their stare might wither away the last of my hope of ever fitting in with people. But I can't leave the elk struggling when I could help.

I glance down. My long skirt covers everything apart from my feet, and they *might* pass for boots. The person is so focused on the rope that they haven't noticed me approaching, so I kneel next to the elk, hiding my feet behind me.

"It's all right," I say gently, putting my hand on his warm, silk-soft snout. The elk's big brown eyes swivel toward me, wide with fear. I wrap my arms around his woolly neck, to prevent him from sliding farther into the river, and his legs stop thrashing. "I'm Yanka," I whisper into his ear. "I'm going to help you."

"Y-Yuri," the elk stammers. "I'm Yuri. Help me up. I'm so cold."

I turn to the person still fumbling with the rope, and my mouth drops open when he looks up at me with familiar gray eyes.

"Sasha! What are you doing here?"

CHAPTER ELEVEN

THE RESCUE

"I came looking for you," Sasha snaps, and I frown, confused by his annoyance. He loops the rope around Yuri's neck and under his front legs again. "They wouldn't let me join the search party, so I—"

"Search party?" My head whips around in panic. I don't want a group of villagers finding me and taking me back now—I have to make it to the bear cave and discover my story.

"They won't have gotten this far yet." Sasha glances up from the knot he's tying. "They were still gathering supplies when I left, and I've been skiing along the riverbank, faster than they'll travel through the forest."

A current swells and tugs at Yuri, and he thrashes against the ice. He kicks Sasha's wrist by accident. Sasha isn't hurt, but the rope falls from his hands.

I lower my arms farther into the river to tighten my grip on Yuri. Icy water trickles into my sleeves and I grit my teeth against the cold. "You shouldn't have come looking for me," I grumble. "I can take care of myself."

"Of course people are going to come looking for you." Sasha picks up the rope again and resumes tying a knot. His movements are quick and jerky. "You went into the forest alone at night. And after you'd been injured. What were you thinking?"

The anger in his voice bites like the icy water. Sasha has never been angry with me before. I groan and try to lift Yuri, but he doesn't budge.

Sasha finishes tying the knot and pulls the rope taut. It digs into Yuri's flesh and he lets out a high-pitched wail. "Don't cry," I whisper into his ear. "I know it hurts, but we're trying to help." I grip Yuri and pull as hard as I can while Sasha tugs on the rope. But Yuri still doesn't rise. "This isn't working."

"Maybe if we both pull the rope?" Sasha edges toward me, to make it easier for me to grab the rope, but I don't want to let go of Yuri even for a moment, in case Sasha can't hold him on his own.

I shake my head. "I just need a better grip." I lean deeper into the water, until it sloshes over the front of my coat and trickles between the buttons. I gasp at the cold but manage to reach my arms farther around Yuri's chest. Strength surges through me, and Yuri rises as I pull . . . But then the ice under me tilts and dips.

"Watch out!" Mousetrap squeals in my ear as a crack

opens between me and Yuri. Yuri screams as he crashes fully through the ice. A wave of freezing water splashes over my face, and for a moment I can't see anything but bubbles and light.

Yuri slips from my arms, and before I can reach him again, a current grabs him and whooshes him away, a dark blur beneath the frozen surface. The rope burns through Sasha's palms and he yells in pain.

I jump to my feet and run after Yuri, across the frozen parts of the river.

"Stop!" Sasha shouts. "You'll fall through the ice too."

But saving Yuri is all I can think about. I pick up speed, moving across the bluer, thicker ice, until I'm ahead of him. Then I choose a place where the ice is thinner, lift a foot, and smash it into the crust.

The ice cracks. I hit it again, and again, until a hole opens. Then I drop to my belly and plunge my arms into the hole, right up to my neck.

I'm so focused on the outline of Yuri flowing toward me that I don't feel the cold. He slams into my arms and I wrap them around him, lock my fingers tight together, and heave. But he's too heavy. The current drags him away. I roar with the effort. Blood and heat surge into my face. But I can't pull him from the water. And I feel myself slipping and sliding into the hole.

Sasha appears at my side. He lowers his arms next to mine and grabs Yuri too. With us both struggling together, gradually Yuri emerges. But his eyes are glazed over and he's worryingly still.

"I think he's dead," Sasha whispers as we pull Yuri's back legs onto the ice.

I shake my head, my eyes burning. "He just needs to warm up." I rub Yuri's chest and move his legs up and down, trying to get his blood flowing. *He asked me to help him.* He told me his name and calmed down when I held him. He already feels like more of a friend than most of the people in the village. *He can't be gone.*

Sasha lowers his face to Yuri's snout. "He's not breathing."

My vision blurs. I should have been strong enough to save him. I thump Yuri's chest, and the ice beneath us wobbles.

"We need to go, Yanka. It isn't safe here."

But I carry on pummeling, trying to wake Yuri's heart. My fist pounds into him, and the ice beneath us splits. A crack spreads in a jagged circle around Yuri, and between me and Sasha.

"Come on!" Sasha shouts, but I can't take my eyes off Yuri. There *must* be a way to save him.

The crack widens and water surges into it. I look up at Sasha in desperation.

But he's staring at my feet, with their thick fur and long dark claws. Above them my skirt is wet, clinging to my legs, revealing their new size and shape.

Sasha's face pales and his forehead crumples. And with that look, everything changes. Any lingering desire I had to return to the village rushes away. Because Sasha, my only friend, the only person besides Mamochka who has always treated me like I belonged, is now staring at me the same way everyone else stares at me—like I don't fit.

My world shatters. Mamochka's too-wide smile. Sasha's look of horror. If the two people I love react like this, how would the rest of the village behave? I wouldn't be surprised if they screamed and drove me back into the forest, the way they drive any bears back that wander too close to the village.

I don't belong in the village, or with people, at all. I never have—and like this, I never will.

My face smolders with shame and disappointment and a million other emotions I don't understand. I roar as loud as I can, from the depths of my lungs, and the great thunderous rumble of an angry bear echoes along the river.

"Yanka, please." Sasha reaches for my hand. "Come with me. I want to help."

For a moment my fingers twitch toward his, but it's a hopeless wish for something already gone. I've changed too much, and everything between me and Sasha, and me and Mamochka, and me and whatever life I had before, is gone.

I reach up to check whether Mousetrap is still curled around my neck, then I smash a foot into the crack between me and Sasha and push hard. The great chunk of ice Yuri and I are on breaks free and the current pulls us away.

"Yanka! What are you doing? Wait! Stop!" Sasha surges up, as if he's going to leap onto the floe with me, but I'm too far away already. He sprints after me along the riverbank instead. But the current speeds me away faster than Sasha can run. I sit, paralyzed by the realization of what I've done. There's no turning back now.

My stomach lurches as the ice floe tilts and sways. It speeds me across the river and around a bend. Sasha is left on the other bank, his arms loose at his sides. I swallow back the urge to shout for help. Another twist around another bend, and Sasha disappears behind the trees.

All the cold comes at once. I'm drenched, right up to my neck. I grab on to Yuri as the floe pitches sideways. He groans, then coughs. Water sprays from his mouth and nose.

"You're alive!" I hug Yuri's woolly neck. He rolls his eyes up at me and shivers. "We need to get off this thing." I look around, desperately trying to think of a plan. But we're sailing far from the shore, and there's nothing I can grab to pull us closer.

Mousetrap runs down my arm and jumps onto Yuri, where the rope is still tied around his neck. "Could you use this?"

I try to untie the knot, but my fingers are too frozen to feel the rope in my hands.

"Here." A moment later, Mousetrap drops a frayed end into my lap. He's nibbled through the rope. I thank him, although my teeth are chattering so much I'm not sure he understands.

We swerve toward another bend. On the far side of it, a thick branch overhangs the river. I gather up the rope in my arms and flex my hands. Blood flows into my fingers, making them sting like nettle burns.

I hold my breath, wait until we're almost directly underneath the branch, then fling the end of the rope into the air. It flies over the branch but tangles in a clump of frosty twigs. I growl in annoyance, because the twigs don't look strong enough to hold our weight.

The floe slides under the branch, and the rope lengthens, then pulls taut. Twigs snap, the branch creaks, and we swing sideways, making Yuri slip toward the water.

I grasp his neck with one hand and hold the rope with the other. For a sickening moment I think we're going to flip into the river, but then we pick up speed, swerve toward the bank, and smash into the shore.

"Quick, get up," I shout. Yuri struggles onto his front hooves, and the floe tips as he scrambles off. He lands in a heap, chest heaving, his back legs dangling in the river.

I rise to my feet, lose my balance, and skid into the icy water up to my waist. I brace myself for the cold, but the fur on my legs protects me from the worst of it. I dig my fingers into the frozen earth and, with a great heave, pull myself up.

"Mousetrap?" I gasp.

"I'm here." His whiskers tickle my ear.

I lift Yuri's back legs out of the water and push him under a pine, where low boughs have shielded the ground from snow. Then I collapse against him to catch my breath. I pull my coat tight around my chest but it's soaking wet and I shiver hard.

"You need to get dry and warm." Mousetrap leans over my face. "You can't rest now."

But I'm so cold and so tired that I close my eyes and can't help falling asleep.

When I wake, it's dark and I'm frozen numb.

"Thank cod," Mousetrap chirrs into my ear. "I've been trying to wake you for hours. We have to go."

"What's wrong?" I wheeze. Ice cracks on my lips.

"Wolves," Mousetrap hisses. "A whole pack of them, circling closer. I think they're after your elk."

CHAPTER TWELVE

THE WOLF PACK

Yuri is frozen stiff, his breathing weak. I rub his neck and chest until he stirs to life.

"Hold him tight," Mousetrap barks.

"Why?"

"Because he'll bolt when he smells the wolves, and they'll run him down easily in the state he's in."

I wrap my arms around Yuri's neck as he takes a deep breath and opens his eyes.

"Wolves!" he squeals. His eyes roll in their sockets and he struggles to stand.

"Prey animals," Mousetrap scoffs. He jumps onto Yuri's head and talks into his ear. "You're all the same, fleeing at the first whiff of danger. But you shouldn't do that with wolves. They'll chase you into a trap—a thicket or a gully—then they'll be on you before you know what's happened."

"Help!" Yuri cries, and his hooves thrash against the earth.

"You're making him panic." I glare at Mousetrap and

tighten my grip on Yuri. "It's all right. I'll protect you. I promise." My voice is steady, the opposite of how I feel. But acting strong for Yuri is like scaffolding for myself.

"You'll be my herd?" Yuri stops struggling and looks from me to Mousetrap.

"For now." I nod. "Come on. Get up." I help Yuri onto his hooves. He's young but already tall enough to look me in the eye. "We'll follow the river." I stare into the shadows upstream, wondering how far away Anatoly's next cabin is. I don't know where we are, and it's too dark to read my map.

Mousetrap points his nose into the pines, away from the river. "I smell food cooking and hear singing on the breeze."

I listen and sniff the air. But I don't hear singing or smell any food. "Are you sure? I remember the map showing Anatoly's cabin on the riverbank, not among pines."

"Of course I'm sure." Mousetrap scowls so ferociously I lower my head and walk in the direction he suggested. My clothes are crusted with ice and I'm frozen to the bone. If I'm going to survive the night, wolves or not, I need shelter. And it's possible Anatoly's cabin might be a little way into the forest but still look close to the river on the map.

Yuri and I make so much noise walking between the tightly packed trees that it's impossible to listen for stalking wolves. And if there are any, they'll know where we are.

Mousetrap reluctantly leads us down a slope, muttering that it's too far to walk around. He orders us to be quiet, but we skid down the hill on slush and collapse at the bottom in a series of splashes and thuds.

Suddenly, Yuri screams—the same deafening, earsplitting noise he made when he fell through the ice. I frown at him, confused—then make out a writhing dark creature on top of him.

A wolf. Teeth flash as they bite into Yuri's rump.

Before I can move, a second wolf darts in and grabs one of Yuri's back legs. Another surge of movement, and a third lands on one of his front legs too.

My gaze flits from wolf to wolf as I try to work out what to do. Panic speeds my heart and fogs my brain. Mousetrap trembles on my shoulder—then leaps into action.

He moves like a streak of copper through the dark, bursting from one wolf to the next. Yelps rise into the air, followed by snarls and barks. Mousetrap bites a nose, tears an ear, nips an eyelid. He moves so fast he's out of range by the time each wolf snaps at him.

Yuri lurches up, kicking out at the wolves as he staggers away. A hoof lands in a stomach, and a wolf yowls in pain. But it jumps back up, baring long, gleaming fangs.

Finally, my muscles surge to life. I push past Yuri, and a roar explodes out of me, so loud that the forest shakes with the force of it.

The wolves scatter instantly into the trees. And I stare after them, lungs burning, unsure if I'm more shocked by the noise I made or them fleeing.

"Come on. Before they regroup and attack again." Mousetrap runs up my arm. He's still trembling, licking blood from his teeth, and I realize he does shake with fury after all.

"You were brilliant," I whisper to Mousetrap as I step over a ditch to Yuri.

"I know." Mousetrap curls around my neck. His tiny body burns with heat. "You needn't sound so surprised though. I told you I've exceptional hunting skills."

Yuri groans and I peer at his wounds in the dim starlight. Spots of blood ooze from bite and claw marks on his back and legs, and there's a nasty open cut on his rump. It's the sort of wound Mamochka would close with aloe leaves and smother with a balsam she makes from beeswax and sandalwood and other secret ingredients. Just the memory of its scent is healing.

"How are you feeling?" I ruffle the woolly fur around Yuri's neck.

"Sore." Yuri snorts. "And cold."

"Keep walking," Mousetrap urges. "It isn't far now."

Guided by Mousetrap on my shoulder, I lead the way, attempting to clear a path for Yuri, who keeps getting tangled in knotted shoots and thorny briars. Though my muscles are working hard, I'm ice-cold. The forest here feels hostile, like it's trying to block our path.

Finally, despite the wind pushing us back, yellow light glows through a snarl of spiky branches ahead. I squeeze between two gnarled old tree trunks, which seem to move closer together to shut us out, and see a clearing and the corner of a cabin.

"Stop." Mousetrap grabs my ear, and his sharp claws pierce my skin.

"What?" I snap. "It's one of Anatoly's cabins."

"No, it's not."

"Of course it is." I try to brush Mousetrap's paw from my ear without knocking him to the ground. "Only Anatoly has cabins in the forest."

"I smell bones." Mousetrap sniffs the air.

"So? You said you smelled cooking before, remember?"

Mousetrap's claws dig deeper into my ear. "You don't understand. I smell human bones."

CHAPTER THIRTEEN

THE HOUSE WITH CHICKEN LEGS

"It can't be real," I whisper, scanning the skull-and-bone fence for evidence it's fake.

"It smells real." Mousetrap's tail tightens around my neck. "I was wrong to lead you here. We should go."

I nod but don't move. I can't pull my gaze from the fence. Icicles drip from long chains of vertebrae strung between upright bones. Skulls balance on top, candlelight creeping out between missing teeth and through empty eye sockets.

The villagers tell stories about Yaga—witches who live in houses with chicken legs surrounded by skull-and-bone fences. In their stories, Yaga eat lost children and steal their souls. But in Anatoly's stories, Yaga aren't cannibals. They're linked with death though, so I've never been sure if they're good or bad.

I look at the house behind the fence. It's a small log cabin, not unlike my and Mamochka's. I can't see any chicken legs, and I picture Mamochka shaking her head and telling me what nonsense that would be. But still, something about the house lifts the hairs on the back of my neck.

The lines of the windows and door curve, making the shape of a face, and as I stare, they change expression.

"Let's go." Mousetrap pushes my neck with his tiny paws. "A fence of human bones is a sure sign you're not welcome here."

I itch with curiosity about the house and ache to rest somewhere warm. But Mousetrap is right. The skull-and-bone fence is not a welcoming sight.

I sigh and turn away, but as I do, the house screws up one side of its wooden face and winks. "Did you see that?" I gasp, but Mousetrap has disappeared into my pocket and Yuri is lying down, facing the other way, quietly whining.

The door creaks open, and a girl steps out. She's about my age, small and slight, with dark hair and big round eyes. I step behind the nearest tree and hold my breath.

"Hello?" she calls. "Are you lost? Do you need help?"

I stand stone-still, hoping she'll think it was an animal she heard. She looks like an ordinary girl, and her words are friendly. But she lives in a winking house with a skeleton fence. She *could* be a Yaga, and she *could* be the kind who eats lost children. I curse myself for not leaving as soon as Mousetrap suggested it.

"Don't be scared." The bone gate rattles open, and footsteps crunch toward me. My heart accelerates like a bird taking flight. Mousetrap trembles in my pocket, and Yuri lowers his head to the ground.

If she's a Yaga, I should run. And if she's not a Yaga, I should still run because I don't want her to see my legs. I can't face another reaction like Sasha's, or any more stares that confirm I don't belong with people.

The girl steps so close I hear her breathing. My leg muscles tighten like springs. Then they release, and I try to sprint away. But my foot slips on slush and I fall backward, smacking my head against a tree and landing hard on the ground, legs in the air. Pain shoots down my spine, and my head rings.

"Are you all right?" The girl leans over and offers me a hand. "I'm Elena." She must see my bear legs, but she doesn't appear shocked or scared. She doesn't look at me like I'm different at all. Elena just smiles a big, wide smile that makes her whole face light up. And for some reason, that makes my eyes sting with tears.

Bones clatter behind me, and the groan and grate of moving wood echoes through the forest. Yuri scrambles to his feet and I try to do the same, thinking a tree is about to fall, or a skeleton is about to jump on me, or both. But my limbs aren't working, so I squeeze my eyes shut and brace for impact.

Light runs across my eyelids but nothing hits me, so I peep my eyes open again and flinch at the sight of one of the house's windows right above my head.

"What are you doing?" Elena hisses at the house. "You'll get into trouble again."

The house swings up and away, and a huge shadow falls over me. It's a massive foot, scaly like a bird's but made of wood, and it plunges straight toward me.

"Stop, you dastardly witch house!" Mousetrap darts up to my shoulder and flashes his teeth.

The foot hesitates. Then a clawed toe unfurls and pokes one of my legs. My muscles jump to life and I roll out of the way, but the rest of the wooden toes spread out and wrap around my waist. I scream as the foot grips me tight and lifts me, like I weigh nothing at all. I'm vaguely aware of Mousetrap growling as he attacks the house's ankle.

"What's going on?" an older woman's voice shouts from the porch above. "House. Put that girl down."

My head spins as I sail through the air toward the porch steps. Floorboards rise impossibly to cradle me as I land. Gray spots cloud my vision and I groan. I don't want to pass out. I can't pass out. Not now. This is a house with chicken legs. The home of Yaga who eat lost children and make fences from their bones. I imagine my own skeleton becoming part of the fence, and for a strange, calm moment I wonder if my oversized bones would fit in with the rest or stand out, like I do in life. Then Mousetrap nips my ear, bringing me back to the present.

"We're meant to be guiding." The older Yaga woman prods the porch canopy with a broom. She's short and round, wearing an angry scowl and a headscarf decorated with skulls. "You should be scaring away living souls, not picking them up and putting them on your porch. When are you going to stop getting distracted by every little thing that stirs your curiosity and start taking your responsibilities as a Yaga house seriously?"

"She needs help." Elena appears next to me and puts a hand on my arm. "She's frozen, and wet through. And look at her elk. It's bleeding."

Yuri is lying at the bottom of the porch steps, still whining. I try to work out what's happened. Yuri hasn't moved toward the house. But the house has moved toward Yuri. I hold my head to stop it spinning. Maybe this is all in my imagination and if I hold my head tight enough I'll wake up in bed, without bear legs, and none of this will have happened at all.

"For spirit's sake." The Yaga woman leans over me and frowns. "Whatever state she was in before, she's worse now. Getting grappled by your great chicken feet is enough to send anyone into shock. Elena, get some blankets and tea. And you . . ." She glares up at the house. "Open the Gate again so I can finish guiding before we bring her inside."

At the mention of being taken into the house, my heart starts thumping like a snow hare's foot. What if my story ends here, with me being eaten by Yaga deep in the forest?

CHAPTER FOURTEEN

ELENA

The Yaga disappear indoors and I push myself up to sitting. But a hot, sickening darkness rushes around me and I collapse back down. Tears flood my eyes with frustration at not being strong enough to stand.

"Come on, human girl. Get up." Mousetrap pushes the back of my neck, like he could lift me himself. I manage to sit up again, but my legs won't work.

"It's all right." Mousetrap stands on my shoulder, his teeth and claws poised for attack. "If you can't run away yet, I'll protect you until you can."

I remember how Mousetrap took on the wolf pack and I can't help but smile. I exhale slowly and focus on trying to move my feet. A sharp cramp seizes one of them and I stifle a cry of pain.

The porch balustrades curl around my back, helping to support me. One of the wooden spindles snaps free and reaches toward my hand before erupting with bright white blossoms. I blink at them in confusion.

"Aww. The house likes you." Elena sweeps back through the doorway with a beaming smile, a bowl balanced on her head, blankets under her arms, and a steaming tray in her hands. She unloads everything onto the porch and tucks fire-warmed blankets around my chest and legs. The cramp in my foot subsides and my body tingles back to life.

I stare at Elena, unsure whether to be scared or grateful. She finishes fussing with the blankets, pours tea into a mug, and passes it to me. I shake my head. The tea could be poisoned, her friendly smile some kind of trap.

"What happened to your elk?" Elena asks, picking up the bowl and a small basket of mushrooms. She edges closer to Yuri, strokes his neck, and places the basket under his nose. He munches the mushrooms before I can tell him not to. "Was it wolves?" Elena takes a cloth from the bowl and washes Yuri's wounds. He stops whining and becomes so calm I wonder if Elena is using witchcraft on him.

"She doesn't seem dangerous," Mousetrap whispers into my ear. "Maybe I was right to bring us here after all."

The roof nods in agreement. "Your house—" I say without thinking, then press my lips tightly shut. I'm still not sure I should talk to a Yaga.

"Our house is special." Elena smiles. "I'm sorry if it scared you. It's young and still learning how to behave." She moves away from Yuri and sits on the porch steps, closer to me. "It annoys my mother because we're supposed to remain hidden in the forest, but the house is terrible at it. It's far too friendly and curious."

"Are you witches?" The question falls from my mouth before I can stop it.

"No." Elena shakes her head. "Not the sort you think we are anyway. We won't eat you." She winks. "I promise."

I glance toward the bone fence.

"Oh, those bones are so old." Elena laughs. "They're just decorations that have been passed down for generations. They beckon the dead."

"Beckon the dead?" A chill runs through me and I wish I had accepted the mug of tea, if only to have something warm to hold.

Elena glances at the door, then leans closer to me. "We guide the dead to the stars," she whispers. "But it's meant to be a secret, so don't tell my mother I told you."

I nod slowly. I'm not sure what guiding the dead is, exactly, but Elena has such an easy smile, I can't imagine it's anything bad.

Music swells inside the house; the excited strumming of *domras* accompanies the rhythmic thumping of dancing feet. The bone fence rattles and the flaming skulls sway as the whole house heaves and bobs in time to the beat. A window slides open and I smell rich creamy food that makes my stomach rumble.

"Are you hungry?" Elena asks. I follow her gaze to the tray. As well as tea, there's a bowl of mushroom stroganoff, a couple of fish rolls, and a thick slice of rye bread.

"I'll sample the foods." Mousetrap leaps off my shoulder and rushes to the edge of the tray.

"Oh! A weasel! Is he your pet?" Elena breaks off a small piece of bread and places it in front of him.

"I'm nobody's pet." Mousetrap scowls.

"He's so cute," Elena exclaims, clearly not understanding Mousetrap's squeaks and squeals. Her finger hovers over his back, like she wants to stroke him, but Mousetrap flashes his canines, steps over the bread, and pulls a fish roll from the plate.

"The food is good," he mumbles. "You should eat."

But I hesitate, still unsure whether we're safe. Then a dog bounds out of the front door and skids to Elena's feet.

"Wolf!" Yuri screams.

"That's not a wolf, it's a dog . . ." My jaw drops open. "That's one of Anatoly's dogs—Nessa." Instantly, I'm on guard. The Yaga must have eaten Anatoly, because he *never* leaves his dogs. "What have you done with Anatoly?" I demand.

"She hasn't done anything with Anatoly." Nessa rolls her eyes and rests her head in Elena's lap. "Elena and her mother are Anatoly's friends."

"Do you know Anatoly?" Elena asks, ruffling Nessa's ears and leaning down to kiss her snout.

"Yes, he's my—" I search for the right word, but can't find one. "How do you know him?" I turn the question around, still suspicious. Anatoly never told me he has friends in the forest.

"Anatoly and my mother have been friends for as long as I can remember. He often leaves his dogs with us when he goes exploring. He likes collecting stories for his bear-child—" Elena's eyes widen. "That's you, isn't it?" She looks down at my feet and blushes. "I should have guessed. I was distracted by you falling, then the house moving, then your elk . . . You're Yanka." She beams. "I've always wanted to meet you. I've heard so much about you from Anatoly, you almost feel like family."

My face burns with annoyance. "He never told me about you."

"Oh, he's not allowed to. My mother made him promise. Yaga—people who live in houses like ours—are very secretive. Because of the whole guiding-the-dead thing." Elena's eyes sparkle. "I bet he's told you a few tales though?"

I nod, thinking of all the stories Anatoly's told that mentioned a house with chicken legs. He said there was truth in them!

"I'd love to hear one." Elena pours a fresh mug of tea and offers it to me. "I could tell you which bits are true."

This time I accept the tea, take a sip, and sigh as heat trickles into my body. "There's the story of the Bear Tsar and the Yaga." I glance up, wondering if Elena knows anything about humans turning into bears.

"I haven't heard that one." Elena smiles and leans back against the porch balustrades.

Mousetrap finishes the fish roll he's been eating, wipes his whiskers, and burps loudly. Nessa, Yuri, and the house's front windows all turn to me expectantly. And so I begin the story, as Anatoly would, with "Once upon a time . . ."

THE BEAR TSAR AND THE YAGA

Once upon a time, the Bear Tsar, the king of the forest, found a crumbling castle hidden behind towering pines. Golden paint peeled from its onion-domed roof, and brambles crowded its great halls.

The Bear Tsar's fat, furry brow crumpled. The castle felt familiar, but he didn't understand why. He was old, and his memories had faded. So he lay down, rested his chin upon his paws, and tried to remember.

Images shimmered at the edges of his mind: dancing with a lady, telling stories to a child. The Bear Tsar felt he had lived here once, with a wife and child. But he couldn't remember when, or where his family was now.

The Bear Tsar longed to know the truth. So he rose onto his huge paws and set off to ask the help of the Yaga, who lived deep in the darkest part of the forest. A witch and a sage, the Yaga was said to hold all the wisdom of souls departed.

"Don't go!" cried the birds. "Baba Yaga has iron teeth that will crunch you up."

"My hide is tougher than iron," laughed the Bear Tsar. "She'll not crunch me up."

"Don't go!" wailed the tree spirits. "Baba Yaga's cooking pot can boil ten bears."

"I'm the Bear Tsar, stronger than twenty bears. She'll not get me into her cooking pot."

"Don't go!" howled the wolves. "Baba Yaga will steal your soul and send it to the other world."

"I'm old." The Bear Tsar sighed. "My soul is leaving this world soon anyway. I want to remember my life before I go." And he stopped before a fence of skulls and bones.

Behind the fence a wooden house rose up on chicken legs and turned to face the Bear Tsar. Its windows blinked like eyes, and its door opened like a mouth yawning.

Out stepped a Yaga, with bony legs and crooked teeth. "What do you want?" she snapped. "I have no time for bears."

"Please, dear Yaga, help me remember my life. I believe I had a wife and child once, and I want to know what happened to them."

The Yaga's eyes sparked with curiosity. "If your soul is more than bear, I can help you remember." A gate in the fence creaked open, but the Yaga held up her hand. "My price is high. I deal in death and souls. If you enter this house, you won't come out."

The Bear Tsar looked back into the forest. He loved the whispering trees and the chattering animals, but he knew it was time to move on. He turned to the Yaga and nodded his great head. "I'm ready. All I want is to remember before I go."

The porch floorboards creaked beneath the Bear Tsar's weight and the door widened to let him through. Inside, the house was warm. A cooking pot, large enough to boil ten bears, bubbled over the fire.

"Sit." The Yaga pointed to a chair growing from the floor. It grew and grew until it was big enough to hold the Bear Tsar, and he sat and rested his old bones. The Yaga brought him a bowl of *kvass* and a basket of berries, and he ate and drank until his belly was full.

Then the Yaga played music on a five-stringed *gusli* that sounded like rain chiming on a pebble-filled brook. Memories flooded the Bear Tsar's mind, clear as the waters of the Silver Stream in summer. He saw a cabin near the forest, smelled the sap of freshly chopped trees, and remembered he'd been a woodsman. He heard his wife singing, felt his child's soft cheek against his own, and remembered he'd been a father, full of warmth and joy.

But then he saw the Lime Tree at the soul of the forest and remembered asking it for more and more. His heart twisted with remorse for his greed, and he felt burning anger at being cursed to live as a bear.

Tears filled his eyes as he watched his child fight the curse and leave to join the human world. He watched, helpless, as his wife's heart broke and she wandered to a high cave alone.

The Yaga stopped playing and held the Bear Tsar's paw.

"I remember," the Bear Tsar whispered. "I remember it all." His great body trembled with memories, bitter with loss and regret but sweet with generosity and love.

"Then it's time to go." The Yaga lifted the Bear Tsar up and he felt as light as a spring breeze. He turned and saw his great bear body lying still in the chair, and he looked down to see his callused woodsman's hands. His wedding band shone on his finger, and a bark bracelet woven by his child caressed his wrist.

"What do you take with you to the stars?" asked the Yaga as she led him across the room to the large black gateway to the other world.

"Memories of my wife and child." The Bear Tsar smiled, stepped through the Gate, and disappeared forever into twinkling darkness.

CHAPTER FIFTEEN

VALENTYNA

"Well, Yaga don't have iron teeth, eat bears, or steal souls." Elena giggles. "But some parts of the story are true. Yaga do help people remember things and celebrate their lives before they go through the Gate and move on to the stars. That's what guiding the dead is. As for the bits about the Bear Tsar, I haven't heard of him, so I've no idea if they're true. My mother might know though."

The front door swings open and the Yaga woman steps out. "All the guiding is done." She blows air from her lips dramatically. "Those that were in the house anyway." She peers into the night, then looks down at me, hands on hips. "I can't imagine any more souls will turn up now. Not with you here."

"This is my mother, Valentyna." Elena glances up at her mother. "This is Yanka. You know, Anatoly's Yanka."

Valentyna frowns. "What are you doing in the forest all alone? Your mamochka will be worried sick."

My stomach twists at the mention of Mamochka. "I grew bear legs," I mumble. "I had to— I mean, I—"

Valentyna looks down at my legs and her face bursts into a radiant smile. "Bear legs!" she exclaims. "How wonderful."

I shake my head, utterly confused.

"I'm not sure Yanka wants bear legs." Elena looks from me to her mother.

"Why not?" Valentyna tilts her head. "They're wonderful. A gift from the forest. A reminder of all that's magical and mysterious in the world. How could you *not* want them?"

"Because I'm human?" My voice wavers, because I'm not even sure of that anymore.

"It's not your body that makes you human. It's your *soul*." Valentyna picks one of the blankets off the floor and wraps it around my shoulders. "Come on, let's get you inside and warmed up—body *and* soul. Elena, help the elk onto the porch and cover him with blankets. He looks like he needs somewhere warm and dry to rest too."

"Yuri," I say to Elena as Valentyna ushers me through the door. "The elk's name is Yuri."

Inside, the rest of Anatoly's dogs—Bayan, Pyotr, and Zoya—are sleeping in front of a roaring fire. The sight of them dissolves the last of my worries about the Yaga. Anatoly's dogs would only relax like this if they felt safe— and if they feel safe, I know I will be.

The mantelpiece curves into a broad smile and the floor-boards roll beneath me. I wobble on my feet. Even after everything that's happened, the idea of a living house is still bewildering.

Valentyna opens the door to a small bedroom. "You can take your wet clothes off in here, and I'll dry them by the fire. Wrap yourself in blankets from that shelf. I'll make more tea."

Valentyna leaves me alone and I peel off my wet clothes. The fur on my legs is cold and damp, and the skin on my arms sticky and wrinkled. It feels wonderful to rub myself dry and cocoon my body in huge woolen blankets.

Valentyna returns, and I sink into the chair I'm offered by the fire. Waves of heat flow over me, making me heavy with tiredness. On the other side of the room, a table is laid with a feast for twenty, but there are no signs of the people I heard laughing and dancing earlier. "Where did your guests go?" I ask, wondering if they really were dead souls who were guided to the stars.

"They left through another door." Valentyna passes me tea and all kinds of comforting dishes from her table that she says need eating up. The mushroom stroganoff that made my stomach rumble earlier is as delicious as its smell promised. There's soft dark bread, *golubtsy* cabbage rolls, and fried potato knish. Everything is delicious, and I feel so much stronger once I've eaten. My muscles relax, and a smile lifts the corners of my mouth.

Elena manages to get Mousetrap eating salmon from her fingers. But when he notices me watching, he lifts his nose into the air and announces he's off to search for mice. He sniffs his way along a skirting board until a knot in the wood widens into a mouse-sized hole. Mousetrap peers into it suspiciously before venturing inside.

Moments later, Mousetrap is darting in and out of holes that open and close as fast as he moves, growling with a mixture of frustration and excitement. Mossy mounds rise and fall around him, and tiny shoots reach up and poke his shoulders when he's not looking.

"Play fair." Valentyna throws a stern look up to the rafters. The house groans and the shoots behind Mousetrap sink back into the floorboards.

"I've never seen a house like this before," I murmur.

"Of course you haven't." Valentyna smiles. "And I hope you don't see another for many, many years. Only dead souls are meant to visit Yaga houses." Valentyna tilts her head and stares at me until I shift uncomfortably in my seat. "You look like your mother," she says finally.

"Mamochka?" My brow furrows. I look nothing like Mamochka.

"No." Valentyna laughs. "Your birth mother."

My eyes widen. "You know my birth mother?"

"I met her once." Valentyna nods. "After she died."

Valentyna's words land like stones on my chest. "After she died?" I repeat, clutching at the thought I might have misheard her. All my life I've wondered about my birth mother—who she was, why she left me in the bear cave, and whether I'd get to meet her one day. I've known nothing about her, not even if she was alive or dead, but that meant that anything was *possible*.

Now the first thing I discover about her is that she's dead. The knowledge burns, deep in my chest.

Elena sits next to me and rests a hand on my arm.

"I guided Nastasya to the stars." Valentyna nods. "About twelve years ago."

"Nastasya?" I reach for my arrowhead necklace. "The Princess Nastasya, like in Anatoly's stories?"

"Princess?" Valentyna chuckles and shakes her head. "Anatoly can't tell a story without embellishing it in some way. Nastasya wasn't a princess, but she was your birth mother. And she was strong and brave and kind. Like you, if what Anatoly tells me is true."

"How did she die?" I whisper.

"She came here fresh from a battle with Smey, the fire dragon in the north."

"Smey is real?" The arrowhead slips through my fingers, slicing a cut in my thumb. The stinging pain is the only thing that makes me sure I'm not dreaming.

"Smey is very real, and very dangerous." Valentyna's eyebrows fall, throwing shadows over her eyes. "He's full of anger."

"Then why would my birth mother go to fight him?"

"She was trying to rescue your father. He was trapped in Smey's cavern. I'd imagine Anatoly has told you the tale of the great battle between your mother and Smey."

I nod, remembering all the details of Anatoly's story. Nastasya's husband—my father—dropped into swirling dragon fire. Grief tearing through Nastasya. Smey, tumbling through the sky and collapsing upon her. I stare into the fire, unblinking. *Could my parents really have been killed by a fire dragon?*

My thoughts churn and clash, like meltwater and ice in a swirling eddy. I don't know whether to disbelieve the story, or grieve for my parents, or be angry with a creature I've never seen. I don't even know what a fire dragon is.

"Anatoly might embellish his tales, but there's always truth in them." Valentyna reaches out and squeezes my hand. "Your mother fought valiantly. But she died."

A tear trickles down my cheek, and as I wipe it away, a vine falls from the rafters and wraps around my shoulders in a strange kind of hug.

"Then your mother came here." Valentyna glances around the room proudly. "We ate and drank and sang and danced. She took courage to the stars, and her only regret was not being able to watch you grow. She loved you dearly."

"She loved me?" Something hard and tight unknots in my chest. I turn to Valentyna, to see if her eyes are honest, but she's blurry through my tears.

"Your mother loved you as the stars light the sky!" Valentyna beams and my heart swells until I think it might burst. "She didn't want to leave you, but she knew your grandmother would take care of you."

"My grandmother?"

"The Bear Tsarina."

I open my mouth, but no sound comes out.

"Are you all right?" Valentyna peers at me with concern.

"The Bear Tsarina is my grandmother?" I whisper.

"Well, of course she is." Valentyna chuckles. "Isn't that where you're going? To visit her and talk about your legs?"

"I was on my way to the bear cave." I nod. "But I didn't know the Bear Tsarina is my grandmother." Stories of enchanted trees and curses and bears and fire dragons swirl through my mind and excitement buzzes inside me. *I'm so close to discovering the truth of my past.* "The Bear Tsarina is my grandmother," I say again, rolling the words around my mouth, to see how they taste and feel. *I wasn't abandoned in a bear cave, I was left with my grandmother.* "So the Bear Tsar . . ."

"Was your grandfather." Valentyna nods. "I guided him to the stars too."

"And their child, the one who was cursed to be a bear, but fought the curse and became human . . ."

"Your father." Valentyna nods again.

Her words are like fireworks, throwing back the shadows in my mind. "These legs are because of a family curse?"

"You could think of them as a gift instead of a curse." Valentyna smiles.

I look down at my feet and frown, thinking about Mamochka's too-wide smile and Sasha's look of horror. "So am I meant to be a bear or a human?"

"Only you can answer that." Valentyna chuckles. "But

if you want to know more about being a bear, then visiting your grandmother is a good idea."

The house lurches sideways, and Valentyna nearly falls over. I grip the arms of the chair, but the whole thing skids across the floor. Anatoly's dogs wake and bark at the rafters. The fence bones clatter and Yuri screams from outside on the porch.

"House. Sit down!" Valentyna yells. "Nobody said we're going anywhere yet."

But the house surges up and up. Plates slide off the table and smash onto the floor.

"What's going on?" I ask, but my voice is lost in the chaos.

"Come and see!" Elena shouts. She beckons me to an open window. I sway across the tilting floor, kneel next to her, and grip the windowsill. Outside, the forest flies past. A branch bangs into the wall and I jump.

"It's all right. Look." Elena points down. "The house is walking, that's all."

The ground is far below, almost invisible in the darkness. The house's chicken feet pick their way between trees. Then its legs extend, lifting us higher. We rise above the snowy treetops, and the moon appears, fat and bright.

My heart accelerates as the house picks up speed. The house jumps and my whole body lifts, weightless. Elena squeals in excitement and I gasp in a mouthful of icy air. I feel the rush of sledding, a thousand times over.

"House! Stop running." Valentyna hits the rafters with a broom. Her face is red and her headscarf is coming undone.

"When are you going to stop being so impulsive and start behaving sensibly?"

Mousetrap leaps onto my shoulder. "I know where the house is going," he trills into my ear.

"Where?" I shout, wind rushing through my hair.

"I told the house we came into the forest looking for cod, so it's taking us fishing."

Laugher bursts out of me. Because although I'm not looking for cod, and I've just found out my parents were killed by a fire dragon and my grandmother is a bear, and I'm not sure what I'm meant to be . . . it feels incredible to know that my birth mother *loved* me, and there's *magic* in the forest, and *truth* in Anatoly's stories. It feels like there are wonders to discover around every bend of the river.

"We're following the Silver Stream." Elena points to a curve of moonlit water shining between the trees. But I've spotted something else in the distance, and a thrill runs through me as I realize we're moving toward it: the Blue Mountain—where my grandmother's cave is. Stars sparkle above its shining peak.

"House! Stop running!" Valentyna shouts, and bangs the rafters again, but the house speeds into a rolling gallop. Anatoly's dogs quiet, Yuri stops screaming, and Elena sits next to me, smiling at the view whizzing past.

Valentyna continues shouting at the house. But I don't want the house to stop running. I want it to carry me into a future in which I know all the stories and secrets of my past.

CHAPTER SIXTEEN

COD FISHING

The house settles opposite a small cabin on a quiet bend of the Silver Stream. Mist rises from the water and glows in the moonlight. And to the west, the ice-capped peak of the Blue Mountain glistens with reflected stars.

I rise to my feet, bursting to find my grandmother. "Thank you, for the food and the ride—"

Elena puts a finger to her lips and points at Valentyna. She's asleep in a chair by the fire.

"I have to go," I whisper, stepping over broken crockery and sleeping dogs to reach my clothes on the drying rack.

"I know this place." Mousetrap sniffs the air. "It's the perfect spot for cod fishing." He jumps through the open window and sprints away into the darkness.

Something between a groan and a growl rumbles in my throat.

"What's wrong?" Elena asks, oblivious to what Mousetrap said.

"Mousetrap's run off to go fishing." I pull on my skirt,

sweater, and coat as fast as I can. "I have to find him; I don't want to lose him in the forest."

"I'll come and help." Elena skips silently after me, stopping to lift a shawl and headscarf from a hook. The door swings open ahead of us and we step out into the cold night.

The Silver Stream bubbles and burbles alongside us. Only a thin line of ice remains clinging to its banks here. The moon and stars are distorted in its waters, throwing silver-tipped shadows into the night.

I take a few steps away from the house, then listen for Mousetrap but only hear the river and Yuri's snores from the porch. "Mousetrap!" I call in the loudest whisper I dare, not wanting to wake Yuri or Valentyna.

"Human girl!" Mousetrap's voice drifts from the black outline of the cabin ahead. It must be another of Anatoly's. The lightless windows and smokeless chimney tell me he's not inside. I'm glad. Right now, all I want is to make sure Mousetrap is safe, then find my grandmother.

"Mousetrap!" I call again, walking toward the sound of his voice. Elena follows, pulling her shawl tight against the damp air. The house creaks as it tries to creep after us, but Elena turns around and throws it a stern look that reminds me of Valentyna, and it slumps back down, its roof frowning.

"Over here," Mousetrap trills, and I spot his silhouette on an upside-down canoe at the side of the cabin. "You can use this to watch me fishing from the water."

"We can't go fishing now. I need to go to the bear cave." I beckon to him, but he doesn't come.

"Fishing is always best by moonlight." Mousetrap shivers with excitement and I realize that although I came into the forest looking for answers, he really did come here looking for cod.

"We could go fishing tomorrow night," I suggest. "You can't be hungry after all the salmon you just ate in the house."

"Are you talking to Mousetrap?" Elena's eyes widen.

I nod. "Ever since I grew these legs, I've understood him."

"That's amazing." Elena beams. "I wish I could talk to animals. What does he say?"

"Tell her that if she listened properly, she might understand." Mousetrap's whiskers twitch with annoyance. "And that it's impolite to disrupt a cod-fishing expedition."

"He mostly talks about cod." I glance up at the Blue Mountain and sigh. My feet are itching to climb it, but Mousetrap is looking from me to the river with shining, eager eyes. I've waited my whole life to find the story of my past. I suppose I could wait a few minutes longer—for Mousetrap. "How do you think you're going to catch a cod?" I ask him. "The ones Anatoly brings us are huge. Big enough to eat you."

"After all we've been through, you doubt my cod-fishing skills?" Mousetrap huffs out an offended snort, leaps off the canoe, and sprints toward the water. "Come on, human girl. Bring the boat."

I hoist the canoe onto my shoulders and turn to Elena. "Would you like to watch Mousetrap catch a fish?"

"I'd love to." Elena lifts a paddle and a five-pronged fishing fork from hooks under the eaves and follows me to the river. "What's that basket for?" she asks.

I lower the canoe into the water and peer at the soot-blackened wire basket dangling from a pole at the front of the boat. I remember something Anatoly told me once. "Freshwater cod are attracted to firelight. The basket must be for a small fire."

"I can get one." Elena rushes off and returns with a skull. "From the skeleton store—the skulls and bones of the fence run into it when the house moves." She lights the candle inside the skull and places the whole thing in the basket. "Will this do? The skull should stop the breeze from blowing the flame out."

"It's perfect." I nod, trying not to grimace at the eerie, glowing skull.

"Come on," Mousetrap shouts from the front of the boat. "I smell cod already."

I step into the boat. It sinks low into the water but feels stable. Elena gets in behind me and pushes off from the bank, and we let the current carry us away from the shore.

Mousetrap's fur shines like brass as he leans over the edge of the canoe, his head tracking movements in the water.

"They're coming," he purrs, flashing his teeth. "There's a plump one lying in the skull light right now."

"What did he say?" Elena whispers.

"He sees a fish." I reach for the fishing fork, but Mousetrap turns and scowls at me.

"*I'll* do the fishing." He scampers along the narrow pole toward the basket, shrieking louder than I've ever heard him.

Then a bird swoops out of the darkness, its wings as wide as I am tall, snatches Mousetrap up in its long, splayed claws, and disappears into the night.

Water slops against the side of the boat; my body sways and my thoughts reel. Mousetrap can't be gone. Not like that. Cold air creeps into my collar and swirls in the space where he always curls up.

"What . . ." Elena's voice trails off.

I listen to the silent night and finally hear a tiny, distant scream. The noise gets louder until it's ringing in my ears, then the bird rushes back out of darkness, straight toward us. It's an owl—the biggest one I've ever seen—with tousled ear tufts and bright yellow eyes. It dives in front of the boat and I spot Mousetrap on its back, his head held high and an enormous grin on his face. Relief rushes through me.

"That one," Mousetrap yells. He grips the owl's ear tufts as if steering it, and they bank down out of sight. There's a splash and another shriek. Then the owl flaps back into view, rises above the boat, and drops a huge cod from its talons. The fish lands at my feet with a wet thud and a chaotic splatter.

"How many shall we get?" Mousetrap shouts, pulling back on the owl's ear tufts until it turns around.

"Amazing!" Elena squeals and claps her hands.

I look at the fish at my feet. It's as long as my forearm. "This is plenty," I call after Mousetrap.

The owl circles around, effortlessly lifts another fish from the water, then lands on the front of the boat, making the bow dip and bob back up again. Mousetrap jumps down. "This is Blakiston the fish owl," he says with a flourish. "I told you how I rode on his back for three days and nights. This is the human girl I live with, Yanka, and this is a new friend of ours, Elena. She's a Yaga girl who lives in a house with chicken legs."

"Pleased to meet you both," Blakiston says in a deep, flowing voice.

"You too." I nod. "This is Blakiston," I explain to Elena.

"You understand me?" Blakiston swivels his head toward me. "It's rare to meet a human who can hear the creatures of the forest."

"My human girl has learned to listen." Mousetrap's tiny chest puffs up with pride, and warmth rushes into my cheeks at Mousetrap calling me "his" human.

Blakiston tears the cod at his feet in two and nudges half toward Mousetrap. "Aren't you eating yours?" he says to me, glancing at the other fish in the bottom of the boat.

"We'll take this one back for Elena's mother, Valentyna," I say, not wanting to offend Blakiston.

"That would be lovely." Elena scoops the fish up into her arms. "She could make a fish soup for the next guiding."

Blakiston gulps down his share of the cod whole, then turns back to me. "What are you doing so far into the forest?" he asks.

"I'm going to see my grandmother, the Bear Tsarina." I smile at my words. I've never had a grandmother to visit before. "She'll be able to tell me about my past, and my legs." I dip the paddle into the water and begin pulling us toward the shore.

"What do you want to know about your legs?" Mousetrap mumbles, his mouth full of food.

"Why they've grown like this." I tap my claws against the floor of the boat, wondering if Mousetrap has even noticed my bear legs. He's never mentioned them. "And whether I'm meant to be a bear or a human," I add when Mousetrap doesn't look up from his fish.

"You don't know?" Blakiston stares at me, unblinking.

I shake my head, and all of a sudden I feel so lost and confused that tears well in my eyes.

Mousetrap sprints up to my shoulder. "You're human, human girl," he squeaks into my ear. But his words only make the tears fall, because they're not true. I'm half bear and half human, neither one thing nor the other. The paddle slips from my hands.

Elena reaches out and steadies the paddle before it falls. "Are you all right?" she asks.

"I will be." I take a deep breath and carry on paddling. "I just need to find my grandmother. She'll know what to do."

The boat bumps into the riverbank and I step out. But even on solid ground I feel like I'm rolling on waves. I don't know who or what I am. Elena follows me, cradling Valentyna's fish, but Blakiston shows no sign of moving, so I drag the boat from the water with him still sitting on the bow.

"I have some cod left." Mousetrap leaps back into the boat and runs over to the remains of his meal. "Would you like some, human girl? It would make you feel better."

"No thanks." I sit on the bank next to the boat and wait for Mousetrap to finish eating. Moonlight dances on gentle eddies, and without thinking, I lower my feet into the water and let the fresh, cool currents swirl around my toes.

Blakiston scratches an ear tuft with his claws. "I don't understand how your grandmother will know what you're meant to be."

"Because she cared for me when I was a cub. Or a baby." I frown, because I'm not sure which I was. "And because she's like me. She was a human who turned into a bear." A story swims into my mind—a story Anatoly told me years ago— that begins before the Bear Tsarina was a bear. When she was a girl, just like me, who felt she didn't fit.

Elena sits next to me and rests a hand on my arm. Mousetrap snaps a fish bone, leans back against Blakiston's thick feathery legs, and picks his teeth with it. And I tell the tale, as Anatoly told it to me, starting with "Once upon a time . . ."

THE BEAR TSARINA'S DANCE

Once upon a time, there was a girl named Anya, who felt like a goose among swans in her village. But when she wandered into the forest, Anya swelled with such happiness that she rose onto her toes and danced.

She spun to the melodies of the wind, twirled to the harmonies of the rain, and bounced to the beat of the woodpecker's beak. Anya spent every spare moment she could in the forest, and by the time she had grown into a young woman, she felt she didn't need the company of people at all. At least she felt that way until she met the woodsman, Dmitry.

He smiled at her. She smiled at him. And they danced together through long summer days and cold winter nights until they fell in love.

They moved into a home at the edge of the forest and made it as comfortable as a feather-down nest. And when a baby boy arrived, all three of them danced together under the towering pines at the bottom of their garden.

Everything was perfect.

Until Dmitry brought strange gifts from the forest: seeds that grew faster than was natural, and jewels that shone brighter than rainbows. When Anya asked Dmitry where he'd found these things, he only smiled and kissed her cheeks.

Dmitry's secret weighed heavily on Anya. She stomped and flapped around their home, frustrated that Dmitry would not tell her the truth.

Then one day Dmitry took Anya and their son to a castle with a golden domed roof, hidden deep in the forest. "This is our new home." Dmitry beamed with pride.

Anya furrowed her brow and asked how this was possible, but Dmitry took her by the hands and spun her around until she felt the pulse of the forest, and her question drifted away.

Dmitry danced with Anya under the golden domed roof, with the song of the wind and the chirp of the birds and a chorus of frogs around them. And they were happy, for a while, living in their castle deep in the forest.

But all too soon, Dmitry came home pale and trembling, and everything changed. Dmitry would not tell Anya what had happened and fell asleep with his head on her lap. Anya burned with annoyance until she too fell asleep. And when they awoke, they were bears.

"How is this possible?" Anya stared at her huge paws with wide eyes.

Dmitry opened his mouth to speak, but no words came out. Guilt and remorse choked him.

"Tell me," roared Anya. "You have kept secrets from me for too long."

"This is all my fault," Dmitry whispered. "We've been cursed because of my greed."

Anya frowned as she tried to remember what she'd heard about curses. "I believe with curses," she said finally, "there's always a choice." And she rose onto her back paws and began to dance. "Dance with me." She beckoned Dmitry and their son. "And maybe we'll remember what it is to be human."

But the sounds and scents of the forest drifted through the open windows, and Anya, Dmitry, and their son were now bears. Their snouts twitched, and their ears swiveled, and they found themselves dancing out of the castle and into the forest. They spun to the melodies of the birds, twirled to the harmonies of the bees, and bounced to the beat of the snow hare's feet.

Anya felt the pulse of the forest stronger than ever before, and she danced deeper and deeper into it, through bubbling streams of silver fish, up mountains tingling with snow, and into caves that smelled of earth and autumn.

For a while Dmitry and their son danced with her, but as the seasons passed, they danced a different way, and Anya found herself in a high cave alone. But with the forest and its music spread out before her, she felt part of a beautiful world.

CHAPTER SEVENTEEN

THE BEAR CAVE

I finish the story, longing to roam deep in the forest, to find all the wonders of my grandmother's world. *My world.* The forest was my home once too. The sky is lightening; dawn is coming. Snow drips and birds fidget in the branches above.

Mousetrap is asleep against Blakiston's legs, a fish bone in his arms and his belly bulging. Blakiston's head is resting on his soft, feathered chest, and his eyes are closed.

My gaze drifts to the Blue Mountain, and at that moment the sun peeps above the treetops and throws a brilliant shaft of glowing sunlight onto its peak. I rise to my feet, the urge to find my grandmother ballooning inside me. The hope that she will know the answers to my questions is like a breeze and a storm all at once, lifting me, tugging me, spinning me around.

"I need to go to the bear cave," I whisper to Elena, not wanting to wake the others.

"What, now?" Elena asks. "You haven't slept all night or had breakfast—"

"I'm not tired or hungry." My feet are burning, the urge to leave now overwhelming. "Would you do me a favor?"

"Of course."

"Take care of Yuri? His wounds need to heal and—" I hesitate, bracing myself for what I'm about to say. "Can you take care of Mousetrap too?" I rush the words out before I can change my mind.

Elena nods, although her eyes are tight with concern. "You know, we could all go together. My house could take us—"

I shake my head. "This is something I have to do on my own." I look into Elena's eyes, hoping she'll understand, because I can't find the right words. I need to figure out who I am. And I love Mousetrap, but he can't help me with this. He only sees me as the human girl he lives with, and that's not what I am anymore.

"All right." Elena throws her arms around me. They barely reach halfway and tears well in my eyes as I think of Mamochka's hugs, but I blink them away. "I'll take Mousetrap to the house." Elena releases me and takes a step back. "But if you change your mind or need anything, just shout. The house senses everything in the forest for miles around."

"Thank you." I force a smile, and despite the doubts crowding in around me, I turn and walk away.

The peak of the Blue Mountain dips out of sight behind the canopy. But I know which way to go. I feel it as a pull in my chest and a tingle in my toes. With each step, excitement rises in me like a swarm of bees.

Everything sparkles in the morning light. Dew glistens on spiderwebs, meltwater glazes rough bark, and new buds gleam like amber beads on the tips of branches. Spring is coming, everything is changing, and the forest feels fresh and new.

When the mountain appears again, above a young, swaying willow, I scan its face for signs of the bear cave. *The Bear Tsarina.* Until now she's existed only in stories and dreams, and memories so old they feel like imaginings. But she's real, and close, and my *grandmother.* She'll know the truth of my past and where my future lies.

I wonder how she feels, waking after her long winter sleep. Perhaps it's a nice feeling, like waking in a sun-warmed bed. Or maybe it will leave her thickheaded and bad-tempered, like when you're pulled from slumber too soon. She'll be hungry after months of not eating, and Anatoly told me at this time of year bears want meat. He always said to be wary of bears in spring. *What if she doesn't remember me? Or what if she's not there at all?*

My nerves crackle as I draw close to the mountain, and by the time I reach the base of it, I'm so charged with electricity I feel like I'm glowing. I gaze up at the peak, which is hidden by mist, and the fur on the back of my legs lifts.

"Yanka! Yanka the Bear!" a bullfinch calls, and I suppress the urge to run. I pick out a rough trail that zigzags its way between the steep rocks and begin the ascent, slowly and carefully. I'm not sure how far away the bear cave is, so I need to pace myself.

My legs are strong, but they're heavy, and scrambling uphill is hard work. Tiredness gathers in my muscles and I think of Elena reminding me I didn't sleep last night or have breakfast today.

The higher I climb, the colder it gets, so by the time I rise above the tree line, it feels like midwinter instead of spring. But I stop anyway, to rest and look at the view. The sky is clear all the way to a distant, glimmering horizon.

Far in the northeast, flares of orange light shine through thick black smoke. That must be the Fiery Volcano, where lava streams down jagged rocks and pools into blistering hollows. Where Smey the fire dragon lives. The dragon who, I know now, killed my parents.

I squint at the light and smoke until my eyes are sore. Part of me longs to catch a glimpse of a fiery tail or wing. But I don't see anything, and soon my nose and ears are numb from the cold, so I move on.

After the next bend, the trail rises steeply. At the top of the slope is a wide, flat ledge. I stare at it, my heart racing like a shrew's. This place looks, and smells, familiar. A faint breeze drifts toward me, carrying the scents of earth and moss, berries and pine nuts. It's a smell I remember from long ago, and it makes me feel warm and safe.

I creep to the top of the slope and peer over the ledge. The sight of the bear cave whips the breath from my mouth. I recognize the shape of its entrance—the arc of rock, worn smooth by the Bear Tsarina's movements, and the tree roots breaking through on one side, forcing cracks into the glossy stone.

My feet carry me up and over the ledge—then I stop, a few paces from the entrance, hands trembling. Hopes and fears swirl inside me. I hear the Bear Tsarina breathing—a familiar, deep rumble.

A pair of eyes flash in the darkness, and my heart stops. The Bear Tsarina huffs out a cloud. A huge, heavy foot pounds onto the rock. Slowly, she walks to me, out into the light, muscles rippling, every movement full of power and grace. Strength radiates from her, and a calm contentedness, as if she knows exactly who she is. And right now, in this moment, I want to be just like her.

Questions die on my tongue. The Bear Tsarina's long brown snout reaches out. Her shiny black nose twitches as it sniffs the air between us. She grunts a deep peaceful greeting, then sits beside me.

The massive mound of her body curves around my back, and I collapse against her. I know the feel of her thick, warm fur. I know the pace of her breath and the sound of her heart beating deep in her chest.

I slide my fingers through the fur of her neck and burrow into her, like I used to do when I was little. I curl up until I'm a tight ball, surrounded by her huge limbs. She turns and licks my face with her soft wet tongue and I close my eyes. All the years that have passed since I was last here melt away until all that's left is a faint and distant memory of Mamochka in our house at the edge of the forest, far, far away, and this moment, in which I finally feel like I belong.

. . .

I'm not sure how long I doze. My coat digs into my shoulders and I wrestle it off. I'm hot and restless, all my clothes too tight. I lift the Bear Tsarina's front paw and pull my sweater over my head. When I try to loosen the waistband of my skirt, it tears. It must have caught on something. But I'm more comfortable now, and I sink back into sleep.

My eyelids open, and I squint against the light. The sun is low in the sky, the shadows long. My fur is damp with dew. I yawn, and a shuddering growl reverberates through my chest and skull. My whole body feels . . . *wrong*. My head is heavy, so heavy, and my mouth sticky, my lips loose. There's a cooler patch on my back where I was leaning against the Bear Tsarina, but she's gone now. I turn to look for her, and my body moves strangely. It's cumbersome, and too low to the ground. I try to push myself up but can't do it.

I stare at my hands, each heartbeat a booming explosion in my chest. My hands are paws, like my feet. Huge and round, with long dark claws. My arms, my chest, my whole body is covered with fat and fur. The weight of my shoulders is a log on my back. I lift a paw to my face but can't bring myself to touch the two together. I already know what I look like. I'm a bear.

CHAPTER EIGHTEEN

THE BEAR YANKA

A groan starts deep in my belly and rolls into my throat. I try to swallow it back, but it turns into a roar that blasts from my mouth. Confused and frightened by how much my body has changed, I lash out at the ground, and my claws scrape scars into the rock. I stare at them, feeling as lost and out of control as a swift in a snowstorm.

My grandmother appears at the cave entrance and ambles over. "What's wrong?" she asks. Her voice is a calm, mellow rumble.

"Look at me. I'm a bear." My breath huffs from my snout in short, hot bursts.

"What's wrong with being a bear?" My grandmother sits next to me and licks the fur on one of her front paws with a long pink tongue. "This is what you wanted. Isn't it?"

My brow furrows. *Was this what I wanted?* My head is full of a thick gray fog. I look up at my grandmother, in the desperate hope that she'll make everything clear.

"You were the happiest little bear cub." My grandmother

rolls onto her side and stares at me with steady, chestnut eyes. Her expression is as familiar as sunshine. "Every moment you were bursting with curiosity and joy. You'd bound through the forest—chasing birds, splashing through streams, digging the earth. You'd climb onto my back when you were tired and curl up beside me to sleep."

Memories swell in my mind, clear as meltwater. Racing after bullfinches, snapping river bubbles with my teeth, snuffling for roots, and the warmth of my grandmother's fur. I lean into her, breathe in her earthy scent.

"It's so good to have you home." My grandmother looks out over the forest. "We used to do this every evening. Sit here together, watching the sun set."

I nod, remembering sunsets of every color. But then my gaze is pulled south. I remember looking that way too. I peer into the distance and see the Great Frozen River, and something nestled on its banks, so tiny and far away . . . "The village!" I exclaim. "I can see the village from here."

My grandmother rises to her feet and yawns. "Let's go fishing."

"Fishing?" I turn back to her, confused. "You want to go fishing?"

"I'm hungry." She steps over the ledge. "Aren't you?"

My belly suddenly feels cavernous and I remember I haven't eaten all day. But there are so many questions I have for my grandmother. Important questions about my past, and what's happening to me now, and what it means for my future . . . I open my mouth to ask her to wait, but she's already gone.

I wobble to my feet and notice my clothes strewn on the ground around me. My coat is ripped apart, my map and Ivan's claw and several dusty apricots spilling from the pockets. The skirt Mamochka embroidered is a torn and crumpled mess. I try to bundle them up, to move them somewhere safe, but my paws are too big and my movements too clumsy.

Growling with frustration, I give up and bound after my grandmother, worried I'll lose her if she gets too far ahead. I stumble on the steep slope, fall over, and smack my head on a rock. I rise onto my back legs and try to walk upright instead. But that isn't any easier. My balance is all wrong, and I buckle under my own weight. I lower myself down and try walking on all fours again.

Finding a rhythm is impossible. My legs keep tangling, and my head is so close to the ground I can't see obstacles until they're right in front of me. My grandmother moves smoothly into the distance while with every step I take, I struggle not to slide or tumble.

By the time I reach the bottom of the mountain, I'm aching from the effort and sore from falling over, and I've lost my grandmother. I lift my snout into the air to search for her scent and breathe in a rainbow of smells. My mind tingles.

As a human, the forest was full of smells, but this is incredible. Otherworldly. Every tree has its own perfume: a mixture of bark and sap, and other scents left by creatures who have crept or scurried across them. Every inch of the forest holds a history of the animals who have visited, the plants that have grown, even what the weather has brought. I smell snow and dew, frost and rain, and the warmth of spring sunshine.

Wrapped in a world of new smells, I forget I'm looking for my grandmother. I weave between boughs, squashing shoots and cracking branches, sniffing everything I find, trying to work out what each scent is.

Then my ears turn to the sound of water gurgling and I tilt my head, confused and delighted by this new sensation. I smell the fresh, cold river and, mixed in with it, the earthy scent of my grandmother. I've found her again.

I race toward her, tripping over my feet with every step, and collapse onto the riverbank. My tongue lolls out as I catch my breath. Drool flows from it and I slop it back into my mouth, flustered with embarrassment.

My grandmother stands in the shallows, staring into the bright, clear water. She takes a few steps, slams one of her paws into the river, dips her head, and pulls out a fish. She carries it to me and drops it at my feet. "Eat."

I look at the raw, dead fish with puncture marks in its side and frown. "I can't eat this."

"Why not?" my grandmother asks. "It's good. It's fresh."

"Because . . ." I shake my head. I want to say something about how it should be cooked, or how I'm human—but before my thoughts can form into words, my grandmother splashes back into the river. She catches another fish, carries it over, and sits next to me, tearing at its head. I remember sitting here when I was a cub, watching my grandmother fish and eat. So many memories are bobbing up from the depths of my mind. They feel like missing parts of me, finding their way home.

I take a deep breath, and my lungs swell to the size of barrels. Suddenly, I'm aware of all the color in the canopy. While I slept the day away, the blanket of white over the forest shrank. Only dapples of snow remain on the conifers, and their needlelike leaves shine a thousand shades of green.

"Isn't it beautiful?" My grandmother leans against me and a smile bursts across her face, revealing pink gums and long white teeth. "Aren't you happy to be home?"

A smile lifts the corners of my mouth as I realize I am. But there are questions burrowing through me too. "Why did I leave?" I ask suddenly. "If I was so happy here, as a cub, why did I leave?"

"That doesn't matter now. What matters is that you've come home." My grandmother blinks lazily, then closes her eyes against the rays of the setting sun.

"Please." I fidget beneath the weight of my grandmother. "I need to understand what happened."

My grandmother sighs. "Sometimes your curiosity was insatiable. You were always wandering off, looking for new stories and adventures. One night you disappeared and returned with a wolf claw. I've no idea how you got it." Her body rumbles with laughter, but then she sighs again and her face falls. "You were curious about humans too. You'd follow hunters and woodcutters and herb gatherers.

You'd stare toward the village at night. When there were festivals, you'd creep far too close. I tried to stop you, tried to warn you, but you wouldn't listen." Her eyes well with tears. "Eventually you were more human than bear, and I had to let you go."

Feelings flow back, making sense of my memories. I chased birds because I wanted to talk to them. I wanted friends. I'd gaze at the distant village because I longed to go there. I loved the sounds of music and laughter. I loved the excitement fizzing in the air.

I remember seeing Mamochka, before she was my mamochka, collecting berries in the forest. I followed her because I wanted to be like her.

"I left because I wanted to be human!" I wriggle free of my grandmother and rise to my feet. My body seems lighter, my head clearer.

"But you've returned now." My grandmother smiles. "I'm so pleased. I never understood the desire to be human. You and your father both had it—"

"My father?" My ears turn toward her.

"Your father." My grandmother nods. "My son. Like you, he kept getting distracted by humans as he grew older. And like you, he turned into one and left."

"Can you tell me about him?" I ask.

"Those memories are gone. Long-forgotten dreams. It's better to forget and just enjoy being a bear. Being a bear is a gift."

"Please?" I try again. "I don't know anything about my

father. If you could tell me something about him, even a little, it would mean the world to me."

My grandmother stares at the river for so long I don't think she's going to say anything else. But then she opens her mouth and begins a story, as Anatoly would, with "Once upon a time . . ."

THE BEAR-BOY

Once upon a time, there was a young bear who was sometimes a boy. He didn't know why. He asked his parents, the Bear Tsar and the Bear Tsarina, but they couldn't answer him. They thought it might have something to do with a wish, or something to do with a curse, but their memories were faded, and they only ever remembered being bears.

They told him to look at the sunlight in the canopy and the moonlight on the streams, to catch fish and forage for berries, to roll in pine needles and talk to birds, and to enjoy being a bear. They said if he did this and wished hard enough to be a bear, he'd stop turning into a boy.

But it didn't work. The young bear was a storm of confusion—one day a bear, the next day a boy. His confusion grew into torment. He couldn't sleep or eat. He was weighed down with unhappiness and ached to know why he was different.

He wandered through the forest, asking every soul he found, "Why am I sometimes a bear and sometimes a boy?"

The birds in the trees didn't know. The animals in the burrows didn't know. And the fish in the streams didn't know. Finally, he came to a house with chicken legs, deep in the darkest part of the forest, and he asked the Yaga who lived there, "Why am I sometimes a bear and sometimes a boy?"

"I'm something of an expert on souls," the Yaga said. "And I see your soul is both bear and human. You need to choose to be one or the other."

"But how do I choose?" asked the boy.

"Well . . ." The Yaga stared at him thoughtfully. "You know how to be strong and independent and live in the forest as a bear. So now you must learn how to live with humans. Then you'll be able to choose."

The young bear thanked the Yaga and wandered north. There he saw a sailing ship, gathering fish from the Green Bay. He swam to the ship and climbed aboard.

At first the fishermen were scared and backed away from him. But when they saw the bear haul up fishing nets and basket traps, they realized he could be useful, and they soon became accustomed to his presence.

The ship sailed the Northern Sea, from the Calm East to the Stormy West, collecting fish and kelp and crabs. And slowly the bear-boy became part of the crew. He learned how to help and be helped, how to depend on others and have others depend on him, and how to be strong on his own but even stronger as part of a group.

Seasons passed, and the bear-boy grew into a human man. He forgot all about his time as a bear, although sometimes he dreamed of talking to birds in a sparkling canopy or rolling in pine needles till his fur smelled of sap. But the sea air blew his dreams away, and if there ever had been a curse, it was also forgotten, buried by his wish to stay at sea as part of a crew.

CHAPTER NINETEEN

THE CRUMBLING CASTLE

My grandmother finishes the story with tears in her eyes. "He should never have left the forest," she whispers.

"But it sounds like he was happy as a fisherman."

"Maybe for a while. But then . . ." My grandmother frowns. "It's too painful to remember. His desire to be human ended in tragedy. He should have stayed a bear. Fighting it only brings heartache and sorrow. But you understand that now, don't you?"

I shake my head, not understanding what she means at all.

"Were you happy as a human in the village?" she asks.

I open my mouth, but no words come out. Frustration ruffles through me. It's such a simple question; I should be able to answer it. "Sometimes I was happy. But . . ."

"You didn't feel like you belonged?" My grandmother

looks at me with such understanding that I feel a weight lift from my shoulders.

"I didn't always seem to fit. But there are people I love in the village. My mamoch—" I stop still. My blood runs to ice, because I can't remember how to say her name. And as I try to picture her, she disappears into mist. I can't remember my friend's name either. The one with the gray eyes. Or were they blue? I stumble from foot to foot, not knowing where to go or what to do. "I can't remember!" I roar. "I can't remember their names."

"It's all right." My grandmother nudges the fish she caught me. "Eat. Rest. Give yourself time to adjust. The change has happened fast, but you're going to be fine. The forest has everything you need."

I sit and stare at the fish in front of me. It stares back with blank eyes. "But I don't remember," I whisper. "I don't even remember what I was trying to remember."

"It's part of becoming a bear. Don't worry."

I close my eyes, desperately trying to remember whatever I was trying to remember. It was something I loved . . . someone I loved . . . All of a sudden, my human memories surge back to me, full of color and warmth and a swell of affection that takes my breath away.

"My family." I gasp. The word takes me by surprise, because I'm not thinking about my birth parents who I never knew, or my grandmother sitting beside me now. I'm thinking about Mamochka who took me in and has always been there for me, Anatoly who makes me smile with his magical stories, Sasha who walks by my side and accepts me as I am, and Mousetrap who fits so perfectly around my neck and calls me "his" human.

I can't believe I've never used the word *family* to describe them before. Regrets crowd in around me as I realize I've been searching for something I already had: a family, a home, a place to belong.

I stare down at my paws. "I can't go back like this." The words feel huge—cold, dark, and empty.

"It's natural to have doubts as memories of your human life come and go. But when they fade away, you'll be happy here in the forest."

"What do you mean, fade away?"

"The longer you stay as a bear, the more you'll forget of your human life," my grandmother murmurs sleepily.

"But I don't want to forget my human life." The thought makes me feel as fragile and formless as a cloud. "My human life hasn't been perfect, and I've often struggled to fit in, but there have been good times too." I'm surprised by how many happy memories jump into my mind: digging in the garden with Mamochka, climbing trees with Sasha and racing him home, helping prepare for the festivals—holding up beams and hauling sleds full of ice. I've been so focused on where I don't fit into the village that I've lost sight of where I *do*. I have a mother, Mamochka, who loves me. A best friend in Sasha, and other fledgling friendships too. I think of all the hands that reached for me before I fell from the ice fort. Little Vanya, who wanted me on his team. Polina's friendly smile. *There is a place for me in the village.* My eyes widen with the realization.

"You'll have more good times here." My grandmother looks at me with her steady gaze. "You'll be as happy as you were as a cub."

"I was happy as a cub, but I wanted to be human." I look south again, toward the village. Knowing about my past explains why I struggled to fit in, but all the things that drew me to the village to begin with are still there, pulling me back. And the family and friends I found there are pulling me even harder. I have to return. I can't stay in the forest and forget them. Life in the village can be a struggle sometimes, but it's full of joys too. "I want to go home," I whisper. And in that moment, I finally know where I belong: with Mamochka, in our house at the edge of the forest. "Can you help me?" I ask my grandmother. "Can you tell me how to become human again?"

My grandmother rolls back onto her paws and shakes her head. "I can't help you with that. I only know how to be a bear." The last pale sunbeams sink into the earth and a shadow falls between me and my grandmother. "I'm sorry," she whispers sadly, and so quietly I barely hear.

A cold breeze ruffles my fur.

"Come on." My grandmother starts to amble back toward the mountain. "Let's go to the warmth of the cave."

I shake my head, not wanting to go to the cave. I'm scared

of forgetting who I was and who I am and who I want to be. I'm scared of losing everything I had forever.

My feet itch and twitch and before I know what I'm doing. I'm running south. Toward the village. Toward *home*. Toward Mamochka, who will wrap me in her arms and tell me this is all nonsense and bring me a mug of *sbiten* and a pot of ointment that will rub the bear off me. Inside this body I'm human, and maybe I just need a little bit of Mamochka's magic to put me back the way I was.

I charge through the forest, crashing through low branches. With every blundering bound, I grow accustomed to the feel of my legs, and soon all four of my paws are drumming the earth in a steady rhythm. My claws sink deep into the ground, and the muscles in my legs ripple and shake.

Birds fly from my racket, and small animals sprint away from me. I feel the wind in my fur, smell heady sap and sour fear in the air. Though the forest is dark and full of shadows, I see everything. The night is so much clearer than it was with human eyes.

I feel huge and powerful on the outside but tiny and weak on the inside. I want to go home, to Mamochka. I want her to hold me and tell me we belong together—no matter what I look like. I wish she'd done that when I first grew bear legs. I wonder if she'll be able to do it now.

Trees crowd around me, but I keep running, faster and faster, until I can't see the moon or the stars and I'm not sure I'm heading south anymore. Panic crashes through me as I realize I don't know where I am. I can't hear, or smell, the river. I'm far from any trail, and I've lost all sense of direction.

I slow down and collapse in a small clearing, my chest heaving with despair. A tiny stream trickles alongside me and I lap up the cool water. A groan rises in my throat at the sight of my long, pink tongue and the reflection of my huge, furry face. Even if I could find my way home, would Mamochka recognize me like this?

Nobody could possibly know it's me inside this body. Apart from maybe Mousetrap. *Mousetrap.* Why didn't I go to find him first? And Elena and Valentyna and their house with chicken legs. Maybe they could help. I rise to my feet, close my eyes, and lift my head high, searching for their scent.

My nose twitches at a rich, sweet smell, and before I know what I'm doing, my snout is buried in a patch of young leaves. Tiny early strawberries are hidden beneath them, and I snuffle along, gathering them into my mouth. It's been so long since I've eaten, and they're so juicy and delicious; all I can think about is finding more.

Clink! My front claws tap something hard. I sniff and scrape at it, trying to work out what it is. It goes on and on, smooth and cold beneath a tangle of brambles. It's like polished marble or . . . *tiles.* It's the remains of a floor. I sit and look around.

Behind the trees are crumbling walls, covered in vines and creepers. There's a thin slice of curved roof, balanced between stone pillars. The star-filled sky shines through gaps where other parts of the roof have caved in. *This is the castle from Anatoly's stories.*

It's where the Bear Tsar and Bear Tsarina lived with their son—my father—before they were turned into bears. Maybe it was a grand castle once, with rainbow walls and a shining golden domed roof, but now it's in ruins. Both the castle and the humans who lived here once have been swallowed by the forest. Leaves rustle above me and I close my eyes. I feel like the forest is swallowing me too, threatening to take away everything that's human about me, leaving only a lost bear. I sink to the ground, feeling as broken and crumbled as the castle around me.

Then a familiar scent shivers up my nose: old rain and leaf litter, with the edge of something rotten. My ears prick up, but apart from the whispering stream, it's eerily quiet. The air is tense, like all the creatures of the forest are holding their breath, waiting for something to happen.

A tingling sense of danger rushes along my spine. Then a howl cuts through the silence. My heart stops. Another howl rises. Then another. My ears turn to track them all. Wolves, at least four of them, surround me. Goose bumps rise like ant bites and my fur stands on end.

I roll my huge shoulders and remind myself I'm a bear. Not even a pack of wolves would attack a bear. *Would they?*

CHAPTER TWENTY

THE WHITE WOLF

A white wolf steps out from behind a tree and flashes his teeth. He's not as big as Ivan, but he's more muscular and there's a coldness in his blue eyes that chills the air. "You smell weak. Like prey." He licks his fangs and prowls forward.

"I'm not weak," I roar as loud as I can, and rise onto my back paws. But I wobble and stumble backward. The white wolf wastes no time—he leaps, lunging for my neck with open jaws. I try to block him, but he slams into me with such force that I fall to the ground, and his teeth sink into my shoulder.

More wolves dart from the shadows and bite at my legs and side. The pain unleashes a great rush of anger. I roll over and swipe at the wolves with my claws. Yelps and snarls split the air, and I press my ears tight against my head to muffle the sounds.

I struggle to my feet. Two of the wolves release their grip, only to jump straight back up and bite a different part of me. And the white wolf's teeth hold firm. He whips his head back and forth, tearing at my flesh, and I roar until my throat is sore. But his teeth only dig in deeper.

Dark spots cloud my vision and I gasp for air. Jaws clamp onto my neck, back, and legs, and scores of teeth pierce my skin. Blood pounds inside my skull and I sink to the floor, overwhelmed by the weight and power of the wolf pack. Pain jolts through me, and my shoulder—still stuck in the jaws of the white wolf—throbs endlessly.

With all my strength I try to stand, but I'm trapped beneath the snarling, writhing wolves. I try to roar, but nothing more than a weak groan trembles from my lips, and my heart slows to a dull thud.

Frustration storms through me. *I want to go home.* My mind fills with thoughts of Mamochka mixing medicines, Mousetrap pattering beneath the floorboards, Anatoly sitting by the fire, and Sasha gliding to the village on his blades like a swallow in flight.

My heart beats stronger. I heave myself up, then stagger across the clearing. Wolves dangle from me, hanging on with their teeth and claws. I slam my body into tree after tree, squashing the wolves against thick trunks and spearing them with sharp branches. One by one, they yelp and fall and cower below me. But the white wolf holds on.

"Let her go." A deep snarl silences the wolf pack. The white wolf stops still but keeps his grip on my shoulder. His hot breath makes my wound sting.

I turn to the snarling voice and recognize Ivan's golden

eyes and his scent that is edged with something rotten. He glares at the white wolf; his eyes are scorching embers.

Finally, the white wolf releases my shoulder and licks his teeth. "What do you want, Ivan?"

Ivan steps closer to the white wolf and looks down on him. "Leave her be."

"Why?" The white wolf tilts his head.

I back away from the wolves. None of them try to stop me. They're all staring up at Ivan and the white wolf, their heads lowered and ears flat.

"Because I told you to," Ivan snarls.

"You aren't leader of this pack anymore. You abandoned us." The white wolf looks around at the other wolves as if for support, and a few of them nod and growl in agreement.

Ivan raises his hackles. He stands head and shoulders above the white wolf. "I'll lead this pack again, once I've proven my strength."

"You're old," the white wolf scoffs. "Your time as leader has passed. But you could still be a member of this pack. If you weren't so proud—"

"I'm not old," Ivan barks. "And I'll only return as pack leader." His eyes flash in the darkness.

The white wolf lets loose a blood-chilling, howling laugh. "You let a bear cub take your claw, and with it you lost our respect."

"True." Ivan nods solemnly. "But I know how to prove I'm strong enough to lead again." He glances back toward me.

"That bear is the cub who took my claw. She returned to the forest two nights ago. I've been tracking her, and I've learned she's no ordinary bear."

The white wolf stares at me with his cold blue eyes. "She smells like an ordinary bear. And tastes like an ordinary bear." He licks his lips and sneers. The puncture marks he left on my shoulder sting like fire.

"I saw her pull an elk from beneath the ice of the Silver Stream and ride with it on a floe along rushing meltwater channels. From the shadows, I watched her weasel tear through this very pack, and I heard the roar from her chest that scared you away."

The white wolf flinches at Ivan's words, and the pack dip their heads in shame.

"I watched her stare into the skulls of the Yaga's bone fence and ride in their house with chicken legs. But more important than all that . . ." Ivan pauses and lifts his head high, enjoying being the center of attention. "I watched her go to the high cave and turn from a human into a bear."

The wolf pack erupts into a chorus of whispers. My ears swivel as I try to pick out their words.

"She has the curse," a sandy-colored wolf growls. "The tree's curse."

"She must be descended from the Bear Tsarina." A small wolf with thick gray fur nods knowingly. "Has she come to face Smey?"

My fur lifts. I'm scared of the wolves and what they might do; my wounds sting and I want to run home. But I'm also bristling with curiosity to find out what they know about me and the curse.

The white wolf barks, silencing my thoughts and the mutterings of his pack. "I fail to see how any of this will help you return as pack leader, Ivan."

Ivan grins, exposing his long white fangs. "You all know Smey is the most destructive and dangerous thing in this forest."

The wolf pack snarls and growls in agreement.

"He makes the northeast uninhabitable," an angry black wolf barks.

"He poisons the air with his sulfurous breath and heats soil into bubbling mud," the sandy wolf grumbles.

"And he melts rocks into blazing lava," the small gray wolf adds.

"He sends fires through the forest, burning our trees, charring our den," the sandy wolf complains.

"He covers our trails with his stinking ash." The black wolf scowls.

"Because of his fires, our prey flee the forest, and we go hungry for months on end," the small gray wolf growls.

"The time has come to defeat him." Ivan's voice rises above the rumblings of the pack. "This bear returning to the forest is a sign. I'll go with her, to break her curse. We'll defeat Smey together. This will prove my strength, and when I return, I will be leader."

My ears lift at the mention of breaking my curse. I don't understand what Smey has to do with it—but breaking the curse would mean becoming human again. *Completely human.* I could go home and not worry about the pull of the forest or turning into a bear ever again. I could go back to the village and fit in, like everybody else.

"Smey can't be defeated." The white wolf snorts. "And wolves do not fight with bears. You've lost your mind, *Old* Ivan."

Ivan's eyes burn with determination. "We *will* fight Smey. We *will* triumph. Then I *will* return, as pack leader."

"*If* you defeat Smey, and *if* you return, I'll bow to you as pack leader." The white wolf nods to the other wolves and they disappear into the shadows, silent and speedy as moths on a breeze.

I glance around, wondering if I could disappear into the shadows too, but the desire to go home human keeps me rooted to the spot.

Ivan turns to me and nods a greeting. "I saved you from being torn apart."

"I was doing fine on my own."

"You owe me thanks." Ivan tilts his head, and a pang of guilt flashes through me. The white wolf did only release my shoulder when Ivan arrived. I open my mouth to thank Ivan, but he speaks again before I get a chance.

"I've proven my strength to you and helped you in a time of need. In return, you'll allow me to fight Smey with you."

"Why would I fight Smey?" I ask, still confused about what Smey has to do with my curse.

"Because Smey guards the tree that cursed your family to

be bears. If we defeat him, you can ask the tree to turn you human again."

I stare at Ivan, unsure what to say or do. I don't know anything about fire dragons. Questions swirl in my mind . . . along with a tiny, distant scream. My ears swivel to the sound. A familiar squeal rises into a screech, and Blakiston the fish owl swoops through the trees with Mousetrap riding on his back.

Blakiston circles around the clearing, Mousetrap whooping and yelling, his teeth flashing like tiny stars. Then Blakiston lands on a branch, and Mousetrap glares down at me. "Where is my human girl and why do you have her necklace?" he demands.

For the first time since I changed into a bear, I feel something nestled in the fur at the base of my neck. I lower my chin and make out the ice-blue arrowhead glinting through the darkness. "It's me, Yanka." I look up at Mousetrap, hoping he'll believe me. "I turned into a bear."

"Oh, I see," Mousetrap replies. "That explains the necklace. It was impolite of you to leave me with the Yaga girl, but we'll have to discuss that later." Mousetrap jumps onto the branch and flows down the tree until he lands on my back. "We've been looking for you everywhere. It's your friend—the human boy . . ."

"Sasha?" I ask. "What about him?"

"I think he might be dead."

CHAPTER TWENTY-ONE

SASHA

Blakiston flies ahead, pale and silent as mist in the moonlight. I race after him, the need to find Sasha a fire in my paws. Finally, my body feels like my own, and I speed through the forest, wanting only to see Sasha alive and well.

I can't hear Ivan, but the smell of him lingers, even after we've left the clearing far behind, so I assume he's following, silently running through the shadows alongside us.

Mousetrap clings to my ear. "The human boy is on the other side of the river. Blakiston and I were looking for you when we found him. He's lying on the bank, wet, cold, and still. And he smells bad."

"What happened to him?" I gasp for air. Sasha came into the forest looking for me and I left him at the Silver Stream. It was half ice and half rushing water, and I abandoned him there, alone. *Whatever has happened to him will be my fault.*

"I don't know." Mousetrap digs his claws tighter into my ear as I surge forward. "But I smell frostbite on his fingers, and he's so wet he must have fallen into the river. Perhaps he succumbed to the cold. Or drowned."

"Please," I whisper, "don't let him be dead. *Please, don't let him be dead.*"

The smell and sound of the river fills the air and I accelerate toward it with no care for how many branches I break on the way. At last, the water appears behind the trees, rushing along, swift and black as the night.

Mousetrap climbs onto my forehead. "There's the human boy." He points with his snout, but I see Sasha already: a small bundle on the opposite bank. Blakiston glides over the river and lands next to him.

I wade in until the water is up to my chin, then lift my legs and kick frantically, worried my huge body will sink. But I'm surprisingly buoyant, and each sweep of my paws pulls me smoothly across.

My thick fur protects me from the icy water, but I shudder at the sight of Sasha. He looks so tiny and frail. I scramble onto the bank and rush to him, but Mousetrap was right. He's cold and lifeless. I nudge Sasha's bluish face with my nose, then rest my head on his chest, desperate to hear his heartbeat, but there's nothing.

I shout for Valentyna, Elena, and the house. Sasha needs help, and I can't do anything in this body. My voice comes out as an echoing roar, and I growl with frustration. *They won't understand me like this.*

"Mousetrap! Blakiston!" I yell, lifting Sasha into my

arms and cradling him like a baby. "Which way is the Yaga house?"

"Upstream." Mousetrap runs to Blakiston and jumps onto his back, and they fly off together.

I stagger after them, along the riverbank, my feet sinking deep into mud. I try to run, but on two paws, all I can manage is an awkward, swaying jog. Moonlight swirls on the river currents. Stars disappear and reappear as they're swallowed and then spat out again by the waves.

The scent of Ivan follows me like clinging smoke. I know he's close, though I can't see him. I try to huff his scent away, because I don't want to think about him or his desire to fight Smey. I don't care about fire dragons or curses anymore. All I want is for Sasha to be well.

But with every step, Sasha becomes chillingly lighter—as if his soul is floating away. He's too quiet, too still. A cave opens in my chest and I lower my head to Sasha's, wanting only to feel his breath.

A thump shakes the ground. Then another. The Yaga house appears, its brightly lit windows higher than the treetops. My heart pounds with the hope that Valentyna and Elena might be able to help.

One of the house's chicken feet steps over a skeletal elm, and its long, clawed toes squish into the mud of the riverbank. The other foot swings down next to it, and the house lurches to the ground with a bump.

Yuri is still lying on the porch, grumbling something about motion sickness, and Mousetrap waves a greeting from the roof, where he's perched with Blakiston. "We brought the house to you," he trills. "The Yaga don't listen, but the house understands us perfectly."

"Thank you." I stumble toward the porch.

Then the front door swings open and my jaw drops, because floating next to Valentyna is the ghost of Sasha.

CHAPTER TWENTY-TWO

SASHA'S GHOST

I stare at the wispy, translucent figure in disbelief. *A ghost.* A real ghost. One that looks exactly like Sasha. *Sasha's ghost.* The world crumbles around me. *Sasha can't be dead.* He's my best friend. Every day we walk together, talk together, climb together, race together . . . we live our lives together. *He can't be gone.*

I look down at Sasha's body lying limp in my arms, and my heart clenches so tight I gasp in pain.

"That's my body!" Sasha's ghost exclaims. His eyes widen in shock and I see through them into the house beyond.

Valentyna steps closer to me and puts a hand on Sasha's real, frozen cheek. "You're freshly dead. Maybe it's not too late." She holds out her arms to take Sasha's body. "Quick, pass him to me."

"Can you save him?" I lower Sasha's body into Valentyna's arms, and my paws tremble as I wait for her response.

"I can't understand you when you're a bear, Yanka." Valentyna glances up at me. "But if you're asking about this boy, I'll do everything I can." She turns on her heel and disappears into the house with Sasha's body, leaving me lost in a tangle of hope and fear.

Sasha's ghost stays on the porch, looking as scared and confused as I feel. "She called you Yanka." He floats toward me and peers into my eyes. "Is it really you?"

I lower myself onto all fours and nod.

Sasha shakes his head in disbelief. "What happened to you?"

Even if I could speak, I wouldn't know where to begin. I stare down at my long, dark claws and shrug.

"Why didn't you tell me what was going on?" Sasha's eyes fill with hurt. "We've always told each other everything. I'd have only wanted to help."

I wish I could apologize. *I've been so foolish.* When Sasha saw my legs, I should have explained. I should have told him how I felt. But I ran away and left him at the Silver Stream and now . . . I look up at Sasha. *At his ghost.* He's dead or dying, and it's all my fault. A groan rolls from my mouth.

"I can't believe you're a bear." Sasha reaches out to touch my face, but his fingers pass right through me. The sensation sends hot sparks along my snout and I sneeze. Sasha pulls his hand back and stares at it in confusion. "And I can't believe I'm . . . This is so weird." He laughs, but there are tears in his eyes.

I shift from one great paw to the other, not knowing what to do to make this right.

"Hey, Yanka." Sasha nudges my shoulder, sending another

flurry of sparks through me. "Whatever else we are, we're still best friends, right?"

I look up at him, blink away my own tears, and nod.

"Sasha." The door swings open and Elena steps out. "My mother wants you inside, with your body." She sweeps Sasha's ghost indoors as if he's made of nothing but smoke.

"Wait!" I call after him. I don't know what my words sound like to him, but he stops and turns around. "I'm sorry." I stare into his misty, see-through eyes and will him to understand. "I'm so sorry. For everything. Please don't die."

"I'll see you soon, Yanka." Sasha smiles. "Don't run off, trying to get a head start on our next race." He disappears into the house with Elena and I stare after them, worries avalanching onto my shoulders.

Mousetrap leaps from the roof and lands on my neck. He scampers up to my ear and curls around it. "I'm sure the human boy will be fine. The house tells me the Yaga woman is both ancient and wise."

The porch steps stretch toward me, and the balustrades open like welcoming arms.

"If you listened"—Mousetrap nips my ear—"you would hear the house inviting you to sit on its porch."

I look up at the house, and the roof curves into a smile.

"Sit next to me," Yuri calls, and shuffles along to make room. "You can share my blanket." He nudges a green woolen blanket from beneath his legs and spreads it out with his snout.

I step as gently as I can onto the porch and edge my way

around to Yuri. The balustrades swell and curve to allow me to pass. "How are your wounds?" I ask, peering at Yuri's back. The worst one has been dressed with aloe leaves and smells a little of Mamochka's beeswax and sandalwood balsam. It's not the same, but just the hint of home makes my eyes sting.

Suddenly aware of my own wounds from the wolf pack, I turn around, and without thinking, start licking the ones I can reach.

"I'm much better, thank you. The Yaga woman and her daughter are good healers." Yuri looks up at me and sniffs loudly. "I was upset by you leaving though. You told me you'd be my herd, then you left."

"It was rude of you to leave without explanation," Mousetrap agrees. "I was frantic when I woke to find you gone."

"I'm sorry." I apologize to Yuri, then try to look up at Mousetrap, but he's out of sight on the very top of my head. "I'm so sorry, Mousetrap. I should've taken you with me."

"Yes, you should have." Mousetrap leans over my snout and I breathe in his familiar smell of dust and earthy musk.

"I've made the same mistake so many times. I left you, and Mamochka, and Sasha . . ." A lump grows in my throat. "And now Sasha . . . because of me, he's . . ."

"Enough." Mousetrap stomps onto my snout. He's so close that my eyes cross when I look at him. "The human boy will be fine. Listen." He lifts a paw to his lips, and his ears perk up.

177

I lift my own ears and hold my breath but hear nothing. "What is it?" I whisper.

Mousetrap shakes his head in disappointment. "I thought you'd learned to listen."

I frown and swivel my ears all around. I hear Yuri's calm breathing, Blakiston grooming his feathers on the roof above us, the creak of floorboards inside the house, and the gurgle of the stream alongside it. I hear the treetops whisper and a squirrel scoot up rough bark. I smell Ivan, somewhere in a shadowy thicket, and I hear one of his paws brush the earth. But that's it. Nothing else. "What?" I ask again. "What can you hear?"

"The house," Mousetrap trills. "The house is trying to talk to you."

I look up at the eaves. "I'm sorry, I can't hear you at all."

"The house wants to tell you a story." Mousetrap climbs back onto my head and curls around my ear. "I'll relay it for you, if you like."

"Please." I nod.

"It's a true story." Mousetrap nestles deep into my fur. "Of how the house and the Yaga woman saved a life once."

"They did?" Hope flickers in my chest that the house and Valentyna will save Sasha too.

"Yes." Mousetrap nips my ear. "Now mind your manners and listen."

THE YAGA HOUSE AND THE FISHERMAN'S SOUL

Once upon a time, a fisherman died. His soul drifted through the forest, drawn to the skull lights surrounding a Yaga house. The door of the house opened, and inside was a warm fire and a cloud of cold dead souls.

"You're dead," said the Yaga of the house with a smile. "You have come here to remember and celebrate your life before you move on to the stars whence you came." The Yaga passed the fisherman a glass of rich, dark *kvass* and a bowl of thick, spicy soup.

More dead arrived, and they all ate and drank by the fire until their souls were warm and full. The Yaga house buzzed and sparked with stories being shared.

The fisherman remembered his childhood with an aching heart, but when he spoke of his time at sea, his eyes lit up and all the souls in the house stopped to listen. The fisherman conjured wide, open skies and deep, dark waters that changed with each kiss of the wind. He drew mountainous waves and shivering ripples and sea-foam as frothy as snow. Monsters and mysteries danced in his words, and adventures tripped off his tongue.

The Yaga house was entranced. Unable to contain its excitement, it rose onto its great chicken feet and galloped through the forest, determined to find its own adventures at sea.

"Stop!" shouted the Yaga, and she banged on the rafters. "We need to guide the dead."

"Stop!" shouted the dead, and they swirled in confusion. "We need to move on to the stars."

But the fisherman kept telling stories, of enchanted waves and shining treasures and creatures that glowed in the dark.

And so the house ran on, all the way to the Northern Sea. It splashed into the surf and waded deeper and deeper, until water seeped through its floorboards and walls.

"Stop!" yelled the Yaga. "We don't know how to swim."

"Stop!" screamed the dead. "We'll be lost in the waves, like the souls of the haunting *rusalki*."

But the fisherman kept telling stories, of sunken cities and forgotten islands and fish that leaped to the stars. And the house paddled on through the water, faster and faster, until it was swimming far out to the sea. It grew a leaf sail that billowed and bowed and swept the house toward the horizon.

The Yaga sighed, because the house would not listen, and she sat to think up a plan. She looked at the fisherman and realized his stories were so full of life that he must be freshly dead—perhaps so fresh that he might be saved. "House," she boomed, "this fisherman is not ready to go to the stars. Quick, paddle back to shore. We must find his body and reunite it with his soul."

The house sank a little in disappointment. But it turned and swam back to the shore. After all, who would not save a life if they could? The house sloshed from the water and shook its feet dry. Then it raced through the forest until it found the body of the fisherman, broken and burned beneath a fire dragon's cavern.

The Yaga grabbed the fisherman's soul and ran to his body. "Get back in," she ordered with such fierceness that the fisherman dared not refuse. He lay down in his body and breath surged into his lungs.

Pain shot through the fisherman's limbs and darted over his skin. But the Yaga dressed his wounds, gave him herbs for the pain, and left him with food and water to recover. Then she returned to the Yaga house, to guide the rest of the dead in peace.

The Yaga house smiled at the fisherman, pleased it had saved his life, and walked calmly back into the forest. But it glanced at the ocean once more before the waves disappeared behind the trees, and promised that one day it would have its own adventures at sea.

CHAPTER TWENTY-THREE

THE HERD

As Mousetrap finishes the story, Elena steps through the door, pulling her shawl tight around her chest. "Sasha is doing much better. His soul is back in his body and he's breathing." Relief floods through me until Elena continues, "But he's unconscious, his breathing weak, and there are mottles of frostbite all over him."

Frostbite. People lose fingers and toes—even whole hands and feet—to frostbite every year. If that happened to Sasha because of me, I'd never forgive myself. I rise to my feet, wanting to do something to help, but there's nothing I can do.

"You should probably stay sitting," Elena says as the house creaks and shifts beneath us. "We're going to move closer to the village—not so close anyone sees us, of course, but close enough for my mother to sled Sasha to your mamochka. Anatoly left his sled here as well as his dogs, and we can make Sasha comfortable for a short journey. My mother says your mamochka is a far better healer than her, and the best place for Sasha to wake is at home, with his family. Not in a Yaga house surrounded by us scary witches." Elena laughs, but it's a hollow sound that doesn't hide her concern. Sasha might be doing "much better" than dead, but clearly he's still in grave danger.

The house lurches upward, and Mousetrap leaps onto my back. "The human boy doesn't look good at all," he squeaks into my ear. The house turns as it rises and I glimpse Ivan stepping out from the shadows. He stares at me with his golden eyes, and my head fills with thoughts of fire dragons and curses, enchanted trees and *wishes*.

An idea sparks into my mind like pine crackling on a fire.

"Stop!" I stumble along the porch toward the steps, though they're high above the forest already.

"What's wrong?" Elena and Mousetrap ask at the same time.

"I can't go back to the village!" I shout.

"Why not?" Mousetrap leans over my face.

"There's no time to explain. Please, just let me down." I look up at the roof and sigh with relief when the house swings back to the ground and I'm able to step onto the riverbank.

Yuri slips and slides along and off the porch and lands in a heap beside me. "You're not leaving me again," he says firmly. "We're a herd, remember?"

I look into Yuri's big brown eyes and finally understand

183

what being part of a herd means to him. It's like what family means to me. Realizing Mamochka and Sasha are my family has given me a home and a place to belong. That's what Yuri is looking for too.

"You're not coming with us?" Elena looks from me to Mousetrap to Yuri.

I shake my head and back away, wishing I could explain.

"It's all right." Elena nods. "I think I understand. There's not much you could do in the village to help." She taps the balustrades. "I know . . . We'll drop off my mother and Sasha, then come back to find you. What do you think, House?"

The whole house nods before surging back up. Blakiston swoops down from the chimney and lands on a branch behind us. Elena waves as the house turns, picks up speed, and disappears into the night. I stare after it, hoping with every breath that next time I see Sasha, he won't be a ghost.

"Are you going to tell me what's going on now?" Mousetrap nips my ear and I flinch.

"Will you stop biting my ears?" I growl.

"That wasn't a bite." Mousetrap snorts. "It was a gentle nibble to get your attention."

"Wolf!" Yuri suddenly screams, scrambling backward.

"It's all right." I step between Yuri and Ivan, who is walking toward us, his fangs flashing in a wide grin. "This is Ivan. He won't hurt you." I glare at Ivan, hoping to make it clear that I won't let him attack Yuri. I roll my shoulders to make myself look bigger, but on all fours I'm not much taller than Ivan.

"But he's a wolf," Yuri squeals. "A wolf!"

"He's part of our herd," I say, hoping the word will calm him. "Me, you, Mousetrap, Blakiston, and Ivan. We're a herd now."

Yuri looks around at us all and lifts his head high. "We're a herd?" he repeats hopefully.

Ivan's eyes flash in the darkness as he nods. "I'll join your herd, to help you fight Smey."

"Fight Smey?" Mousetrap runs down my snout and turns to stare at me. "Smey the fire dragon?"

I shift my weight on my paws, suddenly unsure of my idea. It made more sense when I was on the house's porch. "Maybe not fight him. I just need to get past him. Ivan says Smey guards the Lime Tree. It can grant wishes, so if I can get to it—"

"She can wish to be human again," Ivan interrupts, shaking his fur impatiently. "Can we go now? It's a long journey to the Fiery Volcano."

"Fighting a fire dragon will be difficult and dangerous. Even for someone with hunting skills as exceptional as my own." Mousetrap inspects his claws in a shaft of moonlight. "Are you sure you want to do this? You're still human in there, despite your current appearance."

"I have a more important wish than wanting to be

human." I look back in the direction the house walked, thinking about Sasha. I need him to recover. He's my family, my herd, my home. I failed him at the Silver Stream and now I need to make things right. "I'm going to wish that Sasha makes a full recovery."

"You can wish whatever you like, as long as we defeat Smey." Ivan walks a few paces north, then glances back at us. "Come on, herd," he growls. "The night is wasting."

I bound after Ivan, worries churning inside me—for Sasha, and for the others too. All I know about fighting fire dragons is that it's dangerous, and I don't want anyone else to get hurt.

"Where's your old herd?" I ask Yuri, wondering if I could get him safely back to them before we reach Smey.

"They don't want me anymore," Yuri grumbles. "The young males always get kicked out before the spring mating season."

"Where do the other young males go?"

"Some wander alone. Some form small groups among themselves."

"Perhaps we could find one of those groups for you to join?"

"But you're my herd now," Yuri says proudly. "You said so yourself."

"We are." I groan. "I just don't want you to get hurt fighting a fire dragon because of me."

"Herds stick together, especially during times of danger." Yuri skids on a muddy patch. "You'll need me."

"The prey animal is right," Ivan growls. "All the members of a pack can be useful."

"But Yuri is just a young elk." My brow furrows with concern. "And Mousetrap a tiny house weasel."

"With exceptional hunting skills," Mousetrap squeaks into my ear.

"You are strong and brave and brilliant, but I don't know what you can do to help fight a fire dragon, Mousetrap." I shake my head. "I don't even know what *I'm* going to do."

"Many years ago, I was asked to fight with an unusual pack." Ivan slows his pace until he's walking alongside me and Yuri. "I was doubtful of the others' strengths, especially the crayfish, but together we defeated the Giant Deathless."

"We've heard this story," Mousetrap trills. "Do you remember, human girl? Anatoly told it to us fifteen seasons ago." I smile at Mousetrap still calling me human girl despite the fact I've completely turned into a bear. Then I try to remember the stories I've heard about the Giant Deathless. They're some of Anatoly's most fantastical tales, and although I've enjoyed them, I've never truly believed in an evil immortal giant rampaging through the Snow Forest.

"Would you like to hear the story again?" Ivan asks.

"Yes, please." I nod. A flush of warmth runs beneath my fur, because whether this story is true or not, and whatever happens next, this moment feels suddenly special. Ivan, Yuri, Mousetrap, and Blakiston all want to stay and help me, and it makes me feel part of something. *Like I belong.*

Walking side by side with Yuri and Ivan, Mousetrap

curled around my ear, and Blakiston flying above, with the river burbling and the leaves whispering, I feel part of Yuri's herd, and Ivan's pack, and even part of the magic of the forest itself.

"All right." Ivan clears his throat with a growling bark. Then he begins with "Once upon a time . . ."

THE GIANT DEATHLESS

Once upon a time, the Giant Deathless came to the Snow Forest. He was taller than the trees, harder than the rocks, and as heartless as the midwinter frost. His breath was so rancid that birds fell from the sky, and he picked and ate wolves like cherries, gobbling them up and spitting out their skulls like pits. He snapped the angelic birches to use as toothpicks, and he drank from the river until the waters were so low that fish floundered and crayfish crawled away to the ocean.

One of the humans who lived in the forest, a great warrior called Nastasya, felt her heart ache to see the Snow Forest plundered, so she vowed to get rid of the giant. First, she went to the Yaga in the darkest part of the forest, to ask her advice.

"The Giant Deathless hid his soul," said the Yaga, "so he could live forever. But without his soul he can't understand the feelings of others, so he's become selfish and cruel. He'll not find peace until he reunites with his soul and moves on to the stars. But his soul is trapped inside an egg that's inside a duck, who is inside a hare, locked in an iron chest and buried deep under the Great Oak on the Isle of Buyan.

And that can only be reached by sailing off the end of the world and through the North Star."

Nastasya then knew that to free the giant's soul, she'd need help. She asked the Bear Tsarina, the strongest creature in the forest, to join her. And she asked the gray wolf who could run the fastest, the golden eagle who could fly the highest, and the thick-clawed crayfish who could dive the deepest.

On the shores of the Green Bay they met a fisherman willing to help, and they sailed in his ship off the end of the world, through the North Star, and to the Isle of Buyan. There, with her immense strength, the Bear Tsarina pulled up the Great Oak and lifted the iron chest from deep underground. She broke the lock and out ran the hare, as fast as the wind.

But the gray wolf ran faster and bit the hare in two. Out flew the duck, up into the clouds. But the golden eagle flew higher and caught the duck in her talons. Out dropped the egg and it fell deep into the ocean. But the crayfish dived after it and brought the egg up in his thick claws.

The fisherman sailed them home and Nastasya tied the egg to an arrow. As soon as the Giant Deathless was in sight, she lifted her bow, pulled back the string, aimed, and fired. The arrow flew straight and true, and the egg smashed into the giant's forehead. His soul poured into his eyes and he collapsed to his knees, overwhelmed with the feelings it brought him.

In the darkest part of the forest, the Yaga and her house

heard the Giant Deathless fall, and the house ran to him. The Yaga stepped out and took the giant by the hand. She gave him food and drink and listened to his stories and danced him all the way to the stars. And there the giant found peace, and he never bothered the creatures of the Snow Forest again.

CHAPTER TWENTY-FOUR

TRAVELING NORTH

We walk north for hours, until night fades away and the dawn chorus blooms. Sparrows chatter in low shrubs, a kingfisher whistles from the river, and chaffinches shake the treetops with their twittering. Usually their music would fill me with happiness, but this morning, all I can think about is Sasha.

I wonder where he is in the forest, and how close to life or death he lies. Elena said the house was going to walk closer to the village, then Valentyna was going to sled Sasha the rest of the way. Their journey could be over by now. Sasha could be waking up, wrapped in healing compresses. Or he could still be unconscious, frostbite creeping over him like a shadow, his ghost drifting in and out of his body.

My legs buckle and I stumble into a gorse bush.

"Are you all right, human girl?" Mousetrap uncurls from my ear and peers over my face.

"I'm just tired, and worried about Sasha." I look up, hoping to see smoke from the Fiery Volcano in the distance, but a mosaic of tall birches blocks my view. "How far away is the Lime Tree?"

"Two or three days' walk," Ivan replies.

"Days?" The forest seems to spin around me. "But Sasha is in danger *now*. What if I'm too late to save him? What if he . . ." My eyes well with tears.

"Focus!" Ivan barks. "We're going to fight a fire dragon. Worries will distract you."

I nod and walk faster. Ivan is right. I need to focus and make a plan to get past Smey and reach the Lime Tree. Sasha is as safe as he can be for now, with Valentyna and Mamoch–. I frown as I try to remember her name. "Mamoch . . ." I say out loud, hoping the word will complete itself, but it doesn't. I growl in frustration.

"What's wrong?" Yuri asks.

"I can't remember her name . . . The lady I live with." I try to picture her, but my head only fills with a thick, dark fog.

"Your mamochka?" Mousetrap squeaks, and with that she's there, back in my thoughts, clear and bright. Her strong, fussing fingers, her matter-of-fact voice, her lime-blossom smell.

"Yes, Mamochka." I sigh with relief, but there's a heaviness in the pit of my stomach. *How could I forget Mamochka?*

"You must be tired." Mousetrap peers into my left eye with a look of concern. "When was the last time you slept? Or ate?"

I think back to when I last woke, as a bear, at the bear cave. I can't believe that was only yesterday. So much has

193

happened; it feels like a lifetime ago. A chill creeps through my fur as I remember my grandmother telling me that as a bear, my human memories would fade. But I've only been a bear for less than a day. I can't be forgetting my human life already. *Can I?*

"We should stop and rest." Mousetrap nods decisively. "I could catch you a mouse. Or a rabbit."

"I'm fine. Let's keep going." I pick up speed, wanting to get to the Lime Tree as quickly as possible. I picture Sasha, long and leggy, his feathery hair sticking up at all angles, and I try to burn his image permanently into my mind. It's essential I remember him, all the way to the Fiery Volcano, so that I can ask the tree to save him. And maybe, once I've saved him, I can ask the tree to save me too.

The sun rises over the forest. Surrounded by trees, unable to glimpse the horizon, I lose all sense of how far we've traveled. Thoughts of Sasha swim in and out of my mind and I'm so tired I almost fall asleep while walking.

"Yaga house!" three bullfinches bellow in unison and flutter off into a pine thicket. The pounding of giant chicken feet shakes the earth, and the shadow of the house falls over us. A fear that it might be carrying bad news about Sasha tears through me like a storm.

One of the house's chicken feet rises high, its claws splay open, and before my mind has registered what's about to happen, the foot darts down, grabs me, and flings me onto the house's porch.

I struggle to my feet as Ivan is deposited to my left, growling, and Yuri to my right, squealing. Blakiston lands gracefully on the roof, and Mousetrap flows along the balustrades, chittering away to the house so fast I can't make out his words.

"Hello, Yanka, Yuri." Elena waves from the other end of the porch.

"How's Sasha?" My question rushes out before I remember Elena can't understand me as a bear.

"Are you asking about Sasha?" Elena edges closer to me while glancing nervously at Ivan. "The house and I left my mother sledding him to the village. He's . . ." Elena's voice wavers. "His breathing is irregular, and the frostbite is darkening despite the rabbit-fat rub my mother used. It's not looking good. I'm sorry, Yanka." She rests a hand on my back. "Perhaps your mamochka will be able to help." But she doesn't sound convinced by her words.

Guilt and despair close around me, but the urgent need to help Sasha burns hotter inside me. "House?" I turn to the front door. "Could you take us to the Fiery Volcano, so I can find the Lime Tree and save my friend?" I hold my breath as I wait for an answer. The house could run to the mountain so much faster than I could travel on foot. And the sooner I get there, the better my chance of saving Sasha.

The house nods, throwing everyone into the balustrades, then surges up and walks along the riverbank, gathering speed with each step. "Thank you!" I roar to the wide-open windows and somehow-smiling door. I'd hug the house if I could.

"Where are you rushing off to?" Elena shouts at the roof in confusion.

The house's legs extend, lifting us high above the treetops, revealing a distant orange glow beneath a dark cloud in the northeast.

"Is that where we're going?" Elena asks. "The Fiery Volcano?"

The house breaks into a sprint, sending Yuri skidding along the porch.

"Why do you want to go to the— Oh!" Elena exclaims, her eyes widening. She turns to me. "Are you going to find the Lime Tree? That's on the Fiery Volcano, isn't it? I've heard so many stories about it—that it can grow birds like leaves and grant wishes. Do you want to wish for something?" Elena looks into my eyes. "Sasha!" She claps her hands together. "You're going to ask the tree to save Sasha!"

I nod, and Elena throws her arms around my neck. "What a brilliant idea! I'm sure the tree can help. I've heard it has more magic in one of its buds than there is in a thousand Yaga houses."

The house bounds into the river and kicks a spray of icy water up and over Elena. She gasps in shock, then laughs, wringing out her shawl. "It wasn't an insult." She looks up at the roof and shakes her head. "That's what it says in *The Book of Yaga*. In fact, it says the very first Yaga house grew from a wandering root of the Lime Tree. So that would make the tree your great-great-grand-ancestor or something, wouldn't it? You'd be made of the same magic."

The house shrugs its eaves in an apology, then its front door opens wide so the warmth of the fire in the hearth drifts out to dry Elena.

"I've always wanted to see the Lime Tree." Elena's eyes sparkle. "I asked my mother if we could visit it once, after I read one of the stories, but she said it's too dangerous because of the fire dragon guarding it." Her eyebrows draw together. "Do you have a plan for getting past Smey?"

I shift uncomfortably, because I don't have a plan at all. I look from Mousetrap to Yuri to Blakiston. Fears sprout and wriggle inside me. Then my gaze lands on Ivan, huge and powerful. "Once we reach the Fiery Volcano, I think Ivan and I should face Smey, and the rest of you should stay safe in the house."

"That's a terrible plan." Mousetrap shakes his head.

"But facing Smey will be dangerous, and Ivan and I are the strongest."

"You need to stop thinking strength is about the size of your muscles or the length of your fangs. *True* strength is something far more delicate. Like spider silk. And you'll need a web of it to defeat Smey. We"—Mousetrap spins around—"are your web."

"I wish I could understand you all." Elena glances at each of us. "I've no idea what your plan is, but maybe I can help? And the house too? It's young, but it's not foolish. It will keep us safe all the way to the Fiery Volcano and back. Won't you, House?"

The house leaps into the air, lands in the river with a splash, and races through it, kicking up so much spray that a rainbow appears ahead of us.

Elena claps her hands together and smiles. "Isn't that beautiful!"

"What do you say, human girl?" Mousetrap trills. "Will you accept *all* of our help with good manners? A nod will suffice."

I want to say yes, but worries buzz around me, as relentless as a swarm of mosquitoes. "What if one of you gets hurt?" I whisper. "It would be my fault. Like with Sasha."

Mousetrap nips my ear. "We'll be hurt if you don't let us help."

The house tilts and I sway, inside and out. Mousetrap is right. Not accepting help from Mamochka and Sasha hurt them and made everything worse. This time I need to make the right choice.

"All right." My head feels heavy as a mountain, but slowly I lift it an inch. "We'll do this together." As soon as my head drops down in a nod, I feel a million times lighter.

A smile tugs at the corners of my mouth. The house is speeding us toward the Fiery Volcano, where, with the help of my herd, I'll find a way past Smey and ask the Lime Tree to save Sasha—and afterward perhaps me too. And then I'll be able to return home, to the family I never should have left behind.

CHAPTER TWENTY-FIVE

THE EDGE OF THE FOREST

The house settles into a steady gallop, and my eyelids droop with tiredness. I straighten my back, take a deep breath of cold air, and shake my head to stay awake.

"I need to make a plan." I look along the porch to where Ivan sits, staring toward the Fiery Volcano with a look of fierce determination. "Will you tell me everything you know about Smey?"

Ivan yawns. "Rest first. Then plan."

Elena bustles through the door, holding a tray loaded with food. "Hungry?" she asks, and my stomach rumbles so loud that Mousetrap jumps from my head in fright. "I also found this." Elena holds out a pot of something that smells like Mamochka's beeswax and sandalwood balsam. "For your injuries." She nods to the claw and bite marks on my neck, back, and legs, made by the white wolf and his pack. I smile at her kindness. It reminds me of Sasha and

Mamochka. *My family*. Now that I know that's what they are, all I want to do is make things right and go home to them.

Elena sets down a bowl of greens for Yuri, plates of smoked salmon for Mousetrap and Blakiston, and a dish of stewed meat for Ivan. Ivan turns away from it in disgust, snarling something about how he catches his own prey. Elena dabs my wounds with the balsam, then goes back into the house and returns with two huge bowls of soup. She sits next to me, spooning hers into her mouth, and I stare at mine, wondering how to eat it politely. But my snout twitches at the scent, and soon my tongue is lapping it up with a life of its own. The soup splashes over my fur and I spill the last bit while trying to hold the bowl with my paw. I lean back, lick my snout clean, and flush with embarrassment under my fur.

When everyone—apart from Ivan, who refuses to even look at the stewed meat—has eaten, we sit quietly, watching the land sail past. Spring fades as we travel north. There's more snow on the trees, and the air grows colder. Elena brings out a blanket, leans against my back, and dozes off. Blakiston snores quietly on the roof, Mousetrap burrows into the fur behind my ear, and Yuri snuffles in his dreams next to me. Ivan continues staring at the horizon, but his eyes are half-closed and his head keeps dropping.

I try to remember the stories I've heard about Smey, hoping they'll help me come up with a plan. But my mind fills with mist. Scared I'm forgetting my human life again, I try to picture every detail: planting seeds in the garden with

Mamochka, her strong, smooth hands tucking my hair behind my ears; Anatoly sitting by the fire, his callused fingers skating over an inky map. I picture Sasha, smiling up at me from beneath his huge furry hat, asking me to race, rolling off his sled laughing.

And I think about what I'll say to the Lime Tree. But I'm so tired that all my thoughts swirl together, and soon the gentle snores of my friends, the rhythmic thump of the house's chicken feet, and the slowly rolling floor rock me into a deep, cave-dark sleep of my own.

When I wake, all signs of spring are gone. Here the trees are weighed down by snow and the river is thick with ice. The sun is pale and distant, descending slowly though a cold gray sky. It's afternoon already. The tip of Elena's nose is blue, and our breath mingles into a big white cloud. I curl around her to keep her warm, like the Bear Tsarina used to do for me. *My grandmother.*

Sadness wells inside me at having left my grandmother behind. She's my family too. But if I'd stayed with her as a bear, I would have lost everything from my human life. Even my memories. And they make me who I am . . . But my grandmother has made me who I am too. I frown, suddenly confused by everything.

I push my conflicting thoughts away and focus on what I am sure of. *I have to save Sasha.* As the day slips away, he could be slipping away too. I stand and search the landscape, trying to work out how much farther we have to go.

Not far ahead lies the northern edge of the Snow Forest. The Silver Stream ends in a wide crescent-shaped bay, frozen over with thick green ice, and beyond that lies a vast navy ocean splattered with huge patches of bright white ice.

To the east, on the boundary between land and sea, looms the Fiery Volcano, its peak hidden by thick black smoke. Blazing reds glow beneath the smoke, and orange and yellow lights crackle and spark within it. I glance up at the roof above me and am suddenly aware of how wooden—and flammable—the house is. "How will we get to the mountain safely?" I whisper.

Elena stirs, stretches, and rubs her eyes, then looks from the house to the ocean ahead. "We've reached the Northern Sea already! Just a short distance around the coast, then we'll be at the Fiery Volcano." She smiles and rests a hand on my back.

The house leaps onto the frozen river and skids along so fast I wonder if it's lost control. Yuri squeals as he slides along the porch, and Mousetrap's claws dig into my ear as he's flung backward.

With a great swoosh and a frightening jerk, the house regains its balance, then skates smoothly onto the thick green ice of the crescent-shaped bay.

"What's that?" Elena peers at a shape in the distance—something large at the far edge of the bay. It grows huge as we approach, and my fur tingles with excitement as it comes into focus, because I think I know how the house plans to take us safely to the Fiery Volcano.

"Mousetrap." I wiggle my head to check he hasn't gone back to sleep. "Look, a ship!"

"I see it." Mousetrap leans over my head and grins. "The Yaga girl said the house would keep us safe. What better way to get to the Fiery Volcano than to sail along the coast?"

I smile, because Mousetrap is right—icy water is the best place to stay safe from a fiery volcano. As we draw closer, I gaze at the ship in awe. It's enormous, big enough for at least five Yaga houses to sit on its deck. Its tall frost-white masts rise high into the sky, and its long, pointed prow twinkles with snow stars.

"It's a frozen ship!" Elena claps her hands together in excitement. "Like the one from Anatoly's story!" She turns to me, her eyes shining as bright as the ship. "Has he told you that story too?"

I shake my head, because although I do have memories of the story, it was another of Anatoly's more fantastical tales that I had trouble believing at the time, and it would be good to hear it again.

Elena picks up her blanket and wraps it around her shoulders, and as the house skates the last stretch toward the still, white ship, she tells the story, as Anatoly would have told it to her, starting with "Once upon a time . . ."

THE FLYING SHIP

Once upon a time, the world was full of flying ships, powered by the heights of imagination and the depths of belief. The ships sailed through the sky like whales through the sea, fishing for adventures and wonders.

But as years passed, imagination and belief became rarer, and one by one the flying ships sank to the sea. They became cargo ships, or passenger ferries, or naval vessels. A few disappeared beneath the waves and became homes for mermaids and sea serpents.

Soon, there was only one flying ship left, captained by a young giant called Koschei. He soared through the sky and skimmed over clouds for one hundred years, until he was furrowed and gray as a blustery sea. The young giant Koschei was now old, and his life was ebbing away. Sorrow engulfed him, because Koschei loved flying his ship so much that he yearned to live and fly forever.

So Koschei devised a plan. He flew off the end of the world, through the North Star and to the Isle of Buyan. And there he hid his soul beneath the Great Oak so he could become immortal and never have to stop flying.

Without his soul, Koschei became known as the Giant Deathless. But without his soul, Koschei found he had no imagination or belief to power his ship, so it fell from the sky and splashed into the Northern Sea. Anger and grief rampaged through Koschei. He snapped the mainmast in fury and stormed away to the Snow Forest, leaving his ship bobbing lonely on the waves.

The ship drifted, alone and forgotten, until it was found by a crew of fishermen. They climbed aboard and fixed the mainmast, then added a second mast and a net winch, and turned the ship into a fine fishing vessel. And they sailed the Northern Sea from the Calm East to the Stormy West, collecting fish and kelp and crabs. Focused on their fishing, the crew didn't have the imagination or belief to make the ship fly.

Then one day, one of the fishermen fell in love on the shore of the Green Bay. His heart lightened until he felt like he was walking on sea-foam. And to his delight, the lady loved him too. The fisherman's crew gave the couple the ship as a wedding gift and returned to their first fishing vessel.

The fisherman and his wife were so full of love, imagination, and belief that when they set sail on their honeymoon, the ship rose into the sky. The ship's sails billowed in the wind, and a smile spread across the bow. They flew off the end of the world, through the North Star to the Isle of Buyan and beyond.

Seven seasons later, the fisherman and his wife steered back to the shores of the Green Bay. They were going to have a child and wanted to build a home together in the forest. So they left the ship alone once more, but before they did, they carved into its gunwales: *For adventurers with belief and imagination.*

Winter came, and Father Frost found the ship, lonely and forgotten. He sat on its bow and froze it into the ice. And there it sleeps, year after year, waiting for a crew with enough imagination and belief to make it fly once more.

CHAPTER TWENTY-SIX

THE FROZEN SHIP

The house approaches the end of the thick sheet of ice in the bay and skids to slow down. Its movements are large and eager, all its windows wide open. I think it would be whooping with delight if it could.

The frozen ship rises above us, glittering and brilliant, and with a massive leap the house jumps onto its deck. Ice cracks and wood creaks beneath the house's feet as it walks along the deck, and the whole ship shifts as if coming to life.

When the house reaches the bow, it sits on the end and stretches its legs down either side of the ship, until they reach all the way to the frozen ocean below. The door curves into a smile so high that it crumples the eaves.

An echoing bang explodes through the air. The ship drops—and my stomach with it. There's another bang, and another, and the ship lurches sideways. Rhythmic thumps roll beneath us, and the ice rumbles like thunder.

I lean over the house's balustrade to see what's going on,

and Mousetrap leaps down and runs off to the rail of the ship. "The house is breaking the ice with its feet," he squeaks over a cacophony of smashing and splashing. "We're about to set sail." A moment later he reappears on the house's roof and leans his whole body east, as if by doing so he might steer the house, and the ship, that way. "To the Fiery Volcano!"

The ice around us splinters and groans like a great monster waking from sleep. Then, with a gut-wrenching lurch, the ship falls through the ice. Glacial waves crash over the gunwales, and for a sickening moment I think we're going to sink to the bottom of the sea. But the ship bounces back up and my heart vaults inside me.

Yuri screams. Ivan growls. Blakiston hoots. Mousetrap trills with glee, and Elena jumps up and down on the tips of her toes.

The house begins paddling. It rocks back and forth as it sweeps its feet through the floe-littered water on either side of the ship. Great chunks of ice bob and drift away as the house steers us into a clear, open channel.

A thick shoot bursts from the floorboards behind Yuri. He jumps up, his already-wide eyes rolling in shock, and staggers away from it, whining. The shoot rises above the porch, and huge leaves unfurl like sails.

"Isn't this wonderful?" Elena drapes her arm around my neck and beams.

I lean into her and smile. It *is* wonderful. The dark blue ocean and bright white ice, shining gold near the horizon, are breathtaking. And the excitement of the Yaga house is infectious—its leafy sails billow and my chest swells.

The channel widens, and the house finds a steady rhythm. It rocks gently as its feet swish and splosh through the water. The sun emerges from behind a wispy cloud, and the sky explodes with light. Dazzling rays shoot across the Snow Forest, and far to the south, the peak of the Blue Mountain shines as bright as stardust.

"Stardust!" I shout, an idea blazing into my mind.

Mousetrap lands on my snout and looks at me in confusion. "What are you talking about, human girl?"

"At the very top of the mountain, where the ancient peak is stained blue by the sky, Nastasya carved six arrowheads. Made from thick blue ice and hardened with stardust, they were strong and cold enough to cool the anger in a fire dragon's heart." I quote Anatoly's story word for word, excitement bubbling inside me. "My necklace is one of those arrowheads! We can use it to fight Smey. Nibble through the cord, please, Mousetrap."

Mousetrap runs to the back of my neck. I feel him gnawing, deep in my fur, then I feel the arrowhead slipping.

Elena catches it before it falls. "This is one of your birth mother's arrowheads, isn't it?" She holds it up to the light. "Anatoly told me the story of her battle with Smey."

I nod, looking at the blue-white rock in Elena's hands. *The last arrow.* In Anatoly's story it sailed over stars, carrying love and strength; it dipped under the moon, picking up moonbeams and magic; and it brought my birth mother's story to me. *The story of how she died.* An image of her forms in my mind. Valentyna said she looked like me, when I was human, but I picture her bigger and stronger. She was a great warrior, but she died fighting Smey. So what hope do we have? My muscles tremble like bee wings.

Mousetrap nips my ear. "A web of strength, remember?"

I take a deep breath and look around at Elena, Ivan, Yuri, Blakiston, and the house. Mousetrap is right. Nastasya was alone. Whereas I have a herd.

"House." Elena pats the balustrade. "Could you grow me a bow and an arrow shaft, please?"

"What an excellent idea," Mousetrap trills. "The Yaga girl can fire the arrow into Smey's heart."

"No." I shake my head, not wanting Elena to be in the center of danger. "I'll carry the arrow between my teeth."

"My attacking skills will be of use." Ivan growls and the fur on his back shivers menacingly. "I'll force Smey into a corner, then you can tear the arrow through his heart."

"Either one of you would be burned to a crisp before you got near Smey's heart." Mousetrap looks from me to Ivan and shakes his head. "You're lucky a creature with intelligence is here."

Ivan bares his teeth and snarls, and Mousetrap darts up onto the roof.

"This is perfect. Look, Yanka." Elena holds a long, curved bow that has grown from one of the balustrade spindles. I raise a paw, longing to touch it. Mousetrap is right; firing the arrow from a distance will be safer than a close battle with Smey. But I wish I could be the one to do it.

A thin, fibrous vine curls down from the roof, and Elena rolls it between her fingers. "I'll string the bow with this." She breaks off the vine and ties it to one end of the bow. "I'm so pleased I can help with your plan!" She beams. "I'll shoot Smey. You can talk to the Lime Tree. Then the house will take us back, and we'll find Sasha safe and well." Elena strings the other end of the bow, then holds it up to admire her work. "I need to practice with something. Any ideas, House?"

Long, thin arrows grow from the floorboards like rye, their heads thickening into sharp wooden triangles. "Thank you." Elena snaps off a few of the practice arrows and steps onto the deck of the ship.

She fumbles with an arrow, dropping it several times before finally managing to draw it back in her bow. Then she closes one eye and aims at some barrels stacked near the stern. She releases the bow string, and the arrow flops to the floor a few feet away from her. But she picks up another arrow and tries again. And again.

Elena keeps practicing and improves slowly, shooting farther and with more force each time. But she doesn't hit the barrels. Most of her arrows skid across the deck. A few sail off the ship and fall into the sea.

"The chance of her hitting Smey is slim," Ivan rumbles as another arrow nose-dives from Elena's bow, skids across the deck, and disappears over the side of the ship.

I nod. Ivan's right, but a plan is forming in my mind. "I'll lure Smey out of his cavern and distract him, so Elena has a clear shot. If she misses, one of us will retrieve the arrow and carry it back to her so she can try again."

Blakiston opens his wings and glides down from the roof to the balustrades. "I can do that." He stretches his claws. "I'll be able to catch the arrow mid-flight, if needed."

Ivan nods. "I'll help drive Smey into the best position and ensure the arrow returns to Elena."

"What will I do?" Yuri asks, rising onto his hooves.

"Your strength is fleeing." Mousetrap drops from the roof onto Yuri's short antlers.

"I'm very good at fleeing," Yuri agrees proudly.

I smile as a perfect idea jumps into my mind. "You can carry Elena on your back and flee with her if things become dangerous."

"I shall do that." Yuri nods.

"And my strength is—" Mousetrap begins with a flourish.

"Your exceptional hunting skills?" I suggest.

"It's rude to interrupt." Mousetrap glares at me. "And actually, my strength is my war dance. It's the best you'll ever see." He leaps onto my snout, puffs out his chest, and sways his head from side to side. "I'll hypnotize Smey with it, to keep him still while the Yaga girl shoots."

The plan clicks into my mind, piece by piece. Yuri will carry Elena and keep her out of danger. I'll draw Smey into the open and Ivan can help me keep him in place. Elena will fire the arrow from a distance, and if she misses, Blakiston or Ivan will return the arrow to her. Mousetrap can do his war dance, whatever that is, and once we get past Smey, I'll talk to the Lime Tree and ask it to save Sasha, and me.

As I let myself believe the plan will work, I feel light as the clouds above. My muscles relax, but I feel strong. It's a strange, new sensation. I always thought strength came from facing things alone, but maybe I was wrong. Maybe working with others can give you strength too.

The house tilts sharply, making everyone lean sideways, as it drags one of its feet through the water to make a great sweeping turn around a headland. An icy wind blasts into my face and I squint against it. When I peep my eyes open again, the sight ahead takes my breath away.

A steep, craggy volcano dominates the landscape. Thin, patchy sections of forest run up to its base, then shrivel away into a graveyard of blackened trees and curling smoke. Veins of bright orange lava glow from fissures in rocks, and pools of iridescent mud bubble in hollows.

"The Fiery Volcano." Mousetrap scrambles up and over my head to get a better view.

My forehead tightens as I trace a path up the volcano, following ribbons of melting snow, hopefully cool enough to walk on, that weave between rocks that shimmer with heat.

About halfway up the volcano is a gaping black cavern, wider than my house and taller than the towering pines at the bottom of my garden. *Smey's cavern.* The thought of him pricks goose bumps into my flesh. Even though I have a plan now, I still don't know what to expect from Smey.

Above the cavern, the volcano's peak is hidden behind

thick, dark smoke, but as I stare, the clouds shift. My heart soars when I glimpse enormous leafy branches that spread wide as a sunset and reach high as the sky.

"The Lime Tree," I whisper, hardly daring to believe it's real. It looks so out of place, growing on the peak of a scorching, smoldering volcano. "How can it survive here?"

"It has little choice," Ivan growls. "This used to be the soul of the Snow Forest. It was a beautiful place, cool and calm and filled with life. But since Smey was created, the Lime Tree has no control over its surroundings. The Fiery Volcano has grown from Smey's touch and left the tree trapped and alone." Ivan glances up at the Lime Tree, barely visible behind swells of dense smoke, and his eyes flash with a mixture of anguish and sympathy.

"You told me before that Smey guards the Lime Tree." My brow furrows. "But now you make it sound like Smey is harming the tree."

"Both are true." Ivan nods.

"I don't understand. Where did Smey come from? Why does he guard the tree in a way that harms it?"

"I'd have thought you would know that story." Ivan turns to me with one ear back and the other forward. "Seeing as it was your grandfather's actions that created Smey."

"My grandfather?" Another gust of wind drives needles of ice beneath my fur and I shiver. "The Bear Tsar?"

Ivan nods again. "Yes, but before he was a bear. When he was still a human—a woodsman called Dmitry. Sit. I have time to tell you the tale before we arrive."

I sit, as Ivan suggests, anticipation trembling inside me. The house paddles smoothly along, past rows of charred trees and jagged black rocks. The evening sun throws long shadows ahead of us and smoke belches from a crack in the ground.

The rotten-egg smell of sulfur seeps into my nose and leaves a bitter taste in my mouth. Ivan snorts out a small puffy cloud. Then he begins his story with "Once upon a time . . ."

THE LIME TREE'S WISH

Once upon a time, there was a lime tree at the soul of the forest, as tall as the sky and as wide as the sunrise. The tree was filled with magic and joy. It danced with the trees around it and sang with the birds in its boughs.

But then the woodsman came.

The tree could have knocked the woodsman's axe from his hands, but the tree was kind and offered the woodsman a wish in exchange for compassion.

The woodsman took the wish and asked for more, and more, until the tree, exhausted and downhearted, refused.

Consumed by greed, the woodsman roared in anger and chop . . .
. . . chop
. . . CHOPPED down a branch.
And the tree cried out in pain.

On the ground, the cut branch writhed and swelled with fury. It cracked and split and grew three heads and reared up as a furious, flaming dragon, burning with the fires of anger and injustice.

The tree trembled in fear, for it had no control over the fire dragon and could only watch in horror as flames and lava spewed from the dragon's mouth. The forest was set alight. Birds flew away, streams dried up, and flowers were smothered with ash.

The tree begged the dragon to stop, but the dragon's flames grew hotter as it vowed to defend the tree from the greed of man forevermore. The dragon roared over the earth, and groundwater exploded into scalding fountains. Mud cooked until it bubbled and boiled, clear pools were poisoned with yellow acid, and noxious gases swirled into deadly mist. The rocks around the tree swelled with magma until a volcano blossomed, with a cavern on its slope for the dragon to live in.

When the dragon grumbled, earthquakes shook the forest, and when he raged, the volcano erupted so violently it drew lightning from the sky.

Above the cavern the Lime Tree stood, alone and sorrowful. Because although the dragon only wanted to protect the tree, the tree was now trapped, far from the forest it loved. Each time the dragon woke and breathed fire into the sky, the tree wept as the forest burned. And although the tree was full of magic, it could not grant its own wish: that one day the dragon's anger would cool, and it could return to the forest it loved.

CHAPTER TWENTY-SEVEN

THE FIERY VOLCANO

"So this is my grandfather's fault?" I stare at the scorched forest, the cracked and blistering volcano, and the Lime Tree, trapped on its peak and choked by soot and ash. "He caused all this by being greedy and selfish and cruel." I look down at my bear feet and shake my head. "My family deserves to be cursed."

"Nonsense." Mousetrap nips my ear. "It was unfair of the tree to punish others for what your grandfather did. Your grandmother, your father, and yourself all did nothing wrong."

"Perhaps the Lime Tree didn't intend to curse your whole family for generations. Curses, like anger and fire dragons, are difficult to control." Ivan glares at the Fiery Volcano, and his muscles tighten, as if he's about to pounce upon it. "What's important is that you're here now, to right the wrongs of your grandfather. Together we can defeat the dragon he created."

I take a deep breath and lift my snout high. Ivan is right. I came here to save Sasha, who is on the brink of death because of me, and to find a way to go home human—but now I realize I can do so much more. I can make amends for what my grandfather did and save the Lime Tree too.

If we can cool Smey's anger with the arrow, we could free the Lime Tree and the Snow Forest from these ferocious fires and this strangling smoke. The Fiery Volcano might subside and grow over with trees once more, and the Lime Tree would be back where it belonged, surrounded by forest. Ivan could return to where he belongs, as leader of his pack. And if the Lime Tree makes me human, I can return home to where I belong too.

"Together we can defeat Smey." I quietly echo Ivan's words, to see how they feel, and my chest swells with a ripple of confidence and a flicker of hope. We *have* to do this, to right all the wrongs of the past.

Mousetrap leans over my brow and grins. "We *will* defeat Smey," he trills, and I smile up at him. Yuri stands and nods his agreement, and Blakiston opens his wings and lets out a low, drawn-out hoot.

The house quivers with excitement and paddles closer to the shore, where a long, flat rock juts out, like a landing jetty. The Fiery Volcano towers over us, a monstrous, red-raw, fuming titan. The dark cavern in its side is so close that I feel the air sizzling inside it. My fur lifts, and my skin tingles. Smey, and the Lime Tree, are just a few breaths away.

Elena emerges from the house. She went inside during Ivan's story to fix the arrowhead onto a shaft, and now she's holding it up, beaming. The triangular ice-blue rock is firmly tied to a long, sturdy shaft with pale, sinewy cord. "It's ready." Elena turns the arrow around in her fingers. Its head glistens like starlight on snow, and the sharp edges flash like Ivan's fangs.

My nerves charge with electricity, and my feet twitch. I'm ready to do this, but at the same time I'm more nervous than I've ever been. I step off the porch onto the boat deck, then turn around and look at the house. "You should wait here, on the ship. The ground looks hot and I don't want you to catch fire." The house's door and windows narrow with disapproval, but it nods grudgingly.

"Oh, wait!" Elena removes a bundle of leather scraps from under her arm. "I thought I could wrap your and the wolf's paws, to protect them from the heat."

Ivan nods and approaches Elena slowly. He holds out his paws one by one, and she binds them with strips of leather and cord. When she's finished, Ivan growls a soft "Thank you."

I let Elena wrap my paws too, and when I stand they feel strange. They might be better protected from the hot ground, but the vibrations through my soles have been deadened, so I feel as though I've lost one of my senses. It occurs to me that if I become human again, I'll lose that sense altogether. *I'll miss my bear legs.* I have to push the thought away before it distracts me.

"My hooves will be fine." Yuri trots off the porch to join the rest of us.

"All right. Let's go." I nod to Yuri, Ivan, Elena, and Blakiston; wiggle my ear to check Mousetrap is still curled around it; and then walk to the gunwales of the ship. There's a carving on one of the wooden planks, almost hidden by frost: *For adventurers with belief and imagination.* I remember Anatoly's story—the one Elena told about the flying ship—and I wonder if this ship ever really flew.

A smile spreads across my face, because that would be ridiculous, like turning into a bear, or fighting a fire dragon, or asking an enchanted tree to break a curse. I might never know exactly which bits of Anatoly's stories are true, but since I grew bear legs, at least I know for certain that *anything* is possible.

Something tightens around my chest, and my feet rise off the floor. For a moment I think the ship has taken flight. But then I realize one of the house's chicken feet is lifting me up and over the gunwales.

I land on the long, flat rock below. It gives slightly and is warm, even through the leather coverings on my paws. A few steps away, water hisses and steams as it laps against a sharp and craggy shore.

Yuri is lowered down next. Then Ivan jumps into the water before the house can grab him, and clambers onto the shore himself. Blakiston glides off the roof, and Elena lets herself be lifted down. She hugs the long chicken claws affectionately. "Wait here. We'll be back soon." She waves to the house, hooks her bow over her shoulder, holds the arrow tight in her hands, and nods to me. "Ready?"

I nod, and gently nudge her toward Yuri until she realizes I want her to climb onto his back. "Oh! I've never ridden an elk before." Elena puts her arms around Yuri's neck and swings her legs up. "I've never ridden anything apart from a Yaga house."

"You'll keep Elena safe, won't you, Yuri?" I ask.

"Of course." Yuri nods confidently. "I'm an expert in fleeing. If things become dangerous for the Yaga girl, I'll run back here, to the ship and the house."

"Blakiston?" I call up to where he's circling above us. He swoops down and lands on my back. "Would you fly ahead and look for a safe place for Elena to fire the arrow from?" Blakiston nods and takes off again.

"I'll stay with you," Ivan growls. "Together we'll make sure the arrow finds its way to Smey's heart."

I nod. "If Elena and Yuri have to flee, it will be up to us."

"And me." Mousetrap scrambles over my ear, somersaults down my forehead, slips, and lands a foot in my eye. "Apologies." He bows and curves his spine from side to side. "I'm warming up, ready for my war dance."

I blink away the pain in my eye. "If you could remain around my ear, that might be safer for both of us."

Mousetrap handstands on my snout, then flips over onto the top of my head. "It would be a shame if you didn't get to see my war dance."

I lead the way up the mountain, across the darkest, coolest-looking rocks. Thick caustic smoke seeps from cracks, and lava glows and flames in crevices. Heat waves distort everything, and I feel as though I'm climbing into a great oven. My mouth opens, my tongue hangs loose, and my breath rasps, short and sharp.

Blakiston circles around and lands on my back again. "There's a platform in the cliff to the left of Smey's cavern. I suggest that Yuri take the Yaga girl there. She'll have a clear view to shoot the arrow at Smey but will be relatively sheltered from danger."

"Can you lead them there?" I ask. "The rest of us will walk closer to the cavern entrance, and I'll lure Smey out." My voice shakes with anxiety that I try to disguise with a confident-sounding growl.

Blakiston nods, opens his wings, and flaps into the air. Yuri follows him, his hooves crunching across brittle rocks. Elena looks confused as we split up, but then she seems to work out the plan and gives me a reassuring smile.

I turn to the dark cavern ahead. "Do you know what Smey looks like?" I whisper to Ivan. "Is he big?"

"Smey can be as big or as small as he likes."

"What do you mean?" I ask.

"Fire dragons are made of fire," Ivan snarls. "They can flare up to the size of a mountain or die down to a candle flicker."

"Made of fire," I murmur. A wave of heat radiates from

the cavern and rolls toward me, but my blood shivers in my veins. I hope Anatoly's story about the arrow is true—I hope it really can destroy a creature made of fire. But whether it can or can't, I know I have to face Smey. I'd face a thousand fire dragons, armed with nothing but a snowball, to save Sasha and find a way home.

CHAPTER TWENTY-EIGHT

SMEY

I walk closer to the cavern, across angry, biting rocks. Mousetrap is on my neck, Ivan by my side. Yuri clambers up a cliff to our left, with Elena on his back and Blakiston flying above.

The air shimmers, and my senses sharpen. Yuri's hooves sound like thunder; Blakiston's wingbeats flash like lightning. Elena adjusts her bow, and the swish of her hair is a gale. Ivan knocks a tiny rock, and it feels like an avalanche. My own heart is an earthquake inside me, because we're about to face Smey.

The cavern is only a few paces away. From deep inside shines a bloodred light, so bright it hurts my eyes. My gaze drifts up and over the cavern, to the Lime Tree peeking through dark shifting clouds.

The tree's bark looks smooth but tough, like Mamochka's hands. The branches reach out, like her arms when she throws them around me for a hug. And for a moment I smell lime blossoms, reminding me so much of Mamochka that tears well in my eyes.

I breathe out slowly and step forward as gently as possible, one foot in front of the other. And with each step I tell myself: *We can do this; we can cool Smey's anger and save the Lime Tree, and Sasha, and me.*

I feel so foolish. I had to walk deep into the forest before I understood what I was leaving behind. I had to lose what I had before I realized how much I loved it. And I had to look back into my past to see what I want in my future—which is a family who loves me. And I already had one in Mamochka and Sasha and Anatoly. Sometimes I struggled to fit in at the village. But now that I'm far away, I miss everything about it. Some struggles, I realize now, are worth it.

Just like facing Smey will be worth it, so I can make everything right.

I stop still in front of the cavern mouth. Ivan is slightly ahead of me. His body, a dark silhouette against the shining light, appears tiny beneath the gaping entrance. The glow from the cavern intensifies and tendrils of thick gray smoke curl toward us. I squint, trying to see what lies beyond them, but can't make out anything.

Then flames lick out and swirl together into a long, writhing ribbon. I stare, openmouthed, as the burning ribbon thickens and rises into a column. A glowing eye and a dazzling fang-filled mouth flash inside the fire.

The mouth opens slowly with a gentle hiss, then darts forward, erupting into a ball of flames that roars like a hurricane.

"Ivan, run!" I shout as I bolt away from the heat. But Ivan doesn't follow. I hear his snarls, all emanating from the same spot. I glance back, and an arrow whooshes past, so close that it parts the hair on my neck.

"Sorry!" Elena shouts from the ledge in the cliff behind us. "Misfired." The arrow soars into the distance and Blakiston and Ivan both chase after it.

The fire dragon grows wider and taller. I gaze in horror and awe as Smey takes shape. Three long necks unfurl and writhe like snakes in the air. On the end of each neck is a jagged, angular head with a pointed snout. With a crack like burning pine cones, a wide grin splits each of the three heads, and my courage fractures too. Three sets of flickering blue-green fangs rain droplets of fire that hiss and sizzle on the ground, and three forked tongues flash out like daggers of lightning.

I back away, anger and fear wrestling inside me. This is Smey, who killed my parents, who sends fires through the Snow Forest every year, and who is now standing between me and the tree that could save both Sasha and myself. I want to defeat him more than anything, to fix my grandfather's mistake and make everything right. But faced with this behemoth of furious fire, I'm not sure how to do it.

Smey expands until he fills the sky. His three heads whip

blindly around, nostrils high as if smelling the air. His eyes are dark and empty—all except one, which is a swirl of color: orange, red, purple, and blue. *It must be true about my birth mother shooting five of Smey's eyes.* The dark and empty sockets are proof that her arrows quashed his flames—if only in those five small areas. My chest swells with pride and hope. Because if Smey's flames can be put out, then he can be defeated.

The colorful eye finds me and flares brighter, then all three heads dive straight toward me. A wall of heat punches the breath from my lungs and I scramble backward on all four paws, heart pounding. I look around frantically, trying to spot something—anything—I can use as a weapon. There's no sign of Ivan, Blakiston, or the arrow.

My gaze settles on a massive boulder above the cavern entrance and I run for it, but the steep slope slows me down and I hear the roar of Smey drawing closer. Mousetrap's claws dig painfully into my ear as he grips me tight, but I'm so relieved he's still with me I don't mind.

Acrid whiffs of charring leather sting my snout as heat burns through the wraps covering my paws. But I keep my eyes fixed on the boulder. At the edge of my vision, I see Smey's heads tracking me, his long necks undulating alongside me. Eels of thick black smoke roll from his mouths and gnaw at my throat.

My heart avalanches into my ribs, and my lungs tighten like pine cones in the rain. But finally I reach the boulder, which is nestled among thick, tangled roots, and I shelter behind it. I tear at the ground, shredding what remains of my leather paw coverings and throwing ashy soil into the air.

Smey's smoke surrounds me, clogging and choking my airways. I hold my breath and dig, faster and deeper. For a moment I think the roots move to help me, but it must be the shifting smoke, or my imagination. When I think I've freed the boulder, I push it as hard as I can.

It doesn't budge. I throw my whole weight at it and roar. Slowly, slowly it shifts, teeters, and, with a final great push, tumbles over the cavern entrance, straight toward Smey's chest. He tries to shift out of the way, but he's too big and too slow.

A thunderous bang rocks the volcano. Spark-filled air rushes up and swirls around me. I edge forward and peer down.

Far below, where the dragon blazed a moment ago, lies the boulder. A tiny ring of orange flames flickers around it.

"I did it!" I'm so amazed that I start to cheer in my roaring bear voice—but before the sound has left my mouth, Smey's flames rise again from beneath the boulder, curling and swirling together even brighter and hotter than before.

Then Ivan, the glint of the blue-white arrow flashing in his jaws, charges toward the dragon. But with every step closer, Smey grows bigger. The dragon's three heads form again and blast upward until they hover over Ivan like angry clouds, howling with a storm wind's laughter.

Ivan lets out a blood-chilling snarl and tears straight through the center of the dragon.

"No!" I shout, and run toward him, skidding and tumbling down the slope.

But Ivan is inside the dragon already, a dark blur engulfed by flames. My heart drumrolls.

Ivan lashes his head from side to side, and the tip of the arrow shines a bright, brilliant white. Smey's flames split where the arrow slices through them, and he bellows in pain. He swirls around, a mass of red fire, and I stare into the chaos, desperately trying to spot Ivan again.

I see him, right in the center of the swirl, still slashing at Smey's flames though his fur is ablaze. "Ivan!" I yell. "Stop! Come back!" But he doesn't hear me, or chooses not to.

I have to get him out of Smey before he burns up completely. So I take a deep breath and run toward him, into the fire.

Flames snap at my snout, my ears, and my eyes, but I grit my teeth and charge on until I reach Ivan. He swings his head once more, and the arrowhead slices a deep, dark gash through the very center of Smey.

A scream surges from the wound and I glimpse a pulsing, beating heart made of fire. Ivan lunges forward, to tear through Smey's heart, but an explosion of light and heat bursts out in all directions, flinging us backward.

Ivan whimpers in pain as he lands awkwardly and the arrow flies from his mouth. I watch it land a few yards away. I look from the arrow to Smey's burning heart, exposed in the depths of a dark wound. I could run to the arrow, grab it, and tear through the heart myself . . . But I look back at Ivan. He's still, his fur smoldering.

I bound over to him and gather him in my front paws. Then I rise onto my back legs and stumble out of Smey's flames. Blinded by the darkness away from the light, I struggle up to the ledge where Elena is calling for us. Behind her is a patch of snow. I collapse into it and throw cold slush over Ivan and myself until our fur stops smoking.

Ivan struggles to his feet. "Did I defeat Smey?" he asks. But as he looks behind me, dragon fire reflects in his eyes, and his face drops. I turn and follow his gaze. My heart sinks. Smey has re-formed and is growing larger with every moment.

"I failed," Ivan growls. His face disappears into shadow as the last rays of sunset sink into the ocean behind us. Darkness rises all around, broken only by the raging flames of Smey.

"You haven't failed." I shake my head, staring into the flames. "Look at him." There's something unbalanced about Smey, and the dark wound Ivan inflicted has revealed his beating heart. "You cut all the way to his heart," I whisper. "I'm sure he'll be easier to defeat now." But I frown and bite my lip, because I don't know how to fight Smey without the arrow.

Then Blakiston swoops toward us, straight out of Smey's chest. The tips of his wings are on fire, but he has the arrow in his claws. Hope surges through me. I hold my breath as one of Smey's heads snaps at Blakiston, but he swerves out of the way and drops the arrow into Elena's lap. Then he lands beside me and rolls over, dousing his feathers in snow.

"This time the Yaga girl will pierce Smey's heart." Yuri lifts his head and stands tall and steady.

I look at Elena, anticipation tingling under my fur. She fits the arrow to her bow and draws back the string. Smey's heart is less than ten yards away and is as big as Ivan. But as she takes aim, Smey swirls around. His heart disappears into the flames and reappears in a different place.

"This is impossible." Elena groans as she tries to adjust her aim. Then she frowns, lowers her bow, and peers at something on the ground in front of Smey. Something tiny. "Mousetrap!" she yells. "Come back."

It's only then that I realize Mousetrap is no longer curled around my ear, but is standing in front of Smey, limbering up.

"Mousetrap!" I cry. "Come back here!"

But he just smiles. And starts to dance.

CHAPTER TWENTY-NINE

MOUSETRAP'S WAR DANCE

Mousetrap springs straight up into the air. His back is arched, his limbs stiff and reaching. When he lands, his body begins flowing smoothly in and out of intricate knots. He darts back and forth, halting abruptly to stare at Smey before continuing with complicated sequences of leaps and backflips.

His fur shines, sometimes coppery, sometimes rust red or burnished gold with the reflections of Smey's flames.

Smey's heads sway as they track Mousetrap's movements, and his flames subside. Mousetrap somersaults, twists, cartwheels, and performs handsprings, and Smey becomes hypnotized.

My own thoughts drift away. There's no rhythm to Mousetrap's movements, but I can't take my eyes off him. And as I watch, I'm overcome with a heavy sleepiness that weighs down every muscle of my body. My eyelids droop.

Smey sinks to the ground, still. The outline of his slowly beating heart is clearly visible in his chest. My eyes pop open again at the sight of it.

"Elena has a clear shot," I whisper.

Elena lifts her bow. Narrows her eyes. Aims . . .

I hold my breath. *She can't miss.*

The bowstring twangs and the arrow shoots through the air . . . straight toward Smey's heart . . .

My jaw drops open. Hope fizzes on my tongue.

Time slows. I blink, fast, and realize it's the arrow that's slowed, not time. The arrow comes to a complete stop, a few inches from Smey's heart. The shaft burns away, leaving only the head, which just hovers in the flames, like it doesn't have the power to go on.

Smey's flames brighten as he wakes from his trance. His one good eye glances down at the arrowhead embedded in his chest, not quite deep enough to have pierced his heart. He claws at it and roars in anger, but the arrowhead doesn't shift. Writhing in frustration, Smey lifts all three of his heads and blasts fire up into the dark sky with the scream and boom of fireworks.

The branches of the Lime Tree high above crack as they catch alight. A few of them fall to the ground amid a shower of sparks. Yuri stumbles backward and whines.

"Retreat to the ship!" I shout as another branch smashes right in front of Yuri's hooves, but Yuri is galloping away already, Elena holding tight to his neck. I step over the sizzling, smoking branch and try to spot Mousetrap. He's poised on two legs, staring at the arrowhead embedded in Smey's chest. "Mousetrap!" I shout—but he leaps straight toward the dazzling triangular rock.

Mousetrap's teeth sparkle, his lips curl back, and he looks more ferocious than a hissing wolverine. He extends his paws to land on the arrowhead, but Smey whips around, and all of a sudden there's a fiery mouth loaded with long blue-green fangs yawning open right in front of Mousetrap.

"No!" I sprint into the blistering heat and lunge for Mousetrap. But Smey's mouth snaps shut over him and smiles, a flickering grin. Mousetrap disappears into flames.

Anger explodes through me. I glare into Smey's luminous body until I see the arrowhead glinting, blue white, like a far-away star. Then I surge toward it, through searing fire, until I feel its cold tremble against my head. I push, forcing the arrow deeper, closer to Smey's heart. But the more I push, the more it resists. Flames curl around me and I smell my fur burning.

Smey roars, so loud that my eardrums shatter. I close my eyes, open my mouth, and roar back. The world seems to still in shock. Except the arrowhead. It slips just a fraction deeper. I lean into it and shove once more. Every muscle of my body strains tight, and the flat end of the arrow digs painfully into my head. Until finally, the tip of the arrow touches Smey's heart . . . and then there's an explosion of white.

I gasp as the air drops to below freezing in an instant. Icy winds gust around me, extinguishing my burning fur, and snow swirls, blinding white. I squint and make out Smey's three heads, his pointed fangs and forked tongues, all turning to ice and snow. He stares at me, and his five dark eyes and single flaming bright one all fade into the twinkling white. Where he burned with anger, he's now cool and calm as a midwinter night. He sways in the air, a cloud of snowflakes dancing, then breaks apart and drifts away, like chimney smoke into the night.

Smey is gone, but I feel no joy. All I can think about is Mousetrap. I call for him, search the ground and sniff the air, desperate to catch his scent of dust and earthy musk.

The Lime Tree crackles above. Some of its branches are still aflame, raining down hot, incandescent sparks. "Help!" a deep and ancient voice creaks overhead.

But I have to find Mousetrap. Panic hurtles through me, because I can't see or smell him anywhere. All around is snow and ash, ice and soot, a confusion of hot and cold and black and white.

Then Ivan barks from somewhere behind me. "Yanka! Over here. It's Mousetrap."

I run to where I heard Ivan's voice and see Mousetrap's tiny body curled up in a mound of snow. I race over and nudge him with my snout. He's as cold as ice, and his fur is as white as the snow around him. Only the tip of his tail still shines copper. "Mousetrap." I nudge him again, and relief washes over me when I feel him shiver. "Wake up. You've got your winter coat."

Mousetrap groans, opens one eye, and looks up at me. "What did you think of my war dance?"

"It was the best I've ever seen." I smile.

Ivan collapses next to Mousetrap. His fur is charred, his muscles trembling, but there's a wide grin on his face. "We defeated Smey." He lifts his chin and howls at the moon, long and loud and triumphant.

I look through the subsiding swirls of debris in the air, to the dark and empty cavern, and slowly our victory sinks in. A laugh rumbles in my throat, then bellows out of me. "We defeated Smey together."

"Help!" the voice calls again. It seems to be coming from the Lime Tree.

"It's the tree." I stare at it in wonder. "It's talking."

Mousetrap groans again as he tries to stand. "I think I've pulled a few muscles."

"I'll take Mousetrap back to the house with chicken legs." Ivan dips his head so Mousetrap can drag himself up onto Ivan's ear. "Unless you want us to stay with you while you talk to the tree?"

I shake my head. "Please, take Mousetrap back so Elena can check that you're both all right." I look up into the boughs of the Lime Tree, and my feet twitch with nervous excitement. I wonder what will be different when I see Ivan and Mousetrap again. *Will all my worries about Sasha be gone? Will I be human again? Will I finally be able to go home?*

I take a deep breath to calm my thoughts and then I turn and clamber up and over the cavern.

As I approach the tree, I hear its voice again, deep and resonant. "Help," it groans. A smoldering branch creaks and crackles, then snaps, and the tree cries out in pain.

I step over roots that sprawl across the ground and finally reach the Lime Tree's trunk. The size of it is astonishing. It's made of hundreds of smaller trunks, woven and tangled together. They spread wider than my and Mamochka's house, and when I look up, the tree seems to go on forever.

"Hello?" I whisper.

"Help," the tree groans again. I can't see where the words are coming from. The trunks creak, the roots whisper, and the leaves, high above, rustle and hum. But the words form in my mind.

"How can I help?" I ask.

"Move me," the tree rumbles. "Move me away from this place, into the forest."

"But . . ." I stare at the tree, feeling tiny as a wren. "I can't. You're too big."

The roots at my feet slither. I look down and watch, as if in a dream, as they turn to water and flow away down the side of the volcano. A burst of noise and movement shakes the air and I look up to see a bellowing of bullfinches take flight, pink chests blushing in the moonlight. "Yanka!" they call as they flap away. "Home in the forest!"

As they disappear into the night, I realize many of the tree's branches are no longer there. The whole tree is shrinking.

"What's going on?" I gasp as streams of water rise and rush around my ankles.

"My roots will flow back to me, and my branches will fly back to me. But you must carry the core of my trunk to the forest, where I can be near other trees again, and watch animals play, and hear birds chatter."

The tree has now shrunk to a fraction of its size, but it is still twice as tall as me and at least as wide.

"I'll try." I tense my muscles and step next to the trunk. But when I try to lift it, it doesn't budge. "It feels like some of your roots are still holding you down."

The tree shakes what's left of its leaves. "All my roots have flowed away. I'm as small as I can be. You must try harder."

I furrow my brow and try to lift the tree again. I remind myself I'm a bear and I try again, and again. But it's far too heavy. I can't even push it over to roll it down the mountain. I lean against the trunk to catch my breath.

"Move me," the tree urges.

"I've been trying to," I wheeze. "Give me a moment to rest, then I'll try again."

I stare down the volcano, to the ship in the distance. It bobs up and down on silver waves, a spray of stars above it. The house with chicken legs sits on its deck, and I can just make out the silhouettes of my friends on its porch. The sight of them fills me with strength.

"Let's try again." I rise back onto my paws, then stop as something—*someone*—catches my eye.

It's another bear, stepping out from a cluster of pines near the base of the volcano. A huge male bear. He moves slowly toward me, and my heart pounds louder with every step he takes. Something about the way he moves is achingly familiar. But I don't know him. I couldn't know him. *Could I?*

He draws closer and I stare at his huge round face. My heart swells. He has ice in his fur and moonlit eyes. He smells faintly of tea with lemon, fresh snow, woodsmoke, and old furs.

"Anatoly," I whisper. "You're a bear." I laugh at the absurdity of it . . . but then gasp as my heart rips in two, because I realize what else he is. "You're my father." I glare at him with burning eyes, the heat of a fire dragon rising inside me. "Why didn't you tell me?"

"I'm sorry." Despite his enormous size, Anatoly looks small and defeated and full of sorrow. "There's so much I should have told you, but each time I visited, stories were the only things that would flow from my lips."

"All these years!" I roar. "All these years you *never* told me. You let me believe my father was dead." I scowl at him. "But you were alive. You abandoned me. You let me be raised by my grandmother, then by Mamochka—by anyone else but you."

Anger tears through me. Being abandoned as a baby because your parents are dead is one thing. But being abandoned because your father can't be bothered to raise you himself, for twelve whole years, is something else. I stamp a paw into the ground and roar into the night sky until my lungs are sore.

When I run out of breath, I collapse against the tree and look up at Anatoly, willing him to say something—anything—that will help me forgive him.

But he sits down and is silent for so long that I begin to

hear the tiny noises around us. The rustle of the Lime Tree's leaves, the hiss of steam on the hot rocks, and even Anatoly's heartbeat, deep and booming in his chest.

Then, finally, he opens his mouth and begins, as he always does, with "Once upon a time . . ."

THE WIDOWER'S FROZEN HEART

Once upon a time, a widower blamed himself for his wife's death. Crushed by guilt and feeling unworthy of love, he could not face his baby daughter.

He followed the cold winds north in a daze and found himself standing on the shores of the Green Bay, unable to cry because anger and shame writhed inside him, hotter than dragon fire.

Out on the frozen sea, the widower saw a sailing ship trapped in ice. Thinking it might cool his burning pain, he walked across the ice to the frozen ship, and there he found Father Frost, sitting on the bow.

Father Frost turned and saw the suffering in the widower's eyes. "Tell me," he said, "what has caused you so much pain?"

"My wife has died, and it's all my fault. She came to rescue me, and in doing so, she lost her life." The widower fell to his knees and clutched at his heart. "This pain is too great to endure."

"I can take away your pain. If that's what you want." Father Frost lifted his hand over the widower's chest, and his fingers glowed a dazzling white. "A frozen heart feels no pain."

The widower looked into Father Frost's ice-blue eyes and

nodded. At that moment, he'd have done anything to escape the agony that was tearing him apart.

So, Father Frost pressed his hand onto the widower's chest, and the widower gasped as his heart froze over. With each stiff heartbeat, ice filled his veins and a numbness fell over him. The widower looked up into the gray sky, and his face became hard and cold as an iceberg. His pain wasn't gone, but it was muffled and distant, as if buried beneath a great snowdrift.

The widower wandered back to the forest and found his baby daughter laughing as she rolled and played in sunbeams. And at the sight of his daughter, so full of love and joy, his heart began to melt.

A sharp pain tore through the widower's chest. His grief and guilt flooded back, and he could not bear the pain. So he left his daughter playing happily under the watchful gaze of her grandmother, the Bear Tsarina, and ran deep into the forest.

There the widower lived alone, avoiding anything that might melt his heart and bring back the pain. He foraged alone, hunted alone, and fished alone. He watched the sky and the seasons change, alone. But he didn't forget his daughter and soon found himself watching her once more.

His heart ached and burned and ruptured, but he endured the pain for as long as he could. And the next day he endured it a little longer.

Every day, the widower watched his daughter from the shadows. And his heart melted, drip by drop, as he built up the courage to talk to her.

CHAPTER THIRTY

THE TRUTH IN THE STORY

"But your heart wasn't really frozen by Father Frost, was it?" I frown at Anatoly, annoyed by the vagueness of his story.

"There's truth in all my stories," Anatoly says softly.

"But they aren't *the* truth. You twist the truth and dress it up. You *embellish* it," I snap, remembering Valentyna's words. "Like how you told me my birth mother was a princess."

"She was a princess to me."

I growl in frustration. "Does Mamochka know?" I ask. "About you being my father?"

"No." Anatoly shakes his head. "I wanted to tell her. I wanted to tell you both. But—" He stares down at his paws. His eyes are huge, silvery pools.

"Explain it to me," I demand. "Explain *everything* to me. Without making it a story. So I can be sure what's true."

Anatoly nods and opens his mouth. Words don't come

straight away, and when they do they're stilted and unsure. Nothing like his flowing tales. But I like them better, because I know these words will be the truth I've been waiting for my whole life.

"When I was young, I lived in the forest with my parents. I only ever remember them being bears, and the other creatures of the forest called them the Bear Tsar and the Bear Tsarina.

"I was a bear too, most days. But sometimes I'd wake as a boy. It might last a day or a week or a month, then I'd wake as a bear again. My parents told me it was a curse, and that I'd grow out of it."

"But you didn't." I look into Anatoly's eyes and he shakes his head.

"As I grew older, I spent more time as a human and less as a bear. Eventually, I left the forest to become a fisherman. Years went by and I stopped turning into a bear altogether." Anatoly smiles sadly. "I almost convinced myself that it had all been a strange childhood fantasy. But then I met your mother, Nastasya, and we had you, and . . ."

"I was a bear?"

"Not at first. You were born a baby girl. We named you Elitsa, because you were strong and beautiful as a fir tree."

My mouth drops open as I realize I had a different name once. Mamochka had no way of knowing, so she called me Yanka, because she thought I was strong and beautiful as a river. I think Yanka suits me better, because a river changes too.

"Five days after you were born, you turned into a bear cub. You should have seen the look on your mother's face." Anatoly's shoulders wobble with silent laughter. "Of course your mother would have loved you no matter what form you took, but I felt I had to do something. All my childhood memories came flooding back. I remembered how difficult it had been to be neither bear nor human, but stuck shifting between the two . . . I wanted to protect you, from this . . ." Anatoly looks at his huge, furry body and frowns. "So, I went to my mother, the Bear Tsarina, and tried to get her to remember her past. It took days, but finally I pieced together the story of the Lime Tree and the curse from what was left of her human memories."

"Then you came here? To find the tree?"

"I thought I could fix everything by myself." Anatoly sighs. "I thought I could fight my way past Smey and convince the tree to lift the curse . . ." Anatoly's eyes well with tears. "But I angered Smey, and then your mother came after me, and . . ." He shudders, as if he's suppressing a sob, or a roar. "Her death was my fault."

Part of me wants to wrap my arms around Anatoly, but I sit still, the freezing air prickling between us, and wait for him to continue.

"I lay, broken and burned beneath the fire dragon's cavern. I'd have died, if it weren't for Valentyna."

I nod with the realization that the house's story—the one about the fisherman's soul—was about Valentyna saving Anatoly.

"Even after Valentyna put me back together and treated my injuries, there were days I thought I'd die of a broken heart. I couldn't face you. Not after what I'd done. But I watched you, every day, my heart slowly mending and my courage building. I hoped one day I'd grow strong enough to be a worthy father for you." Anatoly glances up at me, memories dancing in his eyes. "Some days you were a cub, some days a girl, but you were always happy. Your grandmother doted on you, and you played with your whole body smiling. You didn't need me, or my sadness."

I open my mouth, wanting to argue with him—wanting to yell at him that of course I needed a father, sad or not, and he should have taken me back and raised me himself. But Anatoly's eyes are so full of grief and regret that my anger cools and drifts away, like Smey in the snowstorm.

"I know I was wrong," Anatoly says sadly. "But by the time I realized it, it was too late. You were with your mamochka and there never seemed to be a good time to tell you."

"How did I end up with Mamochka?"

"One day, I came to visit you, but you were gone." A tear rolls into the fur of Anatoly's cheek and freezes there, reflecting the starlight. "Your grandmother told me she had given you to a human lady who was full of love."

"My grandmother gave me away?"

"Not because she didn't want you," Anatoly rushes in. "She only did what she thought was best. You were spending more time as a human, so she thought you'd be happier living with a human mother. She chose your mamochka carefully. She watched her for months, collecting herbs for her medicines in the forest, and when your mamochka finally wandered close to the bear cave, your grandmother nudged you toward her.

"As soon as I found out what had happened, I tracked down you and your mamochka. I was determined to tell you both the truth, to take you back and raise you myself. I should have. But—" Anatoly sighs and shakes his head. "You were happy with Mamochka. You were loved. The bond you two had, right from the start, was so special and beautiful I didn't want to interfere with it. I felt inadequate, unable to give you what your mamochka could. And no matter how hard I tried, the truth wouldn't come. I'm sorry. Please don't think I didn't love you or didn't want you . . . because that's not true. I do love you and want you in my life more than anything."

My heart softens, but another wave of anger flows back as I remember waking as a bear. "You could at least have told me about the curse," I grumble. "You could have prepared me for this." I stare down at my paws and shake my head.

"It's no excuse, but I believed you wouldn't change into a bear again. After you moved in with your mamochka, you stayed human, so I thought living with her, away from the forest, had cured you."

"Clearly not." I dig my claws into the ashy soil. "Do you know why I've turned into a bear now?"

Anatoly shakes his head. "I've never learned to control the changing. But I've learned to recognize the signs of it coming, and there are some patterns to it."

"Like what?"

"When I was a fisherman, living with a human crew, I stopped changing into a bear. And when I was with your birth mother, Nastasya, I was always human. But after she died, and I was alone in the forest, I became more bear."

"My grandmother told me that as a bear, my human memories would fade. Is that true?"

"Yes, but they never go away completely. Your grandmother is all bear, and even she remembers sometimes. When I'm a bear, my human memories come and go. But I've never forgotten you, or how you make me feel. I think even when specific memories fade, you remember something of the people you love. They pull you back, to your human life."

"How often do you change now?" I ask.

"A few times a year. I've changed less since I've grown close to your mamochka. She makes me want to be human too." Anatoly smiles his shy, lopsided smile and I notice his fur is patchy where his beard would be if he were human. "Perhaps both of us have more control over what we become than we realize."

"But I didn't want to be a bear at the festival, so why did I grow bear legs?"

"If you want a life as a human, you have to reach for

them, let them into your world. I think we both struggle to do that sometimes. But it's never as hard as it seems to ask for, or accept, help."

I think back to the moment I fell from the ice fort, before I started turning into a bear. There were hands reaching for me, but I was too scared to take them. I thought they wouldn't hold me. I was worried they'd drop me, or I'd pull them down.

I look at the ship in the distance, where Mousetrap, Yuri, Ivan, Blakiston, the house, and Elena are waiting for me. "That's something I've learned on this journey. Without the help of my friends, I could never have gotten here and defeated Smey."

Anatoly follows my gaze. "It sounds like in the last few days you've learned more than I have in a decade."

"I've learned where I belong," I whisper. My feet twitch with an overwhelming urge to run back to my friends on the ship, to thank them for helping me, then to run all the way home to Mamochka and Sasha. But first, I need to move the tree. Then I can ask it to save Sasha, and myself.

I rise to my feet and turn to Anatoly. "I need your help with something."

"Anything."

"Will you help me carry this tree to the house with chicken legs? It's heavy, but we can do it. Together."

CHAPTER THIRTY-ONE

THE LIME TREE

The Lime Tree creaks and groans as Anatoly and I lift it onto our shoulders. It's awkward edging down the steep slope on our hind legs, and almost impossible to balance. After only a few paces, Anatoly, who is walking in front, skids on loose rocks and pulls us down too fast. The last few leaves are whipped from the tree, and before they hit the ground, they turn into bullfinches that flap around in panic.

I struggle to keep a grip on the tree as my feet slide out from beneath me. I dig my claws into the ground, but they just rake through brittle gravel. We surge forward and fall backward at the same time but manage to keep hold of the tree as we shoot down the mountain like a sled over snow. Sharp rocks tear into my calves and I yell out in pain.

Anatoly desperately scrambles, trying to slow our descent, and my eyes widen with horror as I realize we're heading straight toward one of the bubbling pools of mud at the base of the volcano.

Sulfurous fumes rise from its surface and thicken as we draw closer, until I'm struggling to breathe. The few short branches and roots left dangling from the tree reach for the ground in a vain attempt to slow us.

Though it rips and burns the skin of my back, I push my spine into the ground. But nothing works. We zoom down the slope, careening out of control. Blood pounds in my ears, and scorching air tears through my fur. I hold my breath and brace myself for a splash into boiling mud.

But something blocks out the starlight, and a cool, dark shadow falls over us. A jagged shape reaches down, dripping icy water. Long, clawed toes splay open, and relief washes over me as I recognize the outline of one of the house's giant chicken feet.

It grabs the tree and sweeps it up. I keep my arms firmly locked around the trunk and am lifted too, my arms straining under the weight of my enormous body. I crane my neck to look for Anatoly and see him dangling from the other end of the trunk.

The next moment we're flung onto the house's porch with a crash and several bangs, squeals from Yuri, barks from Ivan, and whoops and applause from Elena. I roll onto my feet and try to get my bearings.

The tree is lying on the porch like a huge cut log. Anatoly is on the other side of it, swaying to his feet. I peer over the balustrade and my heads spins. We're high above the smoking ground. The house's legs are fully extended, its movements jerky as it picks its way across snow-streaked rocks between glowing fissures. "Please be careful." I wince at the thought of the house burning its feet.

Elena throws her arms around my neck. "We saw you skidding down the volcano. I was so worried, and the house was bursting to help. Finally, it leaped off the ship to get to you." Elena squeezes me so tight it hurts, but, relieved we're all safe on the house together, I don't pull away.

Mousetrap sprints along the balustrade and leaps onto my snout.

"Your pulled muscles are better, then?" I laugh.

"I was just a little stiff, from my war dance." Mousetrap holds his arms out and spins around, like he's showing off new clothes. "Look at my winter coat," he trills.

"It's beautiful." I smile. "Though you'd look wonderful in any color."

I glance back at the ship, alone on a moonlit, icy sea, and wonder what adventurers will find it next. Then I turn to the house. "Thank you, for coming to get us."

The house smiles, with its windows and door and eaves.

"Is this the Lime Tree?" Elena stares at the tree on the porch. "What happened to it? Is it all right?" Then she spots Anatoly on the other side. "Oh! Another bear. Hello, bear," she says nervously. "You look familiar . . ." She narrows her eyes. "Are you related to Yanka?"

"He's my father," I say, although I know Elena can't understand me. I look at Anatoly and a smile lifts the corners of my mouth. Anatoly smiles back, the same shy smile he has when he's human, and a swell of love warms my chest, like a hot drink on a cold day.

The tree's branches and roots flail between us. "Help me up."

"Did the tree say something?" Elena kneels next to the tree and peers at its trunk.

"Help me up." The tree groans, louder.

"I understood it!" Elena claps her hands together in excitement. "I understood the tree. Oh! Can you help it, House?"

Vines curl down from the rafters and thicken as they coil around the tree. Gently they lift it, like it's no effort at all, and carry it up, over our heads. The tree sighs with satisfaction as it settles next to the chimney pot, and its short roots lengthen as they burrow between mossy tiles.

"Is the tree going to save Sasha?" Elena asks, and I flush with embarrassment, because I didn't want to ask the tree for anything until it is safely back in the forest.

"You want me to save someone?" The tree's branches elongate. New buds swell, and fresh leaves unfurl.

Hope flutters inside me. "I have a friend, Sasha, back in my village on the southern edge of the forest, who's injured because of me. I was hoping you could help him make a full recovery."

A branch dips and three leaves grow from it. They're different from the other, heart-shaped leaves. These new ones are star shaped and patterned with dark red veins. They break free and float toward the floor. Three bullfinches swoop after them, and each one grabs a leaf in its beak before flapping away. "The birds will take the leaves where they need to go"—the tree rustles—"and your friend will be well again."

"Thank you." A huge smile spreads across my face. I feel light as the birds flying south. "Also, I wondered if . . . there's a curse and . . ." All of a sudden, the thought of asking the tree to make me human again sends a quarrel of sparrows fluttering through my body. I frown, confused by the feeling.

"I'm sorry," the tree creaks, "but I can't undo old curses."

Anatoly moves closer, until he's standing by my side. "I'm sorry, Yanka." He shakes his head sadly.

"No, it's fine." I sigh with relief, realizing what the fluttery feeling meant. *I don't want the curse to be broken.* I don't want to be only a human forever. I like being a bear too. I look at Anatoly, the truth sparking in my mind. "You said we have control over what we become."

"Well, yes." He nods. "But it's difficult; it can be a struggle—"

"Some struggles are worth it." I look down at my feet and feel a rush of affection toward them. They're a gift from the forest, like Valentyna said. A reminder of all that's magical and mysterious in the world. "I want to keep this gift and learn how to control it."

Anatoly lowers his head to mine, until our foreheads are almost touching. I feel our fur merging together. "I'm so proud of you, Yanka," he murmurs. "You really are the most precious treasure in the Snow Forest."

"That's very touching." Mousetrap nips my ear. "Now, perhaps you could ask Anatoly where he keeps the key to that cod store we found on the roof of his cabin."

"How do you know this is Anatoly?" I ask.

"I'm not sure why you humans find it so difficult to read souls." Mousetrap leans over my eye and frowns. "Somebody's external appearance doesn't change what's inside."

"You're right." I nod. I recognized Anatoly as a bear, so I shouldn't be surprised Mousetrap did too. I wonder if Mamochka would recognize me like this.

Yuri squeals as the house picks up speed. We're heading south, toward the village, and for the first time since I grew bear legs, I understand that what my body looks like doesn't change who I am or where I belong. Nothing will stop me from going home. Not even looking like a bear. Somehow, I'll show Mamochka this is me.

CHAPTER THIRTY-TWO

THE FOREST

The house draws alongside the crest of the Fiery Volcano. Already it looks smaller and less angry than before. The gently glowing streams of lava and the smoke pluming from cracks seem beautiful now that they aren't threatening to burn my paws or snout.

I glance down at my fur. It's as patchy as the forest surrounding the volcano, and raw streaks of scorched and grazed flesh glare back at me like they're on fire. I wish Mamochka were here, with some of the goose fat and cucumber ointment she makes for burns. My smile widens as I picture her riding on a house with chicken legs, telling me how ridiculous it is.

Excitement and wonder burst through me. I've seen so many amazing things on this journey, made so many friends, and found a grandmother and a father. But above all, I've learned the importance of going home to the people you love.

"Where's Blakiston?" I ask, suddenly realizing he's not with us.

"He's flown ahead, to wind-wash the smell of burning feathers from his wings," Mousetrap trills into my ear.

"Oh no!" Elena gasps in dismay and her hands rise to cover her mouth. Ivan bolts to her, his ears pricked up, and Mousetrap scrambles frantically over my snout. I follow Elena's gaze, and my heart stops. The house has passed the peak of the volcano, giving us a view of the other side.

The entire south slope is a smoking, black scar. The trees there must have caught alight during the battle with Smey, starting a blaze that has already swept for miles.

I stare at the path of the fire. It's torn through the forest in a wide, curved line, leaving a charcoal-filled trail of destruction that runs all the way to the Silver Stream. On the shores of the river, flames flicker into the sky.

"What can we do?" Elena grips the balustrade tight and the house tilts and swerves in the direction of the blaze, then surges forward as it picks up speed. It gallops through the parts of the forest that have been spared by the flames, leaping and lurching as it rushes toward the Silver Stream.

I look from Elena to Anatoly, to Ivan and Yuri, desperately trying to figure out a way to stop the fire. All of them are standing by the balustrades, as still as figureheads, darkness and flames reflected in their eyes.

"No one can stop a blaze this size." Ivan scowls at the fire ahead. "I need to warn my pack before it crosses the river." Ivan throws a heartrending howl into the air that slices through the wind. Before Ivan's howl finishes, replies surge toward us, eerie and echoing, all coming from the direction of the Blue Mountain. "Let me down, House," Ivan barks. "I need to find my pack."

The house slows as it approaches the Silver Stream and veers north to avoid the flames that flicker all along its banks. It steps into the river and sighs as its feet sink into the cool water. Then it dips down until its porch steps hover above the water's surface, a few feet from the opposite bank.

"Are you sure you want to get off here?" My chest tightens. I don't feel ready to say goodbye to Ivan.

"It's time for me to return to my pack." Ivan nods. "You should all stay near the river as you head back to the village. It's the safest place for the house."

"Will you return as pack leader?" I ask.

Ivan leaps onto the bank and turns back to me. A smile curves his lips. "I've realized being leader isn't so important after all."

My eyes widen in surprise. "But you were so sure that's what you wanted."

"Things change." Ivan shrugs. "We defeated Smey, together, as equals. That's shown me I don't have to be leader to feel strong. I can be strong as part of the pack." He grins, revealing his long, shining fangs. "I'll see you all again." He dips his head in a small bow, then disappears into the shadows.

I lift a paw as a gesture of gratitude and goodbye, but I know Ivan is right: I'll see him again. I'm not sure when, but

I'll come back to the forest. My fur shivers with excitement at the thought, because it's not only Ivan I'd like to see again. It's my grandmother too. I only got to talk to her for a brief time, and I was so confused and emotional at having woken as a bear. I want to visit her again and get to know her properly, because having a bear for a grandmother is as magical as having Mamochka for a mother.

"My grandmother!" I exclaim. "Should we warn her about the fire too?"

Anatoly looks at the Blue Mountain. "She'll see the fire coming from miles away and have plenty of time to retreat farther up the mountain, if she needs to. We should carry on south, to the village. They might need our help."

The house surges up and Elena points downstream. Her face pales. "The fire is crossing the river. There, look." She waves her finger frantically and I peer in the direction she's gesturing.

Sparks fly across the river, and low shrubs burst into flames on the other side. Within moments the fire blazes up and away, following a long row of pines. The air glows orange behind thick clouds of smoke, and air rushes to fuel the rising flames.

"The wind is sweeping the fire toward the village." Anatoly frowns. "So fast the villagers won't have much time to prepare."

The house takes off, picking up speed as it splashes through the river. Yuri squeals as he skids backward, and Elena grips the balustrade tight. "Faster," she urges. "We need to get to the village." Her eyes well with tears, and I realize Elena is worried about her mother, Valentyna, trapped in the village without her house.

Mousetrap's claws dig deep into my ear, and wind gusts through my fur as the house sprints and splashes through the Silver Stream. The house's chicken legs are long, its steps huge and bounding. We travel faster than I've ever moved before. Faster than a sled over ice, or a twenty-strong dogsled.

We speed past the Blue Mountain. I stare at it until my eyes blur, but I finally see the dark shape of my grandmother, walking calmly over snow, toward the peak. For a moment I think I see her stop and glance back at me with a smile on her face. But she's so far away, and we're traveling so fast, it's probably only my imagination. Still, I smile back, just the thought of her safe like a blanket for my soul.

We speed on, my chest tightening as I watch flames leap from tree to tree, blazing through the forest. I can't believe how far the fire has traveled already, and now that it's reached the drier, snowless trees, it's zooming, swifter than a storm wind. It will be at the village in no time.

"My house!" I roar as I spot my and Mamochka's home in the distance. Huge flames are darting toward it. "Please." I lean on the porch balustrade. "I need to make sure Mamochka is safe."

The house splashes out of the river and swerves into the forest, toward my home. But after only a short distance, we run into a cloud of thick black smoke. Heat crackles in the air and a flock of panicked crows scream as they flap away. Yuri coughs violently and the snap of burning branches echoes around us. Shards of burning wood and tangles of smoking moss dance in the air.

"Back to the river," Elena shouts. "It's not safe here."

The house tilts sharply as it veers back to the river. My heart lurches. I know the house must go back to the water so it doesn't catch fire, but I need to get home, to Mamochka.

So before the house retreats any farther or I've had the chance to think through what I'm doing, I clamber over the porch balustrades. And though we're high above the burning forest, I jump, the only thought in my mind of getting home, to Mamochka.

CHAPTER THIRTY-THREE

THE FIRE

I fall through smoke, vaguely aware of Mousetrap screaming as he clings tight to my ear. Branches smash into me,
collapse and crash around me. But I don't feel any pain. All
I can think about is making sure Mamochka is safe. I land
with a thump onto hard, hot ground and wrestle my way
out of a tangle of flaming brambles.

Soot and ash dance in the air, obscuring my view and
filling my nose with a suffocating stench that blocks all
scents of home. But I know the way. My heart pulls me
there. I run faster than ever before, feet searing, eyes stinging, and throat burning.

I grit my teeth and swallow back coughs that cramp my
lungs. Fires rage around me, leaping from tree to tree and
scurrying through the undergrowth like a living creature.

Finally, I surge ahead of the flames and reach a stretch of
bare earth that's cool under my paws. I breathe a sigh of relief
but keep on galloping toward home.

Trees fly past and I recognize some of them: the fallen

cedar I climbed over when I first entered the forest, the aspen with the deeply curved trunk.

"We're nearly there," Mousetrap trills. His encouragement lifts me, until I feel like I'm flying.

My feet drum the earth. I flow between birches and leap over bushes until I see the dark outline of my home. I skid to a halt in the garden, my heart thundering in my chest. There's no light from the windows. The house is quiet and still.

Blakiston glides down from the roof and lands in front of me. "When I saw the fire, I knew you'd come here. So I flew ahead, to see if I could help."

"Where's Mamochka?" I gasp. "Sasha? Valentyna?"

"I hooted outside the window until they looked out and saw the smoke. As soon as they did, they left for the village square, on a cart pulled by dogs."

"Thank you." I sigh with relief. Everyone will be much safer in the village square, next to the Great River. "How's Sasha?" I ask. "Was he recovered?"

"He's fine. Bullfinches brought star-shaped leaves to your mamochka and she made tea with them. As soon as she spooned some into his mouth, he woke." Blakiston opens his wings. "We should get out of the path of this fire."

I nod. Hearing Sasha is well lifts such a weight from my shoulders I could float into the air. I glance around the garden, wondering if there's anything I can do to keep our home safe.

Mamochka has turned the earth already, so it's smooth

and bare. There's nothing that could burn, but a few of the pines at the bottom of the garden are so tall they could fall onto the house if they caught alight.

I bound over to the tallest one, rise onto my back paws, and push with all my might. It creaks, cracks, and smashes to the ground, away from the house. Mousetrap darts into the forest and I move on to the next tree.

An orange glow flares to life a short distance away and creeps along parallel to the garden. I call Mousetrap and he sprints back, carrying a flaming twig in his mouth. He drops it, kicks earth over it, and leaps onto my shoulder.

"I set fire to some dry branches, to block the fire coming the other way."

"Good idea." I slam into another pine, forcing it over, then follow the trail around to Sasha's house.

The fire line Mousetrap lit is burning bright. Mamochka does the same thing in summer—burns the dry under-growth near our home to stop fires from coming too close. We've never needed their protection before though. The for-est fires have never burned this close to the village. Not since I've lived here anyway.

I knock over three larches at the back of Sasha's house, then race toward the village. Thick black smoke plumes into the air above it, and long before I see the village hall, I can tell the linden trees behind it must be on fire. I trip over my feet and skid all the way down the hill into the village square.

It's bursting with people. The older babushkas and

dedushkas sit with the youngest children and the sled dogs at the far side of the square, closest to the Great River. All around them, people rush back and forth, pulling carts stacked with water barrels and buckets. The busiest area is around the roaring linden trees, behind the hall, so I stagger to my feet and run in that direction.

"A bear!" Several of the children shriek as I dart past.

I round the village hall and run straight into searing air alive with sparks and embers. People are backing away from the nearest tree, scarves tied around their mouths and axes in their hands. But it's too late to cut it down. Already the trunk is sizzling with flames, crackling in the heat. The tree creaks and leans over the village hall. Someone shouts a warning, and everyone sprints away, toward the square.

Except me. I squint at the tree, wondering how I can stop it falling onto the hall. The flames curl into the shape of Smey, with his three heads and forked, flickering tongues, and I smile, because it's like a sign I can defeat the fire.

"It's too hot," Mousetrap yells into my ear. "You'll burn yourself."

I race past the tree to the river on the other side and plunge into the icy water. When my fur is soaking wet, I run back up to the blaze.

"Yanka!"

I turn to the deep, rumbling roar and see Anatoly galloping toward me, his fur dripping as he rushes out of the river. Behind him I catch a glimpse of the house with chicken legs, almost invisible in the darkness. The house is standing in the waters of the Great River, the silhouette of the Lime Tree on its roof reaching up to the star-filled sky.

"Help me push that linden tree back before it falls onto the village hall," I shout to Anatoly, then rush into the flames. The heat makes me gasp and hold my breath as it burns the back of my throat. I rear up and slam my front paws onto the linden tree. The skin on my pads sizzles and I bellow in pain as I lean all my weight into the trunk.

Anatoly rises next to me. He's so enormous that his front paws land on the tree above my head. The tree pitches backward. "It's falling!" he shouts, and with an earsplitting creak the tree splinters and crashes down. It lands on the tree behind it, and three trees domino to the ground in quick succession. They all fall away from the hall. My heart lifts, until one last tree wobbles and leans, farther and farther, the opposite way—toward the hall.

"Run!" Anatoly roars, but before I've turned around, the tree collapses onto the roof of the village hall.

The roof buckles and the wooden walls curve outward. With a deafening bang and a fountain of flames, the whole hall slams down on top of me. Anatoly disappears behind an avalanche of roof panels and wooden beams.

My back explodes with pain. Claps and booms sound all around me and I press my ears tight against my head. "Mousetrap!" I yell, panicking because I can't feel him on my ear anymore. I thrash around, struggling to get out from beneath the jumble of wood on top of me, so I can find Mousetrap.

"I'm here, human girl," Mousetrap squeaks weakly from my shoulder. Flames curl up and singe the fur on my cheeks. "Get up," Mousetrap squeaks louder, and I fill my muscles with every drop of strength I have and heave myself up. The rubble on my back slips away and I crawl out from beneath it.

I squint against the blinding light and heat, my gaze darting around as I desperately try to orient myself. The hall has fallen over me, and I'm surrounded by the remains of burning walls and broken roof panels. My heart races and my toes twitch, but I don't know which way to run. I can't see a way out.

"Anatoly!" I yell, but there's no sign of him, and if he does shout back, I can't hear him over the roar of flames.

"Over there." Mousetrap clambers down my snout and points to a far corner. Flames surge up a section of upright wall, but in the center is a large, dark window. I glimpse my reflection: the image of a huge brown bear with a tiny white weasel on her snout. But then I see Sasha and his parents, and Mamochka, on the other side.

I run through the flames, focused entirely on wanting to be with them. But I slam into the window and fall to the floor. I shake my head, confused. I was sure I would smash through the glass.

Then a long brown face bursts toward me. Glass and shards of wood rain down from Yuri's short, velvety antlers. His legs stamp through the charcoaled wall as if it's a patch of brambles, and he lowers his head to me. "Grab on!" he shrieks, his eyes bulging with fear.

"I'm too big," I shout. "I'm too heavy for you." But as I lift a paw, I see fingers, blistered and burned. I gasp for air but can't catch enough. My lungs have shrunk.

"Come on." Yuri dips his woolly neck into my arms and I cling on tight as he pulls me back through the window and out into cold air.

"Yanka!" My name echoes around me, scores of voices saying it all at once. A blanket is thrown over me. Sasha's father prizes my hands from Yuri's neck and lifts me into his arms. I wonder how that's possible when I'm a bear, huge and heavy, but then I remember seeing my fingers in the fire.

I crane my neck to look down at my legs, but they're covered with blankets, and smoke is thick in the air. Then Mamochka appears at my side, saying my name over and over as she cups my face in her hands and kisses my cheeks, and I realize I don't care what I look like anyway, because I've finally found my way home.

CHAPTER THIRTY-FOUR

THE GIRL WITH BEAR LEGS

I'm bundled onto a cart in the village square and wrapped in so many blankets I can barely move. I struggle to stand, because I want to find Anatoly, but my body feels weak and wobbly as a spring fawn.

Then I spot Anatoly in the shadows, behind the flaming ruins of the village hall, and I finally relax because he's fine. He gives me a nod, turns, and disappears into the darkness.

I know Anatoly wants to leave because he's a bear, but that doesn't stop me from feeling disappointed. For as long as I can remember, Anatoly has arrived like a shooting star, filled my imagination with fantastic stories, and then left— always too soon and without ever saying goodbye.

And now I know he left me as a baby too. And for all these years never told me he was my father. Despite understanding his reasons, I still feel a sting from his abandonment.

Mamochka sits next to me and tries wrapping an arm around my shoulders, then settles for fussing over me when it doesn't fit. She dabs goose fat and cucumber ointment on the burns on my hands and face. "Yanka," she whispers, tucking my hair behind my ears, "I'm so glad you're home."

I wrap my arms around Mamochka and realize, for the first time, that although I've grown too big to fit into her arms, she fits perfectly into mine.

Tears prick my eyes, but strength surges through me, pushing away all thoughts of being unwanted and abandoned. Mamochka has loved me and cared for me every day since she found me. I can't believe it's taken me so long to realize how much strength that has given me.

Every time I've wobbled, she's been there to stop me falling. Her, and Sasha, and Mousetrap. And a few other people in the village too: some of the babushkas and dedushkas; Sasha's youngest cousin, Vanya; and Polina, with her friendly smile. Together they've supported me, but I've been too blind to see it.

I kept thinking I needed to do things on my own to feel strong, but sitting here, enveloped in Mamochka's love, with Mousetrap on my shoulder and the villagers all around, I feel stronger than ever.

Mousetrap snores loudly into my ear and Mamochka

271

leans back and peers at him. "Is that Mousetrap?" she asks. "With a winter coat at the start of spring?"

"He's very proud of it." I nod and beckon Yuri closer. He's hovering a short distance away, nervously watching the sled dogs gathered farther along the riverbank.

I pat the side of the cart I'm sitting on and Yuri lies down next to it. "This is Yuri." I rub the top of his head between his antlers, and he looks up at Mamochka with wide eyes.

"Is she part of our herd?" he asks.

I nod. "This is my mother."

Mamochka strokes Yuri's silk-soft snout and frowns at the cuts and burns on his cheeks. She rises to her feet and pulls pots of ointments and powders from her pockets. After she's finished smearing Yuri's burns with her remedies, she turns to me. "Do you need any more?"

I stretch my arms and legs, to see if any of my burns are still sore. The fur on my legs rustles and my claws splay wide. "Oh!" I look down at my legs. The blanket doesn't hide their shape. "I still have bear legs." A smile tugs at the corners of my mouth as I think of walking through the forest, feeling all the vibrations running into my soles. But then I remember why I went into the forest in the first place. I turn to Mamochka, words cascading from my lips. "I don't want to go to the hospital, because these legs don't need a cure. They're part of who I am. In the forest, I found my story and learned these legs are a gift. I want to keep them."

"So you did need a story, not medicine, after all." Mamochka smiles as she tucks another blanket around me. "I just saw you turn from a bear into a human," she whispers. "I don't think I can say the stories of the forest are only fanciful tales anymore. Clearly, there's magic in the forest, and in you." Mamochka puts a hand on my cheek. "I'm sorry, Yanka. I should have listened to you. I was just so scared."

"You've always been scared of the forest, but it's beautiful, Mamochka. And I know how to be careful in there and keep myself safe."

"I've never been scared of the forest." Mamochka shakes her head. "I've only ever been scared of losing you."

"We won't lose each other." I put my hand over Mamochka's. "Because we belong together, don't we?"

Mamochka nods. "We belong together, no matter what." Her eyes well up and she laughs. "Oh, look at me on the brink of tears. There's no need."

Sasha appears with three mugs of steaming tea and we all sit, close together, and watch the villagers douse the last few fires with barrels of water. I want to get up and help, but Mamochka insists I sit and rest, and tells me everything is under control now anyway.

Some of the older babushkas and dedushkas amble over and scold me for running away and worrying my mamochka, but they smile and kiss my cheeks too. Little Vanya bounces up and demands to know everything about where I've been.

As I tell him a few stories, I notice Liliya and Oksana staring at me, their whispered words buzzing like hornets. Liliya points at the bottom of the cart. There's a bear claw poking out from underneath my blankets.

I wiggle it and laugh. Their words can't sting through my bearskin. I know now it doesn't matter how they see me. It only matters how I see myself. And I know I belong here, in the village. No matter where I came from, or what legs I have.

I look around until I see Polina, a friendlier face, and I wave at her and smile. She smiles and waves back, and warmth flows through me. One thing I've learned on my journey is that it isn't as difficult to make friends as I thought. And I already have more friends than I realized.

The sky pales in the east, announcing the coming dawn. But over the Great River the sky is still dark and vast and deep. There are scattered stars, wispy clouds, and a pale, sinking moon. All different, but there's room in the sky for them all. Just as there's room on earth for all kinds of people. If I believe I belong, I'll find my space.

Mousetrap stirs in his sleep and nuzzles against my neck. I reach up and give him a stroke. We don't have to be the same to fit together.

I scan the darkness above the water, looking for the house with chicken legs, but there's no sign of it. I can't see Valentyna in the village either, and I wonder where she and Elena have gone. I shake my head and sigh. I didn't get a chance to thank them or say goodbye.

Soon, there are only a few people left in the village square.

One of the babushkas brings me a *rubakha* tunic and a warm reindeer-skin coat and hat. Mamochka pulls a long skirt from one of her bags and I recognize the embroidered pictures on the hem.

"My skirt!" I exclaim. "The one you decorated for me."

Mamochka nods. "The search party found your clothes outside the bear cave. They returned to the village, thinking a bear had gobbled you up."

"Oh no." I shake my head, thinking of all the grief and worry I must have caused.

"It's all right." Mamochka squeezes my hand. "I never believed that for a moment. And when I sewed your skirt back together I could tell it hadn't been torn by a bear. The seams were just split open."

Mamochka helps me dress under the blankets, and as I slide my skirt over my bear legs I smile. My legs feel right—like this is how I'm meant to be. Because my home is in the village, but a part of me will always be at home in the forest too. I reach into my skirt pocket, and my hand closes around my map and the wolf claw. *Ivan's claw.* Maybe next time I see him, I'll give it back to him.

Mamochka bustles around, trying to load too many things onto the cart, and I stand and sway as I find my balance on two legs again.

"I'll walk back with Sasha and Yuri," I say, rearranging the cart so that Sasha's parents can sit inside instead.

Mamochka shakes her head. "You should ride back. After all that's happened, you need to rest."

"I'm fine, Mamochka." I stand tall and pull my shoulders back. "I want to walk." I beckon Sasha over and we harness Anatoly's dogs to the cart and help finish loading it up.

"See you back at home," Mamochka calls, and I wave as she scoots up the hill ahead of us. The sun peeps over the horizon, throwing peach and violet ribbons across the sky, and I smile.

CHAPTER THIRTY-FIVE

HOME

"Hey, Yanka." Sasha punches my arm as he falls into step beside me.

"What's that for?" I punch him back.

Sasha wobbles away from me and laughs. "Running away in the first place. Leaving me in the forest while you sailed away on an ice floe. Letting a Yaga sled me home without you. But mostly"—he punches my arm again—"for not letting me help you." He looks down at my feet and smiles. "How is that possible?"

"It's a gift from the forest." I wiggle my claws and smile.

"Will you always have them?"

"I don't know." I punch his shoulder again and run away. Yuri gallops after me and we make it all the way to the edge of the forest before we slip on a patch of muddy ash and skid into a meltwater puddle.

Sasha catches up and Yuri sits at the bottom of the gnarly old elm while Sasha and I climb up it, until we're so covered in soot it irritates my nose, and the taste fills my mouth. Mousetrap keeps complaining I'm dirtying his new winter coat, so finally we clamber down and take the forest path home.

All my favorite trees are blackened and burned. I look up into the forest canopy and feel its pain, like a rawness in my lungs. "How long do you think it'll take the forest to recover?" I sigh.

"I don't think it'll take too long." Sasha bites his lips and follows my gaze. "There's always loads of new growth in summer."

The dawn chorus rises around us and echoes Sasha's words. The birds sing about new leaves and flower buds and the promise of berries to come. Then one of them shouts, "Yaga house!" and a cloud of crossbills flutters away. The pound of giant feet shakes the earth, and a shadow zooms through the trees alongside us.

My heart leaps at the sight of the house with chicken legs. "Come on!" I shout to Sasha as I race after the house. It sprints through the trees and skids to a halt at the bottom of my garden.

"Yanka!" Elena beams as she rushes down the porch steps. She throws her arms around my neck and squeezes me until it hurts. "You're human again."

"Mostly." I nod, glancing down at my feet.

"I always loved your bear legs." Elena smiles. "Do you still understand Mousetrap?" She reaches up and dusts the ash off Mousetrap's coat, and to my surprise, he not only lets her but thanks her. "Yuri!" Elena skips over to Yuri as he appears behind me, then I hear her shout a greeting to Sasha too. But my gaze is drawn to the house.

Vines extend from the roof and lift the Lime Tree gently down to the ground.

"Here," the Lime Tree creaks. "I want to grow here."

The vines place the tree between the fallen pines at the bottom of my garden.

"You're going to grow here?" I ask. "But I thought you wanted to be deep in the forest."

"Here is good." As soon as the tree's roots hit the ground, they spread out, thickening and lengthening as they burrow into the earth. Branches stretch into the sky and bullfinches flutter down onto the boughs and turn into brilliant green leaves.

The burned trees around the Lime Tree glow. Ash and charcoal fall from their trunks, and their bark shines, clean and new. Leaves unfurl. The smell of pine cones splaying drifts into my nose. Birds sing, animals rustle over and under the ashy soil, and I look up into the canopy and feel the forest bursting with joy.

The Lime Tree pulses and grows larger with each breath. "I like it here." The tree sighs with satisfaction.

"Yanka!" Mamochka runs down the garden and stops still at the sight of the Lime Tree and the house with chicken legs. I expect her to pale, or faint, or ask a million questions at once, but she just pulls me into a hug and my heart swells with love.

Valentyna emerges from the house's front door and waves

a greeting. Mamochka waves back. "Thank you again for bringing Sasha home."

"You're welcome." Valentyna shoots me a smile. "I'm glad you found your way home too, Yanka." She looks up at the roof and puts her hands on her hips. "Now, House," she says sternly. "We have to go back into the forest to prepare for tonight's guiding."

The house's eaves droop and it puffs a small dark cloud out of its chimney, but then it nods.

"Come on, Elena," Valentyna calls. "It's time to go."

Elena hugs Sasha and Yuri, then wanders over to me. She slides a hand into her apron pocket and pulls out my birth mother's arrowhead. "Mousetrap left this on the porch. He must have found it after the battle with Smey and brought it back."

"You keep it." I smile.

"I couldn't." Elena shakes her head. "It was your birth mother's."

"I want you to have it." I press it into Elena's hand. "To remind you of our adventure."

"As if I could forget." Elena laughs.

"Anyway," I say, letting go of the arrowhead, "it's a symbol of my past, and right now, I want to focus on my future."

Elena pulls me into another hug. "Come and visit, whenever you like. I'll keep the arrow safe, and you can have it back anytime."

"Thank you." I nod. "For everything. You too, House." I smile up at the house as Elena steps onto the porch. A spindle snaps free of the balustrade, reaches toward me, and erupts with bright white blossoms. One of the flowers falls into my hands as the house straightens its legs and steps away. And within moments, the house, Elena, and Valentyna disappear behind a tangle of tall larches.

A flash of pink on a glistening branch catches my eye. "Yanka!" the bullfinch calls. "Come back to the forest!" But Mousetrap launches himself from my shoulder and dives straight at the little bird. The bullfinch flaps away just in time and Blakiston swoops down and catches Mousetrap in his claws.

Mousetrap twists and leaps onto Blakiston's back and they fly off between the trees, shouting something about freshwater cod. In the distance, bobbing up and down above the canopy, is the house with chicken legs, heading north, deeper into the forest.

"Come on." Mamochka links her arms around my and Sasha's elbows. "Let's go inside for a hot drink."

As we walk toward the house, there's a knock on the kitchen window. I glance up and a smile bursts across my face at the sight of Anatoly, in our kitchen. He's a man, with soot in his beard and a twinkle in his eye.

"*Sbiten?*" He mouths the word, holding up my favorite yellow mug.

"Who's that?" Yuri asks. "Is he part of our herd too?"

"That's Anatoly." I smile. "He's part of our herd, although he isn't always strong enough to admit it."

Yuri stares at me in confusion.

"Not everyone is born as brave as you." I ruffle the woolly fur around Yuri's neck. "It can take a lot of strength to admit you need a herd."

My muscles relax as I let Mamochka sweep me into the warmth and smells of home. We drink *sbiten* and take turns telling stories by the fire—some with more truth in them than others.

Anatoly and Mamochka sit close together, with wide smiles and bright eyes, and although Anatoly flushes pink when he smiles, he doesn't always look down. Sometimes he looks at Mamochka, and sometimes he looks at me.

I see the bear glistening in his eyes, and I wonder how long he'll stay. But I know we belong together, so even if he leaves, he'll come home again.

When the sun is high in the sky but we're all yawning with tiredness, I walk Sasha to the door and step outside to say goodbye.

"Call for you tomorrow?" he asks.

I smile and nod. "We could go to the village to help with the cleanup and repairs."

"That would be good." Sasha waves as he runs down through the garden. He stops to stroke Anatoly's dogs, who are settled into the shelter, and Yuri, who is lying in the shade beneath the Lime Tree. He glances back at me and smiles. "While you were in the forest, did you find out who you are?"

I look down at my feet and smile. "I'm Yanka the Bear. Same as before."

"I could have told you that." Sasha laughs and waves again as he wanders away.

I hesitate before I go inside, to be near the forest a few moments longer. The treetops rustle and the wind whispers secrets. I turn my head to the sound, wondering what other stories from my past lie in the forest. My heart races and my toes twitch. But then I turn and open the door. Because more important than the stories of my past are the stories of my future. And those—with a little help from my family and friends—I can write for myself.

EPILOGUE

I climb the Blue Mountain slowly. The summer sun is high in the sky, the rocks are warm, and the air is alive with the hum of insects and the scents of pollen. Vibrations run into the soles of my bear feet: grasses swaying, crickets jumping, and rabbits burrowing into soft soil.

I walked here through the forest, with Mamochka and Anatoly by my side. But they've stayed at the bottom of the mountain, to picnic by the river.

Mamochka said I could wander up to the bear cave alone. She doesn't worry so much these days. She knows I'll always come home.

I find my grandmother sitting on the ledge in front of her cave, her eyes half-closed against the light. Sunbeams play in her thick brown fur, and the forest, a thousand shades of brilliant green, spreads out before her. In the distance, the Fiery Volcano glows emerald with new foliage, and white fluffy clouds gently drift across its peak.

My grandmother grunts a deep peaceful greeting. I sit and lean into her sun-warmed fur, and the massive mound of her body curves around my back. "It's good to have you home," she murmurs. "I missed you."

I slide my fingers through the fur of her neck and rest my head on her chest. The sound of her heart beating is as familiar as my own, and her scent, of earth and moss, berries and pine nuts, makes me feel safe. "I missed you too."

We sit together as the sun slowly sinks through the sky. I tell my grandmother about my life in the village: how the garden I planted with Mamochka is now bursting with color, and the Lime Tree is alive with bullfinch chicks, all hiding from Mousetrap's hunts. I tell her how me and Sasha built a shelter for Yuri and made a dugout canoe together, and how I've been swimming in the river with Polina. And I tell her how all the villagers worked together to carve and paint the new village hall roof.

My grandmother tells me about life in the forest: about the politics of the wolves, and all the new cubs, kits, pups, fawns, and boarlets born this year. She tells me how the river has shifted shape and made new pools and curves to fish in. And she even tells me a story about my birth mother, Nastasya, and another from her past, from when she was a young woman named Anya, living in a castle with a golden domed roof.

"Isn't it beautiful?" My grandmother smiles as the sun begins to set in the distance.

I nod, rise to my feet, and stretch. "It's time for me to go."

A breeze flows up from the bottom of the mountain, carrying the sounds of human voices. It's Anatoly, telling Mamochka a story about a flying ship. She's laughing, asking if he'll take her for a ride in it. My gaze drifts to the village in the south. *My village.* I feel its pull.

It's the summer festival soon. I want to help build the stage for the festival show and race in the canoe with Sasha. And at the end of the night, I want to jump into the starry waters of the Great River with all the other children, and splash and laugh until the sun rises. Mousetrap said he would come to the festival this year, as long as he could stay curled up around my neck, and Anatoly said he'd come to help Mamochka with her stall.

"Will you visit again?" my grandmother asks.

"Of course." I nod. "I'll be back before autumn."

And as I walk away, down the mountain, toward home, my grandmother's deep, rumbling snores echo after me and I smile, because I know something of our souls will always be joined together.

GLOSSARY

babushka: an old woman or grandmother

dedushka: an old man or grandfather

domra: a musical instrument with a round body, a long neck, and three or four metal strings

golubtsy: rolls made by wrapping cooked cabbage leaves around a savory filling

gusli: a musical instrument with many strings, played by plucking

kalyuka: a type of flute with no playing holes, traditionally made from a hollow plant stem

knish: a baked, grilled, or fried pastry with a savory filling

kvass: a sour, tangy drink made by fermenting bread or grains

mamochka: a term of endearment for a mother

piroshki: baked or fried puff pastries with a sweet or savory filling

pryaniki: sweet breads or cookies flavored with spices

rubakha: a long, tunic-style shirt, often decorated with embroidery

rusalki: water-dwelling spirits from Slavic mythology

samovar: a metal urn used to boil water for tea, traditionally with a fire in the middle and a tap on the bottom

sbiten: a hot honey drink made with spices

stroganoff: a dish made from meat or vegetables cooked in a sour cream sauce

sushki: small, sweet, crunchy bread rings

tsar: a male ruler, like a king or an emperor

tsarina: a female ruler, like a queen or an empress

ACKNOWLEDGMENTS

The Girl Who Speaks Bear spent many moons wandering aimlessly through the forest, and I owe mountains of gratitude to the kind and patient guides who led Yanka, and me, to the paths we needed to follow:

For their wisdom, insights, and encouragement: my agent, Gemma Cooper; and my editors, Rebecca Hill and Becky Walker at Usborne and Mallory Kass at Scholastic. I am truly blessed to have you in my life. You lift me and stretch me until I feel like I can reach the stars and sprinkle their dust over my words.

For bringing Yanka, the Snow Forest, and the creatures inside it to life in ways more beautiful than I ever imagined, my endless admiration and appreciation goes to Kathrin Honesta, whose magnificent illustrations blanket and bestow the UK edition with pure magic, and to Maeve Norton for designing and Chris Sickels at Red Nose Studio for creating the stunning US cover. I am astonished by the brilliance of your work.

For their passion, talent, and dedication: the great herd of publishing professionals at Usborne and Scholastic. My thanks to you all, with an extra hug for Sarah Stewart,

Katharine Millichope, Sarah Cronin, Josh Berlowitz, Katarina Jovanovic, and Stevie Hopwood (for hand-stamping nine hundred gorgeous proofs among other feats of awesomeness).

For calling me home from the forest, to the place where I belong, my endless love goes to my husband, Nick, and our children, Nicky, Alec, Sammy, and Eartha. You are my everything.

For their love and support: my parents, Karen and John, and my brothers, Ralph and Ross; my grandparents, especially Gerda, whose stories live on and inspire me every day; the family I have been gifted through Nick, especially Frank and Sheila; and my soul sisters Lorraine and Gillian.

For their inspiration and kindness: James Mayhew, Kiran Millwood Hargrave, Michelle Harrison, Cerrie Burnell, Sarah McIntyre, Onjali Rauf, Liz Flanagan (with extra thanks for the early feedback), Yaba Badoe, Kieran Larwood, Candy Gourlay, Robin Stevens, Catherine Doyle, Samuel J. Halpin, Gabrielle Kent, David Almond, Hilary McKay, and the many other authors and illustrators who have welcomed me into this enchanted story-filled world.

For helping me with my use of Russian words, huge thanks to Galina Achkasova-Portianoi; and to Galina Varese, for creating delicious story-inspired recipes.

For their incredible, invaluable work putting books into readers' hands and promoting a love of reading: all the booksellers, librarians, teachers, book reviewers, and book bloggers. Heartfelt thanks to each and every one of you, with an extra hug for the Waterstones booksellers, whose support of *The House with Chicken Legs* has been truly career making; librarian and chair of CKG judges 2019, Alison Brumwell, alongside all the other judges, and the teachers, librarians and young people involved in the Carnegie shadowing scheme; *The Bookseller* children's previews editor, Fiona Noble; children's book editor for *The Sunday Times*, Nicolette Jones; writer, school librarian, and book blogger, Jo Clarke; and teacher bloggers Ashley Booth, Scott Evans, and Steph Elliott.

Above all, thanks to my readers, for taking *The House with Chicken Legs* into your hearts, and journeying with *The Girl Who Speaks Bear* on her adventures through the Snow Forest. You, readers, make word-filled pages spring to life like trees blossoming after a long winter, and by creating that magic between us, I believe something of our souls will always be joined together.

ABOUT THE AUTHOR

Sophie Anderson grew up in Swansea, studied at Liverpool University, and has worked as a geologist and a science teacher. She currently lives in England's Lake District with her husband and enjoys the freedom of homeschooling her four children, walking, canoeing, and daydreaming. She loves to write stories inspired by different folklores, cultures, and landscapes. Her first novel, *The House with Chicken Legs*, was a Kirkus Best Book of 2018, a Waterstones Children's Book of the Month, and an American Booksellers Association "Indies Introduce" selection, and it was short-listed for the Carnegie Medal.